Modern
Hebrew Literature

mhl
MODERN HEBREW LITERATURE

EXECUTIVE & ENGLISH EDITOR:
Dr. Deborah Guth

LITERARY CONSULTANT:
Gitit Levy-Paz

TRANSLATIONS OF REVIEWS
FROM THE HEBREW:
Miriam Schlusselberg,
Leanne Raday

PUBLISHER:
The Toby Press LLC

COVER DESIGN:
Tani Bayer, *The* Toby Press

Published by *The* Toby Press for
the Institute for the Translation
of Hebrew Literature

CORRESPONDENCE

Submissions & Editorial, please
contact:

The Institute for the Translation
of Hebrew Literature
POB 10051, Ramat Gan 52001,
Israel

Telephone: 03-5796830
Fax: 03-5796832
Email: litscene@ithl.org.il
Website: www.ithl.org.il

For sales & subscriptions, please
contact *The* Toby Press

The Toby Press LLC
POB 8531 New Milford,
CT 06776-8531, USA
& POB 2455,
London WIA 5WY, England
Website: www.tobypress.com

Modern Hebrew Literature is
published with the generous

assistance of the Culture
Authority of the Israel Ministry
of Science, Culture and Sport
and with the generous assistance
of the Department for Culture
and Scientific Affairs of the Israel
Ministry of Foreign Affairs.

© 2007 The Institute for the
Translation of Hebrew Literature
Modern Hebrew Literature is
indexed in the MLA International
Bibliography of Books and
Articles on Modern Languages
and Literatures and in the Arts &
Humanities Citation Index.

Typeset in Garamond Pro by
Koren Publishing Services

Printed in Israel

Modern Hebrew Literature
New Series
Number 4, 2007/2008
ISBN 978 159264 208 3

Acknowledgements

Reviews and articles reprinted by courtesy of:

Maariv, for "In Times of War" by Osnat Blayer, first pub. *Sifrut ve-Sfarim* (13.04.07). Copyright © *Maariv*

Yedioth Ahronoth, for reviews first published in the Literary Supplement:"A Frustrated Othello" by Haya Hoffman (15.09.06); "Under the Knife" by Yaron Frid, (9.4.06); "The Legend of The House of Tott" by Liraz Axelrod (22.12.06); "What a Meeting!" by Ofer Dynes (8.12.06); and for "He Helped to Birth" by Amos Oz, first pub. in the Saturday supplement (5.1.07).

Ynet, for an excerpt from "An Interview with Ayelet Shamir" by Omri Herzog, first pub. on Ynet (6.9.07). Copyright © Yedioth Ahronoth

Haaretz, for "Don't Envy the Author" by Avirama Golan, first pub. in the Literary Supplement Sfarim (2.4.07); "Suburban Oblivion" by Haim Weiss (Haaretz Engl. Ed., 6.7.07); "The Immigrant from 'No Other Place'" by A.B. Yehoshua, first pub. in the Literary Supplement *Sfarim* (3.1.07); "Remembering" ("Suddenly We Could See") by Ariel Hirschfeld, first pub. in *Tarbut veSifrut* (5.1.07). Copyright © Haaretz Daily Newspaper Ltd.

Thanks to the following for permission to include excerpts and poems:

A.B.Yehoshua for an excerpt from *Friendly Fire*

Hava Pinhas-Cohen, for "Woman Breaking," "The Last Autumn," "In the Rhythm of Love"

Sara Friedland Ben-Arza, for "Be'er Lahai Roi," "Suddenly light," "Shtukit"

Special thanks to Savyon Liebrecht and *Images of the Middle East*, Denmark, for "Women in Israel: The Stated Truth and the Hidden Truth"

© 2007 The Institute for the Translation of Hebrew Literature
Modern Hebrew Literature is indexed in the MLA International Bibliography of Books and Articles on Modern Languages and Literatures and in the Arts & Humanities Citation Index.

Modern Hebrew Literature No. 4, Fall 2007

WOMEN IN WORDS

Contents

FROM THE CLASSICS

A STORY

ESSAYS

NEW NOVELS OF NOTE

POETRY

REVIEW ESSAY

REVIEWS

It is with deep regret and sorrow that we announce the passing of Professor Gershon Shaked, Editor-in-Chief of *Modern Hebrew Literature* for the past seventeen years, scholar, advisor, friend and supporter and, for us, far more than the sum of all these.

Fortunately, we still had time, before his death, to plan and discuss this issue, which includes part of a long essay on women writers that he was working on at the time.

It is to his memory that we dedicate this issue.

The Institute

Introduction

It is already a long time since the Western world became aware that, far from being a subgroup of the species "Man," women constitute over half of the world's population, previously known as "mankind." Women's new self-awareness may even have been an unwitting early trigger behind the modern debate on Levinas' Other. Today, however, at least in Western literature, women are no longer "other" at all; they are "self."

The title of this issue—"Women in Words"—was carefully chosen to allow for a range of perspectives. Its first half deals with women's voices: with their words, with the literary as opposed to the spoken word, the inner versus the outer, also with the words of men newly sensitized in response. Indeed, as altered perspectives take root, it seems time to reconsider the notion that *only* woman can write woman, and for this reason we include two excerpts in which female characters appear through the eyes of male authors. Some of these women write consciously "as women," others do not. Some are clearly postmodern, others use more traditional narrative conventions. Conversely, one of the authors presented here, Ayelet Shamir, rejects the notion of "women's literature"—in its modern as well traditional connotations—and sets out to write "as a man." Finally, three women poets have been selected for the current issue, and include a new and interesting aspect of the contemporary literary scene: the rise of a new generation of religious women who actively study the religious sources (previously a male preserve) and are progessively adding their unique voices to Hebrew literature.

Contemporary Hebrew women's writing, it should be noted, is not necessarily synonymous with feminism. And this is not by chance. Rather than aiming to throw out the proverbial baby with the bath water, Israeli women seek to expand their range of choices while still maintaining the importance of family, a central value in Jewish and Israeli culture. Thus, a significant part of their writing relates to exploring mother-child relations in all its complexity, as in Zeruya Shalev's recent novel, *Late Family*,* where the narrative of separation and new couple-love is interwoven with the story of the woman's young child, or in the work of Shifra Horn (e.g., *Four Mothers*).

Needless to say, this issue of MHL does not present the work of all the major, indeed, of all the richly rewarding women writers in Israel today. However, it is hoped that the range of viewpoints provided here contribute to a sense of plurality rather than to any new, restrictive female orthodoxy.

Deborah Guth

---

* See MHL 3, 2006

In Memoriam:
Gershon Shaked

photo © Dan Porges

PROFESSOR GERSHON SHAKED (1929–2006) was born in Vienna. In 1938, with the Nazi invasion of Austria, his father was incarcerated in the Buchenwald labor camp and he himself was sent as a nine-year-old, alone, to pre-state Israel. There, he was educated in various homes and institutions for youth. Shaked started studying in 1950 and rose to become chairman of the Department of Hebrew Literature at the Hebrew University of Jerusalem, chairman of the Theater Department at Tel Aviv University, and a member of the Israel Academy of Arts and Humanities. He was also Visiting Professor at major universities throughout the world. Shaked published innumerable scholarly essays as well as book-length studies, among which, *A New Direction in Hebrew Narrative* (1971), *The Narrative Art of S.Y. Agnon* (1973), *Generations in Hebrew Fiction* (1985), and his five-volume work, *Hebrew Narrative Fiction 1880–1980* (1977–98), for which he was awarded the Bialik Prize (1986) and the Israel Prize (1992). He also received the Bahat Award for Non-Fiction (2004). His books, considered milestones in the historiography of Hebrew literature, have been published both in Israel and abroad. Most notably, a one-volume version of *Hebrew Narrative Fiction 1880–1980* has been published in English, German and Turkish, and will also appear in Chinese.

Remembering

Gershon Shaked—one of the greatest scholars and teachers of modern Hebrew literature—taught for over forty years in the Department of Hebrew Literature at the Hebrew University, and his presence there gave it a center and a direction. He led the department, endowed it with momentum and prestige and left a deep impression on it and its many students. His numerous studies—he wrote over twenty books and innumerable articles—are among the pillars of modern Hebrew literary scholarship, and it is impossible to imagine the field without the historical map he provided in the volumes of *Hebrew Literature, 1880–1980* and without his interpretive insights, which touched on almost all the writers of Hebrew and Jewish prose from the mid-19th century to the present.

I will never forget the first lessons in Shaked's Introduction to Modern Hebrew Literature, which I heard as a first-year student at the Hebrew University, alongside introductory courses in other departments. From the first moment, Shaked's lectures were characterized by something that was always present: complete, genuine and captivating passion, and a kind of existentialism or fatalism, as though to read and understand a story by Mendele or Agnon was to make contact with the very existence of the Jewish people. He believed that these stories could constitute a vital and necessary addition to the rest of this nation's life in the world. Compared to the other lessons in the university at the time, his seemed like strong and concentrated drama. Only in them, I felt, did knowledge join "life;" only in them did knowledge go beyond the academic ivory tower and become important to the world. His lessons tipped the balance and turned Hebrew literature, for which I had felt no affinity whatsoever, into the most important thing in my life too.

Even today, after having the privilege of meeting and hearing other, equally gifted teachers, after also being exiled among scholars who were not gifted with any special teaching charisma, what radiated from him seems to me the essence of what turns knowledge, including scholarly-academic knowledge, into something crucial to cultural life. I presume that I am not revealing any secrets if I say that not everything done in universities is worthy of being called knowledge and research. Knowledge is much more than a wealth of information, more than its integration and more than a method. It must penetrate in camouflage, must go beyond intelligence: knowledge must penetrate knowledge. And it cannot be touched without some profound, totally emotional involvement. Only this involvement, if it is genuine, may turn the archive of things and words into knowledge. Without it everything is dry bones.

Shaked, both in his teaching and in his research (and they are of a piece in this sense) was a prime example of knowledge. There was nothing that touched him that did not enter his blood and guts, that he did not turn into a part of his most personal experiences. This does not mean that he was necessarily "personal" or "subjective," but that he understood that there is no intellectual world without man, and any pretense of presenting it as a thing in itself is a lie. That was the source of his passion and his irony. Nor does it mean that everything he said and did is on the same plane, and that everything stands the test of time. But at its best, his contribution is among the high points of scholarship in the Hebrew liberal arts and the study of Hebrew literature.

Not all his historical ideas are equally convincing and not all his interpretive viewpoints are suited to all the writers he touched upon. But there are several areas in which his insights are indispensable, and I will mention only the most prominent. The first, in the historical outline that he contructed; in other words, the basic idea of a meta-narrative that activates all of modern Hebrew literature, from the hiding place that he called "the Zionist meta-narrative." And within it: his perception of the dual movement of literature, its dialectical nature—literature as the innocent supporter of the Zionist goal, as opposed to the literature that criticizes and undermines it, but without negating it (a duality that, following Brenner, he called "genre and anti-genre"). And the second, in the interpretation of Hebrew and Jewish writers—his studies of works of Mendele Mokher Sefarim, Brenner and Gnessin, Berkowitz and Hazaz, A.B. Yehoshua, Amalia Kahane-Carmon, Amos Oz, and primarily Agnon.

Shaked was one of the most important scholars of Agnon's work, and his two books on him, particularly the first one, *The Narrative Art of S.Y. Agnon* (1973), are basic building blocks for understanding Agnon's work. His chapters on the process of Agnon's consolidation, "The Struggle Against a Surfeit of Sentimentality;" on the undermining of the causal foundation of his plots, "Parallels and Assignations;" and on the pattern of the romantic element in his work, "The King's Daughter and the Mother's Meal," are masterpieces of critical penetration, diagnosis and cultural linkage.

None of his students will forget his humanity, his passion, his simplicity, his biting directness, his vulnerability, the great sorrow reflected in his eyes, the generosity that could quickly turn into a squad drill, the wicked and eager spark in his eye when he heard some gossip, his occasional flashes of intellectual brilliance, as well as a kind of annoying "vulgar" brusqueness. None of his readers will forget his memoir, *The Period of Anxiety (What Motivates the Speaker)*, which recounts what he saw as a foundation of his emotional and intellectual world—his childhood in Vienna during the rise of the Nazis and mainly after the Anschluss, a time when he personally experienced anti-Semitic beatings and harassment, and saw his parents totally helpless.

This memoir reveals a tremendous tension at the base of his personality, between an autonomic, spiritual-emotional existence on the one hand, and a humiliation and ugliness that threatened him both from the direction of the non-Jewish stranger, and—maybe primarily—from that of his parents, with what was impressed on Jewish experience as a type of acclimation to humiliation. In light of this essay, it is fascinating to see how Shaked's world found other dimensions, totally divorced from this personal experience. His escape from his traumatic beginnings is not a model of nationalism or Zionism (as he himself understood it), but one of genuine enlightenment, an ability to lift himself above the personal and to abstract the trauma into narrative-cultural elements. For all his emotional Zionism, there was no direct causal connection in his emotional and intellectual life between the "motive," as he put it, and its results. His vision was far richer than what is defined as a "Zionist motive," and his personal presence also held a tremendous range, full of contrasts and shades of emotion and style.

His teaching differed in one respect from his writing—its entirely personal, childlike and truly touching spark of playacting. This spark was not evident in his public lectures, but only in his seminars, those wonderful hours when young people have the privilege of sitting with a great teacher and reading a text in depth. Shaked's seminar on Nissim Aloni or Hanoch Levin, Kafka, Fogel or Hazaz was an amazing event of textual performance. Shaked would read out a sentence and add some tic or sidelong glance, and suddenly the one text would join hundreds of years of culture. Suddenly Falstaff could be seen in a gesture of Levin's; suddenly a painting by Bosch or Georg Grosz could be seen in a paragraph by Vogel. During those hours Shaked's profound sophistication opened up; it was not necessarily a result of his being from Vienna, but of that same autonomy and a sensual talent for shaping emotional connections and human situations out loud. At those times he demonstrated great finesse.

Shaked was amazingly diligent and productive, and his prolific output speaks for him. But what has disappeared with his death cannot be found in his writing. He contained entire spheres that were not words, and for which there will be no witness except what is imprinted on his family, his students and his many friends—and this imprint is incomparably powerful.

Ariel Hirschfeld

He Helped to Birth

I loved him almost from our first meeting. Gershon Shaked was a kind of father figure to me and to other young writers who were his students in the literature department at the Hebrew University in Jerusalem in the early 1960s. Over the years he became a close friend.

When I came to study literature in Jerusalem I brought with me several short stories, which I showed him with a trembling hand. Gershon was a precise, tough, ironic and loving judge. He was a warmhearted and hot-tempered person, a devoted friend, but a totally objective reader of literature.

In the forty-six-year dialogue between us there were parts that hurt me—but they were a lover's injuries. Each time I finished writing a book, I asked myself anxiously: What will Gershon say? We have lost a great teacher and a great midwife. The midwife of entire generations in Hebrew literature.

He called one of his books *No Other Place*, whereas he called his autobiographical novel *Immigrants*. But Gershon the immigrant was well aware, more than any of us, that there definitely are other places. He came here from another place, and did not leave the other place until his dying day and his last book: Austria-Hungary, Europe, America—he saw them as a threat, but as a temptation as well. When he said "there is no other place," he may have been trying to protect himself both from the threat and from the temptation.

Gershon Shaked, the great midwife, was also the great cartographer of 20th-century Hebrew fiction. For about fifty years he left a clear personal seal on literary scholarship, on the historiography of literature, on criticism and even on the literary debate. The map of 20th-century Hebrew literature as it confronts us today was to a great extent drawn by Shaked. Not only did he draw the map, to a certain extent he shaped it as well: His books *A New Wave in Hebrew Fiction* and *Wave After Wave in Hebrew Fiction* were authoritative books, which determined the place of writers and of works on the literary scene.

However—and this is the most important thing—a very personal secret underlay all his critical, historiographical and scholarly activities. In Hebrew literature, from Mendele Mokher Sefarim to Gabriela Avigur-Rotem, Shaked found the reflection of his personal biography, of the persecuted Jewish boy from Vienna, the boy who was harassed in his childhood by anti-Semitic bullies named Ribak and November. This is the boy who came here as an immigrant-refugee, as an "outside child," and asked us to love him.

There is therefore something intimate, almost confessional, in all his academic work: He talks about Agnon and Brenner, about Amichai and Kenaz—and in all of them he finds himself, his life, the life of an outsider child who hung on tooth and nail to Eretz Israel, which he saw both in its wonder and its ugliness, loving it even when he couldn't stand it. From his first book, *Between Laughter and Tears* until his last, *Identity*, one can read the entire series of Shaked's works as one complex autobiography, which tells us the story of the love and attachment, the fears and anger of one immigrant child who found in Hebrew fiction a mirror to his own soul.

Generations of students, myself among them, will remember him with admiration and with great love.

Amos Oz

The Immigrant from "No Other Place"

Although the absolute borderline between life and death is usually very clear to me, I still permit myself to turn to you, my dear Gershon, in the second person. Only a week ago to the day, Ika and I sat with you in the hospital for a long conversation, and its memory is so alive in us that I allow myself to continue it a little longer, even after your death.

The time has not yet come, at least not for me, for assessments and summations of your great and extensive literary activity. That time will come in the near future, and we will yet discuss it at length. Now I still want to speak to you personally, with love and pain. Since I found out yesterday about your sudden death as a result of complications from the surgery, I can't stop thinking about you, and to tell the truth, although over the years you almost "forced" me and your other friends to imagine your death, and although I was tempted into presenting a small variation on it in one of my novels, I did not imagine that your actual death would hit me so hard.

Death was always present in our conversations, not only because during the almost fifty years of our acquaintance you shared your physical suffering with me and others, but also because I was maybe a good partner for you in the dialogue about death. You called the critical essay you wrote about my first collection of stories "Death at his Window," and with sharp intuition, which was always your strong point, you discerned the important place that death had and would have in my works, including my latest novel.

"It's all psychological," I would say, trying to repulse the descriptions of your physical suffering and illnesses. And you, in your ironic and direct way, would both repulse me in return, and cooperate. Because to your great credit, you were indefatigable when it came to understanding yourself. It's true that even the most introspective person apparently cannot understand himself fully, but with a kind of tortuous and complex honesty you did not make any concessions to yourself—you dug and examined yourself using both psychological and physical therapy, in order to repair, to improve and to help your surroundings. Your famous self-irony was well known, and was beneficial even at moments when you made your friends uncomfortable. It is easy to be ironic towards others, but it's not easy to be ironic—especially so openly and unsparingly—towards onself. Thus you turned the self pity we all have into ironic pity, and that held a great attraction for me, both personally and in terms of literature.

A week ago, on the tenth floor of Sha'arei Tzedek Hospital, with your bed standing alone in a huge and sunny room, after loving words to Malka, to your daughters Dalit and Efrat, you spoke about your parents. After describing them with grotesque humor, you suddenly said how much you miss them and how, like them, and in spite of the roots you have struck here, you still carry the experience of immigration with you. I remember my surprise when I saw that you had called your autobiographical novel *Immigrants*. Slightly pained, I asked you how, towards the end of your life, you could still insist on the identity of the immigrant, when you came here at the age of ten and completed all your studies here.

You served in the army, you raised a typical Israeli family and above all, you dealt with the innermost codes of the literature of Eretz Israel with authority and profound identification. You understood and interpreted the most Israeli of works, from S. Yizhar to Gabriela Avigur-Rotem. So why do you insist on the identity of the immigrant?

Is it only because your parents sent you to the country alone at the age of ten, and you stood alone for a few hours with your suitcase at Haifa port, waiting for an aunt who was late picking you up? Will that experience dominate your entire identity? After all, you are also the author of *No Other Place*, which is influenced by Brenner's feverish Zionism.

I remember that you nodded your head with a little smile when you heard my strange reprimand, and you said: "What can I do? That is still my formative experience, I cannot betray it." In fact this formative experience gave you, alongside your profound Israeli-ness, the breadth, flexibility and curiosity to be in all kinds of strange places—such as Tierra del Fuego—as well as a deep and continuous connection to the Germanic culture from which you came. Perhaps it was this sense of being an immigrant that fueled the constant irony, and said to the Israelis: It's true I have no other place than here, but in spite of its importance and vitality, this place can never make me forget that I came from somewhere completely different.

A.B. Yehoshua

Gershon Shaked

Thoughts on Orly Castel-Bloom*

Orly Castel-Bloom is one of the pioneers of postmodernism in Hebrew fiction, and *Where I Am?* (1990), one of her first works, is a trailblazing book of the 1990s. If I had to point out someone whose work stands in total contrast to that of Amalia Kahana-Carmon, the principal writer of the "new wave," I would choose her. While Kahana-Carmon writes dense and lyrical prose, Castel-Bloom liberates prose from cultural allusions and from any lyrical metamorphosis. In fact, she is closer to the grotesque stories of Hanoch Levin than to women writers of the previous generation: Kahana-Carmon, Almog or Hendel. The metaphors in her work serve mainly a comic-absurd function, and most of them create incongruous contrasts. Take, for example, for following passage: "When you dive—all people are equal you dream that you are flirting with a tall black man the way you flirt with your first husband. The minister of police looked into my

---

* Excerpt of a longer essay which Gershon Shaked left unfinished at the time of his death. Our thanks to Malka Shaked for making it available to us.

computer and spoke to me in a friendly manner." The connections between the black man, the husband and the minister of police create a humorous fabric, because they are presented between spheres that do not overlap. Such connections, which appear frequently in her microtexts, also appear in the macrotext, that describes divorce, marriage, work as a typist, cousins from France, the attempt to be accepted to drama school, university studies, a rape attempt, the pimp who tries to entice the girl into being a call girl for some secret figure, and the meeting with the prime minister, for whom she is also designated. Here too, the sequence of events is incongruous.

The same is true of the heroine-narrator's journey in the Tel Aviv area, between Afeka and Ramat Aviv. In the main, Castel-Bloom uses materials taken from Tel Aviv reality, from its local newspaper, the university campus and even the local underworld (or the secret services that operate like an underworld), and here too, the incongruous connections contribute towards the absurd-grotesque effect that the author seeks to achieve. In fact, the absurd emptiness that surrounds the girl is the predominant meaning in the text, endowing it with its postmodern character.

On another level, the novel expresses no desire for true love, nor does it describe erotic situations. It is full of descriptions of apathetic sexuality that resembles the activity of the girl in front of the computer. In a word, what we see here is the antithesis of the romantic desire for significant human contact that is found in the work of Amalia Kahana-Carmon. Castel-Bloom's character is swept up by her prose—prose on a prosaic, anti-lyrical level, which seeks to achieve a dead end in language as well as in plot. The author succeeds in saying in many words that the world in which she lives is meaningless. The world of computers, newspapers, politics, imaginary husbands and imaginary loves lacks any emotional experience, and the absurd text is a suitable correlative of the emptiness in which Castel-Bloom's heroine is immersed, an existential emptiness that expresses profound despair. Kahana-Carmon's heroines were disappointed and suffered from recurring failures in their struggle for emotional contact, but Castel-Bloom's character lives without contact, and represent the despondency of the metropolitan person, whose emotions are totally paralyzed and whose relationships with others are a form of imaginary contact: "It was, I think, at the beginning of winter. Outside a thunderstorm was raging, but it had no connection to my psychological state, which was as apathetic as a dry well in the desert."

As a result of this, the plot of the novel is not a drama of pain but a sequence of unfortunate existential encounters, which have to be accepted as they are. Although Castel-Bloom's materials are blatantly Tel Avivian, her Tel Aviv is no more Israeli than is Youval Shimoni's Paris, in *The Flight of the Dove*. The practical and political materials—the secretaries who dream of emigrating to the United States, the prime minister, the minister of police, the police or the Mossad agent who tries to hand her over as a female body to the secret emissary or the prime minister, the campus and the professors at Tel Aviv University, the flying husband—none of these represent political experiences; they are cold synecdoches of a meaningless world. They do not signify a particular object, with whom one has to make contact for good or for ill, but rather objects of a kind that the girl encounters without knowing "where she is."

Also the social materials lack any direct social significance. The characters are simply planted within them, and the story describes the loss of contact between them and the girl racing around within them. The novel does, however, have a social significance, which can be understood from the conflict between what these materials signify to the potential reader and the meaning they acquire in the text. The reader, who is aware of the real existence of these materials, understands that the entire Tel Aviv reality has lost its meaning, and becomes a negative of reality when it is absorbed by people for whom reality has lost its concrete actuality.

Where Am I? is one of the sharpest expressions of a desperate youth that has lost its connection with the positive of the picture and is dealing with its imaginary negative, in other words, with a reality in which man is not even a wolf to his fellow man, but an object, a pathetic mirror that absorbs the confused experience, which is conveyed to him without requiring any emotional reaction. All he does is flee from one point to another, where he once again encounters other negatives.

In Castel-Bloom's recent book, *Textile*, most of the familiar phenomena from *Where I Am?* have been consolidated and reinforced. Here, too, the plot is postmodern and Aristotelian rules of storytelling do not apply. The structure, which is supposed to be composed of a beginning, a middle and an end, is very fractured, the diversions from the main storyline are greater than the linear sequence and the subplots are as important as what seems to be the main plot. In keeping with this, *Textile* does not end, it merely stops. The final events do not conclude or clarify anything, but merely signal the end of one of its stories: "In spite of [Bahat's] superficial cleaning, Gruber's smell was still in the room, so she got up and dripped geranium oil in all the corners...and was able to forget him." In other words, the plot ends when Irad is about to return to Israel and Bahat McFee, the third side of the ménage a trois, is left behind and removes the "vestiges of the plot" with an overall cleaning.

Textile is a social and political satire of Israeli reality in the early 21st century. And as such it parodies a number of genres, such as the family saga and the Zionist narrative. As a family saga, it centers around the Grubers: the mother Amanda (Mandy) Gruber, daughter of Audrey Greenholtz, her husband Irad Gruber, and their children, Dael and Lirit. Audrey Greenholtz immigrated to Israel from Rhodesia and founded Nighty-Nite, a factory which manufactures pajamas for the ultra-Orthodox community. However, she despises the State of Israel, and says that it was only her husband's sudden death that forced her to leave Rhodesia and come to Israel. Her daughter Mandy expanded the factory, while the third generation, Lirit and Dael, squander the family wealth and their father tries to escape his family and remain in the United States. The parody results from the distorted relations we see between the generations, and is also reflected in other families, who appear in connection to the Grubers—the family of Dr Yagoda, Mandy's plastic surgeon; the family of Bahat McFee who is supposed to be Irad's lover, and the McFees, the family of her former husband.

There is also the outline of a science fiction plot: Irad Gruber has, it seems, invented a "textile" made of spider webs, to be used for security protection. Towards the end the text turns into a parody of a detective or spy story. The spies are Gruber, a confused and megalomaniac scientist, and his partner Bahat, a frustrated and unfortunate woman who is willing to sell American state secrets in order to promote her certification as a Reform rabbi. The two are apparently engaged in something pointless—trying to produce flak suits out of spider webs (Hassan Nasrallah's metaphor). The parody also hints at an extra-literary event, the Jonathan Pollard story. "Every beginning spy knows that he has to be aware of the government's absolute denial in the event that he is caught," refers both to the parody and to the extra-literary event.

As in Sara Shilo's *No Gnomes Will Appear*, and *Heatwave and Crazy Birds* by Gabriela Avigur-Rotem, in *Textile*, the political and security situation—terror attacks and the fear of them—permeates the text. In fact, the entire novel centers around this issue. Irad Gruber's work for the defense establishment—the protective fabric he is trying to make—and his journey to the United States to get security secrets from Bahat McFree, a former Israeli, have already been mentioned. His son Dael is a sniper who attacks terrorists and carries out targeted assassinations. The author also relates to his army work when she describes a conversation between him and a psychologist concerning the stress of sniping. In order to overcome the problem of impersonal shooting, the psychologist suggests that while Dael is shooting, he should think of people he hates and towards whom he feels a slight revulsion. Dael then expresses hatred of his father and admiration of his mother, so when he is shooting he often imagines his father standing in front of him. In this way, the author combines the son's Oedipal complex and the security situation in which he finds himself.

Amanda, too, expresses security-related anxiety stemming from all the wars and intifadas in Eretz Israel. In a conversation with her daughter Lirit about terror attacks, Amanda says that she suffers when she hears news of wounded soldiers, but she is referring mainly to her concern that her own son will be among the victims: "when a soldier dies, I die. I think about his mother of course, after I make sure that I'm not his mother. If that happens to my son I'll commit suicide on the spot."

The author uses other current political materials. The relationship between Dael and Lirit's partner, Shlomi, clearly reflects the political problem behind attitudes toward Arabs: Dael is the right-winger and Shlomi is the leftist. Dael the rightist fights Arabs and Shlomi the leftist protects them. And in line with this perspective, Shlomi disparages the "nouveau riche" neighborhood of Tel Baruch North, while Dael defends it. The author, however, treats both with sarcasm: "Dael, who reads good literature, knows how to identify with the other," she states, "yet he does not identify with those he shoots;" and she concludes that both Dael and Lirit are "products of corrupt Tel Aviv society."

Generally speaking, *Textile* does not contain any characters from Israel's social margins, such as Mizrahim, Haredim (ultra-Orthodox), Arabs, and so on. Nor does it present any "ordinary" Israelis, but only characters identified with the new social class—"the nouveaux riches who live in the new luxury neighborhoods in North Tel Aviv, such as Tel Baruch North." These are snobbish bourgeois Ashkenazim, including Israeli *yordim* (emigrants). In spite of the security situation, or perhaps because of it, this elite class are spendthrifts who try to shape an artificial image for themselves by means of plastic surgery. Surgical procedures, wasteful spending and emigration are meant to compensate for this class's social and personal insecurity.

On the other hand, many characters uphold the values of global 21st century culture, virtually all of which are imported from the United States. In this culture we find a mélange of modern fashions and values "imported" from the Far East—plastic surgery and technological innovations on the one hand, and hippie-like values, an organic diet and yoga on the other. Phenomena such as the great scientist, ostensibly a cultural hero, who uses science for security purposes, and cheap labor in a textile plant run by a woman also form part of this portrait. In fact, *Textile*, the title of the book, refers both to Mandy's work and to that of her husband.

Overall, the plot describes the downfall of the Ashkenazi class—the Zionists of an earlier time—and banishes the world of Eretz Israel values characteristic of the 1930s and the 1940s. Clearly, the world shaped by Castel-Bloom is free of all the values about which Amalia Kahana-Carmon waxed nostalgic, and she describes the flourishing of emptiness with a certain enjoyment.

The satire relates first of all to the disintegration of the seminal family. Mandy Gruber, the first character we meet, is the ailing product of the new Zionist civilization, which is based on artificiality and forgery: she tries to improve her external appearance by means of incessant plastic surgery, which in the end leads to her death. Clearly, her phsyical degeneration as well as attempts at artificial preservation symbolize the increasingly unstable social body. Mandy's husband, Irad Gruber, is a kind of absurd genius of this civilization—"Gruber was dying to leave his imprint on eternity, like Copernicus, Galileo, and so on." He is an arrogant Israeli megalomaniac, "well aware that the Nobel Prize for the invention of the ultimate protective uniform was already waiting in Scandinavia." However, his lunacy differs from the one that afflicts his wife. During his stay with Bahat, his research partner, and afterwards his bed partner as well, he becomes a hopeless and superfluous nudnik, whose cowardly flight from confronting his wife's death and attempt to delay his return to Israel arouse contempt in Bahat. He deteriorates from a hero-genius to a pathetic Israeli anti-man-antihero, who wets his bed and pleads for his life, until Bahat calls a psychiatrist. This in turn reveals the admired genius who represents the defense establishment as a hopeless impotent. Gruber's reaction to his condition—"It's hard to believe that I'm a widower, this description doesn't suit me at all. After all, I'm the most vital man in the world"—is clear evidence of his weakness of mind and his helplessness.

The daughter, Lirit, who inherits the factory founded by her grandmother and her mother ready-made, is the new stereotype of 21st-century Israel. "Her behavior is typical for her age. Blond streaks—which a woman like that does by herself for NIS 9.90, or in the Mikado beauty parlor when she has time. She is thin but not ascetic, quite tall and most important, self confident beyond what one would expect of someone her age, as though most of her accomplishments were already behind her, and now she only needs to become stronger." Living with her unusual partner Shlomi, she shares his politically correct, organic seclusion in the Negev. Yet when she stays in her mother's apartment in Tel Baruch North, while Mandy is undergoing surgery, she plans a birth in a dolphin pool or a Jacuzzi. All her thoughts are a stockpile of materials taken from women's magazines, and it is this stockpiling as well as the combinations that turn the trivial into the grotesque. This third-generation heroine expresses the revolution in values when she ponders the death of her mother from the suburban society in which she finds herself: "Lirit actually thought that because Tel Baruch North had not an iota of Zionism, it was international, and because there was no socialism, progressive."

The Grubers pursue 21st-century values to the point where they don't have time to educate their children or give them proper attention. In addition to Mandy's disgust with her egocentric husband, the text describes the uneventful separation of Lirit and Shlomi, which takes place over the phone when Lirit is at her parents' home in North Tel Aviv and Shlomi at the isolated farm in the Negev.

Bahat McFee, originally from Ramat Aviv, also comes from a dysfunctional family. The crazy behavior of her parents and her sister are also imported from the United States. As opposed to the materialistic Grubers, the Bahats are hippies who believe in Sivananda yoga and vegetarianism. After losing his job, the father Theodor becomes a yoga teacher, and together with his wife Madeleine practices *asanas* to release their blocked energies. They are so immersed in the sacred work of yoga and everything related to it that they neglect their daughters, who frequently go to friends but do not bring friends home, for fear they will discover their parents' strange behavior. In any case, the family does not last. Theodor and Madeleine go to India for a yoga course; Theodor falls in love with Helen, the daughter of British colonialists, while Madeleine, his legal wife, returns to Israel. The disintegrating family is a synecdoche for Israeli society, in which a certain elite lives like American elites, between capitalist materialism and a Far Eastern-style ascetic spiritual revolution.

What is so interesting about Castel-Bloom's semi-grotesque presentations is their proximity to extra-literary parallels. The reader who is aware of the contemporary social situation is familiar with the characters portrayed by the stereotypes, and with their customs, lifestyles and values. In spite of the multiple special effects that distort the reality from which characters and situations have been drawn, these effects do not blur the reality and the realistic factors that are reflected between the lines.

Yerida (emigration from Israel), and *yordim*, the people who emigrate, are also part of the new Israeli reality, and Castel-Bloom is legitimately concerned with their way of life and mentality, including that of potential emigrants. Her work is less sophisticated and cultured than Bernstein's autobiography *A Dubious Life*, but it is also far more original and outspoken. The writer keeps track of the customs and values of Israeli emigrés in the United States, describes their ties with the local community, how they make a living and their ties to the homeland. The emptiness typical of Israelis in Israel is typical of the *yordim* as well.

Bahat in the United States and Dr Yagoda in Germany are two types of *yordim*. In each case, the explanation for leaving Israel is different, but the reasons are drawn from the realistic lexicon of Israeli society. Yagoda is an arrogant man who serves as the deputy director of the plastic surgery department in the main hospital of Dresden. The medical profession has become a profession for export, in which the doctor—the wandering Israeli—sells his talents to the highest bidder and occasionally visits the homeland, also in the context of his work. Like most of these characters, Yagoda is quite pathetic even though, in terms of the values accepted by most of the characters in the novel, he is a success story. Castel-Bloom portrays mainly successful *yordim*, according to the social criteria of the chronotype, but her viewpoint is ironic-grotesque. Yagoda's way of life is characterized by marriage, divorce, dispersing his children all over the territory of his exile, and making money by imitating the human body. Of him and those like him, Castel-Bloom is asking whether this is the path to happiness or a worthy goal, as the characters in her novel believe.

Another type of *yored* is Bahat's friend, Professor Profeta, who teaches at Berkeley and is an expert on Hebrew slang. His *yerida* is ideological-leftist: he is disgusted by Israel the occupier and by what he sees as its superficial culture. "Every day outside Europe is a waste of time," he declares. He tends to have a very sober view of Israel's situation and of Hebrew in the United States, and he understands that the livelihood of emigrés who teach Hebrew depends on the political situation in Israel. In the spirit of "Berkeley's political correctness" (particularly in the 1960s), Profeta is pro-Arab and anti-Israeli. He is presented as a typical left-wing emigré whose "posture was bent but slight; it wasn't clear how far his spine contributed to his stability." He met Bahat at Berkeley when he stood out by disturbing an Israeli lecturer and accusing him of being a murderer. He believes that anyone who doesn't leave the country is a partner to murder. As he puts it: "Anyone who doesn't leave the country—as I did, incidentally—bears moral responsibility. After seeing for several years how the occupation has an adverse effect on Israelis, I picked myself up and moved to France, and only there did I begin to live."

For this reason he admires the convert Serling, a Reform Jew who has gone over to the Unitarian Church, and believes that everyone should imitate him. His friend Bahat also admires Serling's recorded lectures. Profeta prefers Europe to the United States, and both of them to Israel. To compensate, he has written a book about international terror and is involved in politics, because Hebrew is no longer popular with the students. His goal is to understand the souls of terrorists. Profeta is the ultimate *yored*, for whom leaving Israel is a moral anti-Zionist solution.

Yordim such as these reflect many extra-literary phenomena. They are the product of Israeli abundance. They leave not due to distress but due to abundance. Yagoda and Profeta reflect two results of Israeli reality: extreme materialism and extreme leftism. The author identifies with Profeta's anti-Israel aggression, but she mocks it as well. With typical postmodern ambiguity, she speaks in the voice of the radical left, but also treats it with great irony. She criticizes the American way of life in general, that of the Israeli emigrés in particular, and describes the emptiness that is typical of both. Bahat McFee is studying to be a Reform rabbi, but her absurd behavior as a rabbi shows her lack of both Israeli and Jewish values.

Beyond the social messages that refer to materialistic Israel trapped in an ongoing security mess in the era of globalization, the author conveys existential disorientation by means of the grotesque, which is the clearest expression of the blurring of values and loss of inner direction. The disintegration of the human body described in the novel serves as a synecdoche for the social situation and as a metonymy for all the characters—it expresses their erosion: "Amanda joked that she had already had her breasts lifted, her tummy tucked, the cellulite in her thighs removed, her eyebrows raised, her cheek-bones implanted, and the bottom third of her face and neck lifted. Only the long, beautiful, full wavy white hair was her own, because she was allergic to all hair dyes." As a result, she is composed of artificial limbs, an assemblage that turns a person into a grotesque robot.

Just as Mandy strengthens her aging body with artificial replacements, she preserves it with large quantities of medicine that ostensibly prolong her life beyond its natural limits. After her death Lirit rummages in her medicine cabinet and finds "about twenty bags of cocktails for anesthetizing feelings, awareness, personality and the body that contains all of these." These artificial medications are the flip side of the plastic surgery procedures. The quantity of medicine, like the number of procedures, constitute a grotesque description of how modern man deals with emotional crises. He needs replacement operations, through which he will presumably overcome the laws of nature, and various medicines for sleeping and for alleviating distress, with which he tries to deal with life as a via dolorosa.

The grotesque in Castel-Bloom is the result of narrative oxymorons, the synchronic existence of things and their opposites, which create effects of disorientation because both the things and their opposites are equally valid. In a situation lacking any moral or ethical decisions, the world returns to the chaos of a whirlpool. A small example of such a contrast is the pajama factory Nighty-Nite. Amanda, an ultra-secular woman, manages a pajama factory for the ultra-Orthodox sector. The combination of these two contrasting semantic fields—secular materialism and the ultra-Orthodox sector—creates a bizarrely comic effect. A similar grotesque oxymoron can be found in the relation between the preoccupations of Gruber Senior and the military preoccupations of his son Dael. The father has invented a flak jacket made of spider webs for the Defense Ministry, and received the Israel Prize for it (the combination of a spider web and a flak jacket is a grotesque oxymoron in itself), whereas the son serves in the army as a sniper whose job is to penetrate the body of the victim.

Professor Profeta, the anti-Zionist *yored* who teaches Hebrew at Berkeley, also incorporates a grotesque oxymoron: the person responsible for the link with the linguistic tradition of the Jews and of Israel, wishes ill to the country on which his livelihood depends. This oxymoron is not simply a rhetorical combination but points to the extra-literary reality that is familiar to most of this group.

Lirit also embodies polar opposites that testify to her grotesque disorientation and that of her generation. When her mother dies, she rejects her partner's ascetic values, which become archaic vestiges of another life. The contrast to Shlomi's artificial asceticism is an indefatigable desire to waste money, and instead of mourning for her mother she is seized by a perverse attack of shopping. She compensates herself with new clothes and throws out all the old ones, the change in metonymic covering expressing a new period in her life. In addition, on her return from the bucolic life of the Negev to the city, Lirit becomes the scourge of the female employees of the pajama factory, who are afraid of being fired. She decides to change her mother's production line and to introduce into the Israeli pajama market a "textile" made of organic cotton B. In this way she tries to combine ideas of "the cultural left and everyday capitalism," and the combination of the two contrasting semantic fields also creates grotesque disorientation.

Thus, the entire novel is basically an outspoken work of grotesquerie. Overshadowed by the security threat, it describes how the children of the nouveaux riches in Tel Aviv suburbia deal with the threatening situation. It becomes clear that their bodies are in the East and their hearts (and finally they themselves) are in the far West. Thus Castel Bloom describes the disorientation of the Ashkenazi elite, whose downfall is liable to lead to the collapse of the entire building it has constructed.

Dr Risa Domb (1937—2007)

The Institute for the Translation of Hebrew Literature mourns the loss of Risa Domb, a fine scholar, deeply committed to expanding knowledge of Hebrew literature, and a great friend of the Institute. Risa Domb held the first lectureship at Cambridge University in Modern Hebrew; she was also the Grace Violet Cohen Official Fellow in Hebrew, Director of Studies in Oriental Studies and a Life Fellow of Girton College. In 1993, she established and became Director of the Centre for Modern Hebrew and Israeli Studies at Cambridge.

Risa Domb was the author of three important books: *Home Thoughts from Abroad: Distant Visions of Israel in Contemporary Fiction* (1995), *Rebuilding Jerusalem: Redefining Jewish Identity in the New Israel* (1996) and *Identity and Modern Israeli Literature* (2006). She also edited *New Women's Writing from Israel*, two volumes of stories by Israeli women writers, the second of which, *Contemporary Israeli Women Writers*, was recently published by Vallentine Mitchell. We had the privilege of working closely with her on this book, completed a few weeks before her death. We extend our deepest sympathy to Risa's family.

Fiction:
Excerpts from Recently Published Novels

ORLY CASTEL-BLOOM was born in Tel Aviv in 1960. She studied film at Tel Aviv University. She has published 11 books for adults and a children's book. Castel-Bloom is part of the "Generation of the 80s" which marked a major change in Hebrew literature. *Dolly City* has been included in UNESCO's Collection of Representative Works; in 2007, it was listed among the 10 most major books since the creation of the State of Israel. Castel-Bloom has received the Alterman Prize (1993), the Prime Minister`s Prize twice (1994, 2001), the Newman Prize (2003), the French WIZO Prize (2005) and the Lea Goldberg Prize (2007). Her books have been published abroad in 10 languages.

In this postmodern classic, Dolly, a young physician with a laboratory for operating on animals, adopts a baby boy she finds in a bag in the road. She inoculates him endlessly, transplants various organs into him, and grafts him onto her back so as not to lose him – a mad variation

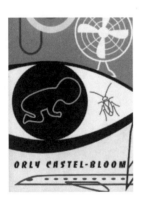

on the Jewish mother. Dolly's love-hate relationship to her son also reflects her bond to her country, through which the author probes Israeli reality. Wildly imaginative and full of black humor.

Dolly City

1992; new ed. Tel Aviv, Hakibbutz Hameuchad/Yavne, 2007. 155 pp.

Orly Castel-Bloom

Dolly City

An excerpt from the novel

One night I woke up at three o'clock in the morning with an intense desire to operate. Once upon a time, when the urge took me, I would find myself in my laboratory, opening and closing animals, but now that my research was shelved and the lab was taboo, there was nothing for me to do, and in any case, there was nothing left for me to operate on since dissecting dead bodies bored me stiff.

At the bottom of my heart, I knew I must not, must not go into the baby's room. He was sleeping soundly. I advanced on him wearing my green surgeon's uniform, undressed him and laid him on his belly on the cold metal table. He shivered with cold. I counted his vertebrae. It seemed to me that there was one missing. I counted them again and again, and after I was one hundred per cent, two hundred per cent—and so on in arithmetical progression up to a million per cent—sure, I started feeding all kinds of data on my child into the computer, until it began to groan like a woman in labor.

The baby was still lying on his stomach. I put him to sleep, even though I still didn't know where I was going to cut. I tried desperately to suppress this drive of mine to mess with the child, I tried to fob it off with a simple enema, but to no avail.

I took a knife and began cutting here and there. I drew a map of the Land of Israel—as I remembered it from the biblical period—on his back, and marked in all those Philistine towns like Gath and Ashkelon, and with the blade of the knife I etched the Sea of Galilee and the Jordan River which empties out into the Dead Sea that goes on evaporating for ever.

Drops of blood began welling up in the river beds cutting across the country. The sight of the map of the Land of Israel amateurishly sketched on my son's back gave me a *frisson* of delight. At long last I felt that I was cutting into the living flesh. My baby screamed in pain but I stood firm. When I had finished marking all the points that my neglected education succeeded in pulling out of the creaking drawers of my mind, I went back to being what I am—a doctor— and I disinfected and dressed the cuts, and sewed them up where necessary.

I contemplated the carved-up back: it was the map of the Land of Israel; nobody could mistake it. At night, when I couldn't sleep, I would go out on to the balcony and try to pull myself together. Dolly City lay below me in all its muddle and ugliness. Dolly City: fragmented city, cross hatched-city, whore's brother of a city.

I tried to ignore the terrible din of the metropolis—the clat- ter of the machines, the screeching and rattling of the traffic which behaved as if Dolly City belonged to it. Cable cars, steam engines, express trains, ships, trams, aeroplanes, automobiles, trucks, motor- bikes—they all criss-crossed each other, collided with each other a thousand times, freaking me out and driving me up the wall in a restless frenzy.

In the middle of the day, the sky was one big traffic jam of leaden planes. I would search for a bit of blue sky and fix my eyes on it. These were rare moments when I would try with all my might and main to feel part of a world far wider than Dolly City, but it was almost impossible. I was my own prisoner, I couldn't escape. All I could do was look at the jet-propelled trains being swallowed up in the black tunnels of infinity, of other people, of the rest of the world.

One evening, I lay on the carpet and surveyed my son's body in detail, as if he were right next to me instead of in the next room. The homogenic computer located trouble-spots in the region of the lower back, and the thought reared up inside me. The kidneys, Dolly. You didn't examine the kidneys! I restrained myself by force. With a thousand tongues I persuaded my folded hands not to touch the baby, to be content with routine tests to check if the kidneys were functioning properly.

The whole of the next day I pored over his urine, trying to discover worrying signs of albumin or clear traces of an infection—the child was healthy. But this had never bothered me in the past and it didn't bother me now. I opened him up. I dug and delved, I poked and prodded and stared and paled—the child had one kidney! I counted fifty times over and the result that came up, more often than not, was one.

I went into a depression. It was a foregone conclusion—a transplant was unavoidable. I racked my brains as to where the hell I was going to get a kidney from and in the end I came up with a five-year plan.

I took a taxi to the B.OFF building in Ben-Yehuda Street. I walked in with measured steps and sat down opposite a diligent clerk who was busy making calculations. She muttered the figures and arithmetic operations aloud to herself, as if she were praying.

I smiled for five minutes until she looked at me inquiringly.

"Yes," I said to her, "that's right. Look at me—go on, look!"

"That'a what I'm doing, isn't it?" she said, and went red. "That's what I've been doing for fifteen years, isn't it?" She stood up, over-wrought.

"Calm down," I said, "take a deep breath, and don't be so sensitive. Don't let things get to you."

"You think it's easy?" she barked rudely.

"You—"

"Look at me," I interrupted her. "Do I look familiar to you?"

"No."

"Look harder, tramp. The features—the nose, pay attention to the nose, especially the lower part—the nostrils. The small eyes, the pale eyebrows. The nervousness, the nerves. How many more hints do you want?"

"The more the merrier."

"My father was an employee of your company."

"I'm delighted to hear it."

"His name was S—"

"Who cares?"

"He was the head of the salaries department.

He died of mesothelioma, an extremely rare form of cancer of the lungs. In the medical literature only…"

"Stop right there!" cried the clerk in alarm. "No talk of illnesses, please. I'm a hypochondriac!"

"And I'm a doctor."

"Seriously?" Her eyes lit up for a moment but were immediately clouded by insanity as she leant forward and whispered, "Shoot a look at my eyes, honey. Give me an off-the-cuff diagnosis. Are the pupils the same?"

"Yes."

"Thank God," she said in relief and her eyes grew clear again, but the next minute they darkened and she pointed to a light brown spot on the back of her hand, "And this mark, is it cancer?"

"I don't think it's cancer."

"Do me a favor. My brother suffers from migraine. Could it be the beginning of meningitis? How long does it take before you know if you've been infected or not?"

"Give me a ticket to Düsseldorf—business class, and I want a reduction."

"Why?"

"Because you've got cancer. You're going to die. You have to fight it. You must never give in!" I clenched my fist and waved it in the air.

"I have to fly," she grabbed her bag and hastily straightened the knot in her brightly colored scarf.

"Where do you think you're going?" called the girl sitting next to her. But she took no notice and rushed straight into the street.

"Actually, I need two tickets," I said to the second clerk. "One for me and one for my baby. How much will I get off if my father worked for B.OFF in the years—"

"Nothing. Your right to a reduction or a free ticket died with him."

She made all kinds of calculations and in the end she threw a sum at me and I wrote a post-dated cheque. When I stepped outside with the two tickets in my hand, I looked at the spiral steps climbing up the outside of the B.OFF building. I reached the roof and was just about to take an Olympic dive when, at the last minute, I saw a B.OFF plane advancing in the direction of the blue sea and I watched it until it vanished into the white clouds.

It took me three days to sterilize all my operating instruments and pack them, and the next day I was fastening my seat belt and that of my son, and we flew away into the unknown. Sitting next to me was a tank who must have weighed two hundred kilos at least, with swarthy skin and a wig on his head. He was suffering from toothache and he cried, and the stewardesses came and went with pain-killers and glasses of cognac to put the tooth to sleep. Nothing helped except the sedative I injected into the lower regions of his paunch, which apparently silenced him for good. I wanted to use the opportunity to take a nap, but suddenly I saw a stewardess running up the aisle and crying in all directions, "Is there a doctor on the plane? Is there a doctor on the pl—" Nobody moved their arse but me.

I said, "I'm a doctor—what's the problem?" "Come with me," she said and tore the baby from his seat. "There's a woman about to give birth."

"Where is she?"

"In the pilot's cabin."

"And who's the pilot?"

"Goldberg."

"Aha." As far as I remembered, there was no Goldberg on the list.

"Is he new?"

"Old as the hills—on his way out. His daughter went to school with me. She doesn't even look Jewish." She looked at the little gold Magen David nestling on my chest. "She's so pretty. She's studying medicine at the Technion."

"Medicine at the Technion?" I said in amazement. "You can't study medicine at the Technion."

"No?" The stewardess shurugged her shoulders.

I helped some woman lying on the floor of the pilot's cabin to give birth. It was a boy-dead and I sewed the woman up, waiting all the time for the pilot to turn round so I could see if there was any resemblance between him and my son, but he kept his eyes in front of him all the time.

The decision to fly with the child to Düsseldorf, Germany, in order to obain a kidney for him from a German baby, was made on purely moral grounds.

Even on the way to the hotel, in a taxi following the minibus containing the Israeli B.OFF air crew, we passed a gang of neo-Nazis who were carrying posters in their language and who waved their fists at the Jewish minibus.

The hotel was incredible; I've never seen anything so grand and splendid in my life. The waiters were clean and scrubbed, the reception clerk was smooth as a baby's bum and he gave me the keys to my room on floor 173.

As soon as I entered my suite, I took care of the baby for a while until he fell asleep, and then I leafed through the German telephone directory. I was looking for orphanages off the beaten track, abandoned institutions in forest clearings or dungeons in God-forsaken villages. I found a few. I packed the child in a perforated suitcase and went out into the pouring rain to hunt for a taxi.

The rain beat down on my thick skull, beat down on the suitcase, got in through the holes and wet the baby, who kept sneezing. I cursed myself for not bringing my x-ray machine along; I would have taken an x-ray of his lungs to see if he was developing something.

The taxi driver was a typical German schmuck—a loathsome creature who made me want to vomit, a sub-human. He criticized the way I was transporting my baby. I didn't even answer him. The day some German tells me what to do and I take any notice will be the day when chickens grow teeth. The imbecile went on passing remarks and I controlled myself. He is my child, and I am entitled to bring him up as I see fit. I wanted to teach him something nobody ever taught me—to live in the privacy of his own four walls.

We entered the forest and it began to snow. After driving for about thirty minutes on muddy paths, next to a lonely, dilapidated old house, I let the driver go, and knocked on the rusty iron door.

I was tense and out of breath. I wanted to get this over with and go back home to Dolly City. I'm not cut out for world travel. The door was opened by a young brunette who announced that her name was Stephanie Poldark and that she was a symphomaniac—but what did it matter?

It wouldn't have taken a genius to guess that Stephanie Poldark was a bullshit name. She brought out a fantastic cheesecake with whipped cream and decorations—it was really something. After I had polished off three pieces—those yellow pills for depression give you a craving for sweet things—I asked her in English if her grandfather on her mother's side had been an officer in the ss.

"No," she replied. "My grandfather on my father's side was an officer in the ss. I'm so ashamed of it, you can't imagine! That's the reason I began to devote my life to serving others," she said and embraced three of her little wards, who clustered round to shelter under her wing. But their kidneys were of no interest to me. I was looking for someone of Son's age.

"I want to entrust this baby to your devoted care," I said and took him out of the suitcase. "He's yours. I don't fancy him any more."

"Hand him over," she said. "He's Jewish, isn't he? It's so obvious!" She stroked him tenderly and kissed his fingers—something I had never even come close to doing.

"But first of all," I said, "I want to stay here for a few days, to check the place out."

"Yes," said Stephanie Poldark, but it was obvious that she was sunk in thought.

"Sometimes I ask myself," she said, in a dense cloud of thought, "How long? How long am I going to go on devoting my life to others? When will I finally be able to start fucking whoever I feel like fucking? How long do I have to go on serving the sentence I passed on myself? I want to be free! Free of these guilt feelings! I can't take it any more." She fell silent and her tears dripped on to my baby's face.

Translated by Dalya Bilu

photo © Dan Porges

JUDITH KATZIR, born in Haifa in 1963, studied literature and cinema at Tel Aviv University. At present, she is an editor at Hakibbutz Hameuchad/Siman Kriah Publishing House and teaches creative writing. Katzir, a bestselling author in Israel, has published two collections of stories and novellas, two novels and two children's books. In addition to literary prizes for individual stories, Katzir has received the Book Publishers Association's Gold and Platinum Book Prizes, the Prime Minister's Prize twice (1996, 2007) and the French WIZO Prize (2004). Her work has been translated into 11 languages.

Gaia, the 15 year-old daughter of two Tel Aviv artists, fails to return from her piano lesson one day. Her parents, Michal and Yiftach, speak to her in alternating monologues while they search for her, examining themselves and trying to understand how far they are to blame for her disappearance. A day later, they discover that Gaia has been writing an internet blog which points to a romantic relationship with an Arab boy from Jaffa, and that the two have disappeared together. Together with the boy's parents, they set off in search of the missing Romeo and Juliet.

Castles in the Air

Tel Aviv, Hakibbutz Hameuchad, forthcoming

Judith Katzir

Castles in the Air
(working title)

An excerpt from the novel

M
ichal
The cell phone chirps and my hand leaps urgently to my bag and gropes like a mole. Purse, umbrella, keys, pens, papers, wipes, aspirin, tampons, lipstick, a half-eaten candy of Yonatan's. And here it is, green light blinking: Reminder-Gideon-one-zero-zero. If I cancel the meeting now, less than an hour beforehand, he'll take the full fee, over four hundred shekels. But I can't sit there as if nothing has happened, wondering aloud for the umpteenth time whether our whole is less or more than the sum of its parts, telling him again about the split, because in fact there are two of us: the Michal who insists on continuing to shoulder the burden, which grows heavier from minute to minute and from year to year, who will do whatever it takes so that what happened to her and her brother won't happen to her children, and so that her man won't collapse into himself like

her father did. Sometimes she even manages to get some enjoyment from it all; from the Sabbath meals, the birthdays, end of the year parties, family hikes organized by the school. And the other, subversive Michal, who already knew in the beginning that one day it would all come apart in her hands, that there was no refuge, and she exposed her chest defiantly to the storm even as she mocked the energetic activism of the first Michal, who was nothing but a sophisticated, self-righteous alibi.

Years ago the first Michal was still big and strong, I had mused aloud at the last meeting, since I conduct most of the sessions in the sunny Ramat Aviv clinic with myself, and the other one only gnawed at her from inside like a worm. But during the course of time the first one weakened and shrank, while the second fattened and swelled like a pig, growing impatient and domineering, a ticking bomb. That's what your father calls me sometimes, a time bomb, sure that one day I'll leave him, just like my mother, as if he himself doesn't give me enough reasons; but it suits him to stick her into my guts like a shard of broken mirror. I don't know anymore, I reflected aloud in front of Gideon's attentive face, if the pact we once made, between two abandoned children, is strong enough to prevent it; perhaps we were naïve when we imagined that one wound can be bandaged by another.

What wouldn't I give to go to the clinic today and hold the same old conversation for the umpteenth time, and sob bitterly, as if I had already left you, as if we were already in the middle of breaking up? But today I'll cry for a completely different reason. I'll choke and mumble, the words will tumble brokenly from my mouth and my heart will still refuse to believe it. Under his inquiring, sometimes skeptical gaze I'll go over the weekend again—the meeting with Yogev, which you may have heard about, the visit from Hava, your argument with Daddy on Friday evening, and the next day the Scouts' festival, where up to now it isn't clear to me whether you did as well as you hoped. Together we'll search for clues, put forward hypotheses about the possible reasons for your disappearance. Gideon will presumably reassure me, and say that from his many years of experience in treating adolescents he knows that sometimes they feel a need to run away, because even the most liberal home can be suffocating, and that in most cases they return.

But where did I go wrong, I'll cry into the scented tissues which I demolish wholesale on Monday afternoons. My whole life is devoted to holding my finger in the dyke and when the hole gets bigger, my entire hand, and in the end my whole self, just so the water won't leak onto them, so they won't get the least little bit wet, everything so as not to repeat my parents' screw ups. Gideon's lips will stretch into the smile of the cat that swallowed the cream, as they always do when he thinks he's about to come up with some particularly brilliant insight, and he'll say that sometimes in our efforts not to repeat our parents' mistakes we create new mutations, which are no better and often worse.

So if it's impossible to repair the damage, I'll cry like a mad-woman, if we can't mend the tear in our bodies and leave our children a clean new page, if we're doomed to pass on the viruses of the soul from generation to generation, to duplicate them in wild mutations till the end of days, if I haven't succeeded in giving my daughter a home she can be happy in and from which there's no need to escape, then what use are you, and all the years you spent cramming at univer-sity and wasted in vain on training? And what use is this damned clinic, with its bookshelves full of fancy books in English and mahogany chairs upholstered in old-rose velvet and scented tissues?

And I'll get up and brandish the chair above my head, and hurl it at the window with its turquoise Belgian glass; the pink chair will hover for a moment in the air, as if making up its mind whether to make the effort to fly or give up, and then it will land with a thud on the well kept lawn, between the flower beds and the broken glass.

I press the speed dial button, knowing that Gideon is busy now with the client before me, and leave a laconic message canceling my session.

A few years ago, the last time we were in therapy with her, Nitza the couples therapist told us about the theory of this Ameri-can psychologist, I forget her name. She claims that marriage vows should be renewed every five years. It seems correct and sane to her not to take anything for granted, but at the same time to promise each other not to start threatening divorce whenever you have an argument. After the first five years I still had hope, and I wanted another child. After ten years Yonatan was still a baby, only two and a half, and I couldn't stand the thought of him being bundled from house to house, wandering from bed to bed with his blankie and his bunny, waking up in the morning and trying to remember if he was in Mommy's house or Daddy's. A year ago, approaching the fifteenth year, which was when my parents divorced, I made up my mind. The sessions with Gideon helped me to give up the illusion that separation would be like a kind of time tunnel, that I would slide down it like a winding children's slide and land up back in the sandbox of my late twenties, and from there everything would open up for me again from the beginning. Painfully I realized that after the separation too I would be a middle-aged woman bringing up two children almost single handed. And nevertheless I imagined myself opening a big window, which had been closed for years, and a strong wind would burst in, and I would stand there intoxicated with freedom, breathing it deep into myself. Yes, I would pick myself up and take care of myself, my true old self, like a wounded kitten; I would bandage its wounds and feed it the best quality food, pet it and cuddle it, until it grew strong and healthy and ready to go out to hunt again, then it would pounce on life and devour it like a tiger.

I spent the months before our wedding anniversary saying goodbye to my old life, hovering over it and observing us all from above, like a soul departing from its dead body; for the last time we celebrated Rosh Hashanah at Aunt Aliza and Uncle Itzik's place on the small holders farm, singing the old Hebrew songs which suddenly brought tears to my eyes. Perhaps with time you'll discover that precisely those were the happiest years of your life, I thought appalled, and by then it will be too late to turn back the wheel.

For the last time we celebrated Yonatan's birthday together, improvising a Born to Dance contest, the boys jumping on the carpet and stamping their feet, the girls twirling their skirts, your father playing the piano, you and I acting as judges. And suddenly, in the lens of the video camera, I caught sight of your astonished look—Mother, why are you crying, this time you've really lost it, it's only a children's dancing competition, what are you making such a fuss about? And I couldn't tell you, that like then, in the last days before my mother left for Paris, when I watched her all the time, photographing her with my eyes—when she woke up and drank coffee, combed her hair, put on makeup, drew nylon stockings up her perfect legs and spoke on the telephone, prepared supper, hung up washing and stared wearily at the television screen—thousands of pictures that would last me for all the years to come that I could project on the screen of my eyelids before I went to sleep, so now too I command myself, remember these moments, burn them onto the hard disk of your heart.

Last summer we all went together for the last time to visit Dubi, Daddy's friend from his old neighborhood, and his wife Nira, at their house in Herzliah Pituah; you and Yonatan in the pool, dropping a coin and competing with each other to see who would dive to the floor of the pool and pick it up first, and for a moment I stopped breathing—you had been down there too long, under the water without any air, but then Yonatan's head emerged with his mouth open, and yours a second later, and one of you was waving it in triumph, shining like a little sun. I turn my head to the other side of the pool and focus on your father, roaring with drunken laughter with his friends, their hair thinning and faces heavy in spite of all the workouts and skiing holidays—presumably they were chewing over old memories from their schooldays, their army service and wild bachelor years— while I am obliged to listen to the women's talk, about this one who had enlarged, and that one who had lifted, and the other one who had been both suctioned and tightened by the latest genius surgeon. I feel like saying to them, how's that for a coincidence, I'm doing the exact opposite, photographing young girls with everything still smooth, erect and tight, and with an upgraded Photoshop program I gradually add expression lines and wrinkles, double chins and sagging skin and cellulitis, and I color their hair in shades of gray and white.

In a matter of seconds I make them age a lifetime, without the pain of surgery and without paying a penny. I really was planning then to hunt young girls in the street and photograph them; I would follow with my eyes the tallest, slimmest sylphs, in low-cut tight fitting jeans with long legs and big eyes and mops of curls, I was going to ask my students at the college to model for me. And afterwards, I knew, I would invite them all to the opening of the exhibition; they would look at themselves aging in the blink of an eye, and be glad that it was only going to happen years later. But the idea, like many others that come to me on white nights when sleep ebbs away like the tide going out, evaporated among all my other preoccupations before I had a chance to realize it. There's no point in anticipating nature, I said to myself, it is more determined and industrious than I am, and can be relied upon to do its job.

The picture of the two of you laughing and shouting in the water, and the sad, aging company sitting round the pool, with their glasses of wine from a boutique wine maker and their expensive cigars, wrapped itself in a haze of alcohol and longings. These are the last days of your marriage, I said to myself again, your last days as a family. Next summer, the three of you will be here without me.

On the fifteenth of November, our fifteenth wedding anniversary, I walked along the promenade to the Jaffa port. I stood facing the sea, under the gallery where we had married, and which had closed down years ago. I took off my ring, a golden hoop entwined with a hoop of white gold, which we had designed together and commissioned Roni the goldsmith, a friend of Daddy's from art school, to make for us. I closed my eyes and raised my hand to fling it into the waves.

Surely you'll notice—I suddenly took fright—not Yonatan, daydreaming in worlds of his own, but you and Daddy will wonder at the sight of the naked finger on my left hand, and I'll tell you that I lost it, yes, I must have taken it off in the studio without noticing and it vanished, maybe it got washed down the drain, such a pity. So I stood there, with my arm in the air and my fist clenched round the ring; a strong wind lashed my face, and after long moments I put it into my coat pocket, my throat choked as if I'd swallowed it, and thus, with my wedding ring churning in my stomach, I turned towards Tel Aviv and went home.

Translated by Dalya Bilu

HADARA LAZAR was born and grew up in Haifa. She holds a BA in history from the Hebrew University of Jerusalem, and also studied literature at the Sorbonne, in Paris. After spending a number of years abroad, Lazar worked with B'Tselem, a human rights organization, during the 1st Intifada. Lazar has published five novels and a non-fiction book, *In and Out of Palestine, 1940–1948*, on the last years of the British Mandate as experienced by Jews, Arabs and the British. Lazar is also the translator of Sartre's major novel, *Nausea*, into Hebrew.

This family saga, whose main events take place before the Yom Kippur War of 1973, take us back to the time of Jewish-Arab coexistence during the British Mandate, and before. Shaul Glickson receives a warning from an Arab journalist not to get involved in an upcoming security situation. While trying to understand the journalist's sudden appearance, his sister Dina discovers a family secret that forces her to review her entire life, especially her father's silence, the memory of a lost love, and the fate of her uncle who was executed by the Lehi, a pre-state, underground military organization.

The Locals

Tel Aviv, Kinneret, Zmora-Bitan, Dvir, 2007.
302 pp.

Hadara Lazar

The Locals

An excerpt from the novel

Neither the gate nor the door was locked, and Carmen, the old German shepherd, followed Dina through the rooms to the last one, the western one that looked out on Meyasdim Street, and sitting there in a new armchair in front of the TV was Rivka, Avinoam's older sister, her eyes closed, her head tilted onto the black plastic back, an occasional snore issuing from her open mouth.

An old lady. She'd already been old the last time Dina had come to Zichron Yaakov, but Carmen the dog had been a lot younger. Judging by Carmen, a great deal of time had passed. Quite a few years since she cavorted around Larry and Rivka kept calling "sit" as her eyes studied Larry brazenly. Now they opened to look at Dina, unsurprised eyes, narrow and penetrating, which abruptly changed the pale face, saving it from looking old. What are you doing here? she asked in her always frightening, scorched voice, and Dina said, I've come.

I can see that, Rivka said, straightening her back into a sitting position and glancing at the wall clock that was ten minutes slow, its hands showing nine twenty-five. Carmen walked slowly away, raising her head resentfully at the narrow windows that once showed the sky over the sea and now revealed only a tall apartment building. Come here, Rivka said, and watched Carmen lumber toward her, head down, still grumbling. When the dog finally lay down at her feet, head on the floor, Rivka turned to Dina and said, why did you come?

Dina knew it would be better not to be roundabout with her and said she wanted to hear about the time the Arabs lived in the farmers' yards, after all, there had been many of them in the town. A great many, Rivka said, not just the tenant farmers, but also the ones who went back to their villages every night and the ones who stayed here even though they weren't allowed to. The tenant farmers, Dina asked, how long were they with the family? A year, ten, twenty. We didn't sign contracts with them, Rivka told her. How long did they live in the yard? Dina asked. Rivka stared at her. Then she took a flat cigarette out of a pack of Dubeks, and as she tapped it lightly on the damask stool, said, What's going on? Why all the questions?

Shall I make coffee? Dina asked after a brief silence. Rivka dismissed the idea with a wave of her hand. You haven't been here since you brought your boyfriend, that Englishman, she said, inhaling deeply and exhaling sticky, sweetish smoke. Then she asked, you know where the coffee is? I'll find it, Dina replied, and went back through the rooms: the small one where Rivka slept, the shuttered one they called Zvi's room, then the dark one that used to be a storeroom she would sneak into when she was a girl, and after she'd let her eyes adjust to the darkness and checked to see that Fatmi wasn't around, she'd open sacks of rice and cracked wheat and beans, lick the fine dust left on her fingers, take the cover off the wooden chest and smell the tea. Sometimes Fatmi would suddenly materialize, filling the room all at once, tall, dark-skinned, wearing one of those loose dresses of hers that always absorbed dampness, and she'd put a handful of dried fava beans down in front of Dina and show her how to play with them, laughing her full-bodied laugh at Dina whether she managed to throw the beans and catch them or not, saying, again *habiba*, and Dina, who just wanted out of there, sensed that she had to please Fatmi, so she would throw the beans again.

From the storeroom, she went into the kitchen that was usually empty; most of the cooking was done outside in the *taboon*, the
stone oven. And yet, when Dina thought about Zichron, she didn't
see the pleasant, western room where everyone used to sit, but that
kitchen at the eastern end of the house, especially what could still
be seen through the window: the abandoned yard that descended
with the hill, Fatmi and Abu Mahar's small yard at the far end of
the slope, and beyond that, the hills that rose high into the sky and
seemed to engulf the place. Distance doesn't create more space here,
Dina thought. Zichron is on the mountain, and all around it's open
to the sea, but there's another kind of all around here, one that closes
in on you.

Returning with the coffee, she found Rivka going through her
purse. I see you don't smoke anymore, she said calmly, not at all like a
person who'd been caught with someone else's purse, and after Dina
took out a pack of Kents and gave her one she said, what exactly did
you want to hear about? Dina was careful now. If she asked another
direct question about the Arabs who had lived in their yard, Rivka
would bombard her with questions of her own, so she said, about
life back then, little things. Like what you used to eat for breakfast.
Same as now, Rivka said, an omelet made with olive oil. Coffee. But
it was more chicory than coffee.

We didn't have much of anything then, she said, taking a long
drag of the cigarette, narrowing her eyes but never taking them off
Dina, the big day was when the mailman came, an Arab on a donkey
who delivered packages and letters from place to place, a kind of
private post office. He didn't know how to read or write and he was
half blind too, but he remembered that this person had a sister in
Rishon and that one had a cousin in Hadera. He wore a big turban
on his head with letters stuck in it in a certain order, and he knew
that the first one on the right was for this person and the second for
that one and the large fifth one for someone else. Avinoam would
always go outside to ask if we had mail, and the Arab would tell him
nothing today. I don't know what kind of mail Avinoam was expecting, maybe he wasn't expecting any and just asked out of boredom,
or maybe he was waiting for a letter from Antebbi, it's a good thing

that Papa was dead already when Antebbi became your father-in-law. It was okay to talk to them, to do business with them, but to marry one of those preening peacocks? What are we to them? Ashes and dust. And don't get me wrong, your husband is a nice person, I have nothing against him, not at all, she said, in clear, polished diction that somehow suited the formal Hebrew of the time the language was revived, when zealous teachers were particular about every word their pupils uttered. Rivka, that firstborn child now surely past eighty, must certainly have been a good and diligent pupil.

Listen to me, she said sipping her coffee warily, it wasn't better then and anyone who tells you it was is simply lying. What could have been good? Stuck here on the mountain, seven hours from Haifa. Today it's how much, half an hour, and no one comes here, not your father, or your brother. Avinoam only calls when I send him bills, goes over them with me, wants to know why there are so many repairs here. I tell him next year there will be even more. Why do we keep this house, I ask him, why not sell it or build an apartment building like everyone else, but he doesn't answer, the only thing he's ready to talk to me about is the repairs, he thinks this house is only his. I've been talking about it for years but he won't listen, he's happy in his villa on the Carmel, but what will he do if I leave here too, who'll look after this house for him, who? she asked Dina, her eyes narrowing to slits, but her gaze dark, shining, alert.

Where have you just come from? she asked, and when Dina said that she was on her way back from her parents, in Haifa, Rivka asked how everything was there, and Dina replied, the usual.

You didn't talk to your father about what it was like here?

You can't talk to him about such things.

He's right. What is there to tell?

Fatmi and her husband, when did they leave?

Too late, after the riots, Rivka said. We should have sent them away years before then, but Mama and Zvi wouldn't let me, how could we send the tenant farmers away like just that after they'd worked here for us so long, and she stopped.

You haven't heard from them all these years?

We heard. Oh yes, we heard all right, Rivka said, the day Abu Maher and Fatmi left was the day they came and ripped out our vineyards.

You haven't seen them since then? Dina asked, and Rivka shot her a mocking look. Now you're an Arab lover too? she said, you married Antebbi and became like them. You look like them too, that bump on your nose from Avinoam and those curls of Zvi's, you look like a real Levantine, she said, her girlish laughter changing her face for a moment.

Don't be insulted, she said, you know what kind of mouth I have, and Dina asked, were their children born here? The children? Rivka repeated her question as if for a moment, she didn't know who Dina was talking about. They left the older ones in the village, in Sindiyani; the younger ones were born here. Right here in the yard. Fatmi used to nurse Zvi because Mama didn't have milk anymore for the son she bore so late. She would nurse him and Shahira, she was so beautiful, remember? How could you, she left years before you were born. Just to look at her. Avinoam would sit on the window sill in the kitchen with his books and she'd be walking around in the yard in front of him. He read *David Copperfield* there, *David Copperfield* and a dictionary. He'd sit on the window sill for hours, looking up every word he didn't understand and memorizing it, that's how he learned English, and Shahira was in the yard the whole time, sometimes with the laundry, sometimes with a pile of twigs on her head for the *taboon*, and Avinoam would watch the slow way she walked, the way she touched the twigs with her fingertips so they wouldn't fall, her raised arms slender and long, like her legs. *La belle* Shahira. She left suddenly. It was during the world war that she married someone from Ein Ghazal.

Her oldest son, she added, was the leader of the village gang, the one who came to rip out our vineyards the day they left, and Rivka stopped speaking and stared at the blank television screen. She probably watches the Arab channels for hours too, Dina thought, never misses the Arab movies.

Rivka's eyes closed. Her fluttering dress suddenly looked so big on her. She'd fallen asleep again, so small in the black armchair, her feet in the heavy brown shoes surprisingly large, as if they'd grown as her body shrank. Their total lack of movement and the dog lying still on the floor gave Dina the strange feeling that they too were inanimate here in this room that had barely changed over the years. Except for the armchair and the television, it still contained Grandma Esther's furnishings, and she should go before Rivka woke up, get up quietly and disappear before her sleeping aunt opened her mouth again and her narrow eyes flickered on her once more. If only a honey-sucker would come to the window and sing a bit, or there were any other small good omen, because Rivka's words are always bad omens.

And yet it was to this house in Zichron that she had brought Larry, and it was here in this room, as Rivka listened, that she told him how she'd visited Zichron during the Hanukkah vacation in the winter of 1941, and when Zvi was leaving for Tel Aviv, she begged him to take her with him. In the early evening, Zvi had parked his Morris on a quiet side street not far from Dizengoff Center, and when they went into an apartment, Zvi left her with the woman of the house and closed himself into a room with someone Dina later realized was a prominent Lehi activist. A while later, an elegant, fairly young man arrived at the apartment wearing a coat over a dark suit, gleaming black shoes and a hat that shaded his piercing eyes. He asked Dina her name, and as they spoke, the doorbell rang again. The woman came to say that it was a mistake, someone had the wrong address, and the man put his coat back on over his dark suit and asked Dina if she would take a short walk with him, and when she got up, he said with a smile, don't go out like that, put on a coat, and that was Yair, Abraham Stern. The Stern Gang, Larry said. They weren't a gang, Dina said. They weren't? he said, so what were they?

Why are you telling him about Zvi and the Lehi, Rivka had said then in Hebrew, tell him about us, how we came here, how we built everything there is here long before Allenby ever dreamed of conquering this country, that's what she said, in exactly those words. Dina could still hear them and the fervor in her voice, could see her sitting on Grandma's couch, the high couch that was still in its place against the wall, still with the same cover in dark reds. Everything was still here, all the furnishings that now seemed to be taking up more and more room, old things still whole, still in the same order they'd been placed in years ago, still everyday things: the narrow cabinets with the glass doors no one ever opened; the tapestries hanging on the wall, separated by family photographs; the heater that was still stoked with wood chips; the unwieldy black bakelite telephone—everything was here just as it used to be, and where was *she*, the girl who'd come here with Larry that day? What had happened to *her*?

She, who told him then about the underground, hadn't actually given any thought to anything, she'd just wanted to come to the family home in Zichron, to be there with him, to go out to the family vineyards with him and make love there. What does your old aunt think of you? he'd asked when they went out to the hills east of the town, her eyes don't miss a thing, and Dina had shrugged. I wanted someone from the family to see us together, she'd said.

She didn't like what you told me about Stern, Larry had said. No, Dina had replied, and you weren't too happy to hear about him either. Larry's eyes had sparkled with laughter as he looked at her. What happened when you went out into the street with Stern? he'd asked and she told him that Yair had whispered, this will only be for a minute, and put his arm around her shoulders. Look at me, he'd whispered, not at the street, just at me, and they'd continued walking like a pair of lovers till they reached the corner, where he stopped, leaned over as if to kiss her, and the brim of his hat, worn at an angle, had brushed her head. Wait here a little while before you go back, he'd whispered before he disappeared between two buildings.

Sounds like you liked him, Larry said when they were sitting on a rock on the sloping vineyard, and Dina told him that not long after—the winter of '41 had already turned into the winter of '42—a young stranger was waiting for her when she came out of school and although there was no vacation at the time, he asked her to come to Tel Aviv for a few days so they could send Yair a pupil that the British secret police didn't know. She would be the liaison only once or twice until they could get Yair out of the city, he said, and several days later she found herself on Balfour Street in Tel Aviv, in a room on the roof, reading books and waiting to be called. Suddenly she was completely alone, but she didn't feel lonely, only tense because the silence around her was strange, as if it were snowing there all the time, absorbing more and more sounds as the time passed. No one came to call her, though, and one night, Zvi arrived, to this day she didn't know how he found the room, who told him she'd been sent to Tel Aviv.

Zvi told her that the CID was closing in on Yair and when they found out where he was hiding, they would kill him and whoever was with him without asking any questions. He'd come to take her home. When she said she wasn't going back to Haifa with him, Zvi said, okay, so I'll stay here, and he slept there. He went out the next morning and when he came back a few hours later, he told her that Yair had been found that morning and shot right there, no one would come to call her, there was nothing for her to wait for.

Translated by Sondra Silverston

photo © Dan Porges

NURIT ZARCHI was born in Jerusalem in 1941, grew up at Kibbutz Geva and studied at the Hebrew University of Jerusalem. She
has worked as a journalist and held creative writing workshops for
children and adults. Zarchi has published a novel, four collections
of short stories, several books of poetry, a book of essays and over
80 books for children. Among her many awards: the Bialik Prize
(1999), the Ze'ev Prize (four times), four IBBY Honor Citations, the
Education Minister's Prize for Lifetime Achievement (2005) and the
Amichai Prize for Poetry (2006). Her books have been published
abroad in 15 languages.

Zarchi's most recent book contains seven poetic stories which blend
prose, poetry, fantasy and essay. At the heart of each story is a female
character—child, adolescent, woman—propelled by loneliness to
the limits of reality, and beyond, into the
strange and fantastic.

The Sad Ambitious Girls of the Province

Jerusalem, Keter, 2007. 119 pp.
short stories

Nurit Zarchi

The Sad Ambitious Girls of the Province

The Egret

There were four hours of guard duty left. He stretched and looked at the morning skies that stretched out above him and led the misty vapor, in which the entire army camp was now resting, to the ends of the earth.

Because he was too young to identify the monster of emptiness by name, the soldier tried to avoid it. With the butt of his rifle he poked through the newspapers on the floor. The headlines were familiar to him from guard duty at the beginning of the week. But beneath them he saw something else, a brochure left by the soldier on duty before him. It was entitled: "Hypnosis in Three Lessons." He looked at it with a lazy mind that by nature showed no interest in what lay beyond appearances.

The guard duty had been assigned to him as a punishment. Thanks to a mistake he had made, the entire company—which was standing in order in the sun, conducting the ritual of getting everything possible to shine: weapons, shoes, beret symbols and buckles—could go on holiday leave without a lottery. Young and cheerful, they hastened to distance themselves from the base, as though the approaching leave would spread like an oil stain on the memory of their entire army service.

The soldier at the gate pretended to himself that he was suffering, but in fact he was relieved at having been punished for something he had done, rather than for who he was. He found it convenient that someone thought it a punishment for him not to go home. He sat here, light as the blades of grass which, without even bending, are spared being uprooted by the stormy winter wind.

The glow that rose from the field of sunflowers opposite flickered until it burned his eyelids, which made an effort to remain open. Disoriented from being half asleep, he heard a rustling. Luckily he didn't cock his rifle. A moment passed, and it seemed to him that from among the reeds, clods of earth were approaching him. No, they were partridges. Hopping along, like a wealthy bourgeois family, they came closer. In the lead were the adults, behind them, with their feet spread, came the fledglings, the color of dry earth. He followed them with his eyes when they passed the guard post and entered the camp, as though there were no fences or prohibitions in the world.

Then another rustling was heard in the reeds, and a partridge emerged, more cautious than the others, perhaps one of those who always live on the edge of catastrophe. Alone it reached the gate, standing frozen in front of the soldier.

By nature the soldier was not accustomed to examining how far the world obeyed him, but that did not preclude his need to use any opportunity to acquire more power. A glance at the brochure, a glance at the victim, and the hen sank into a state of profound unconsciousness.

The sergeant who passed by afterwards and found the soldier asleep on his watch, kicked the frozen hen and woke up the soldier. Poor guy, he thought, one punishment is enough.

And so the soldier arrived on the following Shabbat, with a cropped haircut and rather pale skin under the layer of tan, to the warm asphalt banks of the swimming pool in the community he considered his home. Like a closed eye, without getting excited, the pool below him was absorbing the midday sun. Casuarina needles and double-bass leaves flew lazily over the matter-of-fact appearance of the water that had accumulated for irrigation. At the other end of the pool, lame M. Perfectionist was hopping back and forth, as was his daily custom, summer and winter. The soldier, like everyone else in the community, knew that his ambition was to execute the perfect dive.

The soldier followed his movements and counted the number of dives, in order to stop himself looking at the three girls lying naked on the bank. He could almost sense the touch of their slippery skin, their legs, their totally exposed arms, dedicating themselves to the sun.

By their appearance you could tell that the girls—even though their thin bodies bore the signs of femininity more as bud than as flower—were on the verge of that age which entitles one to a bathing suit. But not according to the outlook of this place, which favored the modesty of naturalness. Because of this denial, they looked like the corrupt fantasy of an observer. The girls had no personal attitude towards their bodies—it was more a principle than an act of self-exposure. Out of the corner of his eye the soldier noticed two of the young Gracias stand up and march towards the houses, saturated with water-scum and sun, their towels wound around their waists.

An afternoon silence was in the air, only the buzzing of the fat wasps and the trembling sound of the dragonflies' transparent motor could be heard. From the basketball court the bouncing of the ball sounded like a heartbeat. Although he followed the girls with his eyes, the soldier did not hasten to get up and go.

He was not entirely alone in the place. After the accident in which his father died, his mother had joined her sister in this community, and she subordinated her schedule and lifestyle to that of her elder sister. Because the soldier came only occasionally, she didn't want to upset her sister's schedule, and he, who couldn't tolerate his mother's frightened subservience, preferred to remain at the pool.

Ooh, came the exhausted call of a bird from the depths of the casuarinas, where poisonous mushrooms could be found bursting forth from the rot. Naked feathers could be found there—the last sign of a small life that had been devoured; even the white skull of a jackal, or a rabbit. The soldier looked at the girl. Now, when only one remained, he wondered why she hadn't gone with her girlfriends. She lay with her eyes closed, which was why he wasn't afraid to express his interest.

Before he rose from his place she got up, and with her body that was whiter than he had imagined—or perhaps it was the stream of sunshine—she entered the water, the only one in the pool, moving around with her eyes closed the way addicts do. Although it was nothing more than an irrigation pool, she was able to float weightlessly. In spite of her thin body, to be expected at her age, she already had a foreboding of heaviness. And for her, to forget her body was to forget everything she didn't want to remember about her childhood. She swam from one end to the other, until it became increasingly clear to her that water was the element that suited her, as though she were a water lily metamorphosed or an ocean nymph. The sky, which had become whiter and higher, was reflected in its entirety in the green pool. She emerged from the water and fell breathless onto the sun-soaked asphalt rim.

The soldier approached in a sitting position, came closer, and even closer. The swimmer didn't move. His nearby breathing restored a sense of her body to her.

A very white egret, rare in our region, came and lightly touched the darkened water with its beak. Had the girl looked at it, she would have seen before her eyes the book of Chinese art that her mother had received as a farewell gift from her fellow teachers on one of the occasions that she left. The soldier was still watching the egret when amazingly, it turned its narrow face the other way, ascended the ridiculous rise, one long leg after another, climbed up the slope of the bank and stood a stone's throw away from him. It stood that way for a long time, or maybe it was only a short time. The soldier, who was holding his breath, looked at it and applied Lesson One.

The egret closed its eyes and turned its neck diagonally. It works! thought the soldier, applying Lesson Two. But the egret spread its white wings, casting its spell and its shadow over the body of the sleeping girl.

Now it is gone, thought the soldier, who didn't actually know what had taken place; there was no point in applying Lesson Three. He looked towards the hills. Sometimes does would appear there, tiny ones, like a long line of small print at the bottom of the page. A wind rose. The pool was turbulent. The soldier shivered in his wet bathing suit and left with an inexplicable sense of dissatisfaction.

When the swimmer awoke there was nobody at the pool except M. Perfectionist, who continued what he was doing. Everything swayed for a moment when she saw him, pulling her heart as though tied to it with a too-short string.

After a while the swimmer left the community with her family. Predictably, she went to the army, where she was careful to wear her pressed uniform with the seam at the side. For a time she lived in rented rooms with a faucet in the living room. She studied at the university to the point of stupefaction. She encountered disappointment when the poems she sent to the newspapers were returned to her. She learned to work at jobs that are not considered important and that don't consider you important. But without being aware of it, she never stopped keeping track of the image of the little soldier, who in her eyes was not graced with any charm or special quality. This was stronger even than the fact of his death, which was announced by a notice on the dining room bulletin board. He was killed by a stray bullet during training exercises. There was no more logic in his death than there was in the searches for him.

And every time she almost got married, and finally did get married—first to a vip in the Labor Party, later to the Swiss minister of finance—it was because of a slight movement of the arm that was similar to his, or a look out of the corner of the eye, perhaps a voice, or a way of breathing. She chose them according to their wishes, and occasionally despite their wishes. Even when she thought that this was the chosen one, it turned out not to be him but the one behind him. With hindsight, the previous beloved would always seem to be the right one, and so on. She understood that she was not seeking love but rather freedom from the need for it. And she continued with this same motion which is like trying to catch a reflection, or eating the image of a meal. She was not stupid, and yet she didn't know how to feel real without giving in to this.

Because she tended to live backwards towards the hypnotic spell, just as birds are guided in their flight towards the right climate, she arrived one day at the last stop. It was the netherworld. She saw the little soldier, although she didn't recognize him, having tea at a round table with others who had come there around the same time.

And still she asked them: "Why am I here?"

She thought it was because of her difficult childhood, unsatisfactory heredity, prolonged childishness or a previous life. For she did not know her secret.

"Have some tea?" the little soldier asked.

The swimmer studied him for a moment, then she said, "I last saw you at the swimming pool, didn't I?"

"It was an irrigation pool," the soldier said. "But you're right. Aren't you drinking?" He moved the cup closer.

All the others sat quietly, watching them.

"No, I only drink coffee."

"That's a shame," the soldier said, "we only get tea here, so we won't wake up."

The soldier had no idea why she was there either, but the more experienced dead said, "An event is the most secret thing that exists, and it can't be touched by understanding. That is why we can't answer questions about what happened. Maybe the living know. The dead, you understand, only see what happens in between things: they see the air between the leaves of the tree, the instant between one moment and the next; their element is air.

You should stay away from here. The living should not immerse themselves too much in this element. Go to the place where you saw the little soldier and hold on to it the way you hold on to the edge of a table. For someone alive, the best way to understand is to hold on."

"You know that M. Perfectionist was there too," the little soldier added.

Some say that the swimmer didn't know how to return to that place. But I saw her again, on the banks of the pool, approaching M. Perfectionist. If I assumed that she asked whether he saw anything special happen at the time, I would be right. Because I saw M. Perfectionist go up the diving board slowly—he hadn't become any younger since then—and dive. Not a forward somersault, but a backward one. He dived repeatedly and all the while the swimmer stood on the bank.

There was total silence. The wasps stopped buzzing and even the sun darkened for a moment. It was clear that this was the perfect dive. And then the egret arrived. It appeared from the darkness of the casuarinas and hovered over the surface of the water with that same Chinese look from the album that her mother had received as a gift from her fellow teachers.

The swimmer went in naked, because she hadn't brought a bathing suit, and swam inside the reflection of the egret in the water. Thus they both went around in a circle—she in the water, the egret in the air. And when she left the magic circle, without knowing that it was one, of course, she freed herself from it and from the backward movement toward the little soldier.

She got out, and with the towel I offered her she dried off the leaves and the transparent algae that had stuck to her body. The egret walked with those same strange steps and stood at the edge of the pool. I saw the swimmer climb on the egret's back, but before that she said to me, "I'm sailing with it to Switzerland." And she made this request: "Call from the secretary's office, and tell my husband to wait for me with a bouquet of orchids."

Of course I didn't phone. The telephone in the secretary's office was always locked, and she knew it.

She waved goodbye to me and was swallowed up in the distance. I looked around me. M. Perfectionist had limped away from the pool. I didn't know whether she sensed that she held a secret—that sense without which you only exist superficially. When she rode on the egret's back, borne on the winds, did she have that sensation which makes you feel mysterious about yourself, as though you were a Chinese landscape?

Translated by Miriam Schlusselberg

AYELET SHAMIR was born in Israel in 1964 and grew up in Israel and Africa. She received a Ph.D in Hebrew literature from the University of Haifa and now lectures there as well as at Oranim College. Shamir has written a collection of novellas and a book—part-fiction, part-essays—with Nissim Calderon. *Piano in Winter* is her first novel.

On a stormy winter night in northern Israel, Joe Ochana, an ex-seaman, is alone in his bar with his pianist and a young Arab kitchen worker, Fadil. A party of go-getting Tel Avivians stop there; they are not made welcome and slowly a quarrel breaks out, awakening the sleeping demons of Israeli society: between prosperous city dwellers and underprivileged periphery, Jews and Arabs, women and men.

In between, as Joe ignores his unwelcome guests, his mind wanders back to his sea-faring days, but to no avail. By dawn the entire bar is in ruins.

Piano in Winter was awarded the Wiener Prize (2007).

Piano in Winter

Tel Aviv, Am Oved, 2007. 315 pp.

Ayelet Shamir

Piano in Winter

An excerpt from the novel

He recalled a voyage south to Durban where they'd unloaded a cargo from which the word "Israel" had been erased so there wouldn't be any unnecessary trouble ("You know, politics," he told them with all the erudition of a young man, and they nodded vigorously as if they knew anything about politics apart from the never-ending squabble between Geshuri, the sanitation contractor, and Sela, the head of the local council). When the unloading was completed they wanted to load a hundred barrels of formaldehyde. Yeah, formaldehyde, the stuff they use to preserve tissue and human fetuses and pitiful animals in sealed glass bottles, and if you touch it the chances are you'll end up with burns, and if not burns, then cancer. It had a terrible stink that formaldehyde; a toxic smell hung in the air and wafted up to them, the guys from the *Netanya*, tears in their eyes and mucus-filled noses, and there was nobody of all the local crew who'd agree to handle it.

So what did they do? What they always did in situations like that, they brought in a gang of prisoners. Or more precisely, thirty black prisoners. In any case these guys breathe the stinking air of the jail, the white port bosses said, and anyway, what kind of life have they got behind bars, it's no picnic that's for sure, and with this never-ending war and the rotten punishments in jail, how much longer have they got to live? A year, two, three tops? Their fucking life's short anyway, so getting out for a breath of fresh air in the port and using their muscles won't do them any harm.

So the prisoners came, escorted by some soldiers to keep an eye on them with cocked rifles. And they worked. Who wouldn't work with a rifle aimed at him? Facing the blue eye behind the rifle sight, did they have a choice? No.

So they started unloading the barrels of formaldehyde from the trucks and slowly rolling them barehanded along the quay to the narrow jetty and from there to the gangway. After they crossed the gangway, they lifted them onto the back of one of the prisoners, who looked the oldest but was still the toughest of them all. He had a back built for carrying a fridge, that one, and a neck covered with frizzy gray hair and bent from effort, and so he went down into the hold with measured steps, sweating like crazy.

They were all standing not far away—the engineers, the maintenance crew, the cooks, the captain, and Joe too. And from the deck they watched the black prisoners working in their place, as if they were in reserved seats in the upper circle.

Joe didn't know what they were inside for or even if they'd committed a crime. Back then he didn't even dream that in South Africa they had crimes without perpetrators and perpetrators without crimes and that putting somebody in jail was no big deal, just a kind of decision that someone in the right military echelon had to make. He didn't understand the seriousness of the situation and didn't speak the language, but he wanted to see. They were all leaning over the deck rail, watching the show.

The prisoners moved slowly, they were in no hurry. Time was the only thing they had lots of, or at least that's what they thought. They spoke to each other dull-eyed, and listened submissively (from the height of the bridge this submissiveness seemed innate, almost like their skin color) to the curt orders issued by the officers and the curses of the troops. The port was quiet for a Tuesday and greenish glints of light reflected onto the ships' hulls close to the waterline, and tiny fish attracted to it leapt from the water here and there, then circled round and round close to the old tires used as fenders.

From the quayside came the metallic noise of the rolling barrels and the swishing of the liquid inside them, and every few moments the heavy breathing of the elderly black prisoner was heard as he arrived with his barrel. He lifted barrel after barrel onto his broad shoulders, carried it onto the deck, then into the hold, and returned to the quay. He didn't even look back to see if they were watching. But they were.

The hours passed. Early morning trundled into almost noon and it no longer seemed like morning; the sun was at its zenith and the two British officers, one a short-haired subaltern and the other a horse-faced major, decided to change their vantage point; they moved from one place to another and then back again, and finally went up onto the bridge.

They stood next to Joe, glanced haughtily at the *Netanya*'s foreign crew, lit two long cigars, chewed the ends companionably, and spat. The aroma of fine tobacco wafted into the formaldehyde- and sweat-saturated air. Rivers of sweat flowed there, and the prisoners worked barehanded. In the meantime thirty barrels had been counted, leaving another thirty. The subaltern urged them along with curses and the major with blasts from a small gold-plated whistle that hung from his neck.

The hollow between the elderly black prisoner's shoulder blades deepened and filled with sweat, and his knees began trembling, but they wouldn't let him rest. He brought his hand up to his chest and it came away damp and sticky; he looked at his hand, wiped the sweat on his pants leg, bit his lip, then wiped his damp forehead and didn't raise his head. His dull glance did not rise above the level of the barrel rolling towards him on the quay, and his full lips moved of their own accord, as if he were murmuring an oath to himself.

"How long d'you think that old mule can last?" joked the horse-faced major. All his teeth showed when he spoke, and as he turned his head slightly his bright eyes met Joe's veiled ones. The major fixed him with an arrogant gaze and Joe shifted uncomfortably. A troubling thought furrowed his brow and his left eyelid began twitching.

The subaltern responded to Horseface right away in a toadying tone, "I think he's managing the show quite well, wouldn't you say, Major?"

"He certainly is, the old mule!" the major chuckled, and stubbed out his cigar on the rail.

He took a greenish banknote from his pocket and waved it in front of the subaltern. "This is good money," he said, scrutinizing the note, "I'll bet you he collapses at forty barrels."

"Fine," the subaltern replied cheerfully with a small gesture, and he took a similar note from his pocket and waved it.

The officers chuckled. It was a familiar game, and they recalled its thrill.

Joe was chilled. He felt the blush rising from his chest and flooding his cheeks, ears and face.

"I not see what so funny in this," he blurted in his broken English. He felt a profound sense of shame and his dry tongue curled up in his mouth, but it was too late to retreat or keep quiet. He straightened up and in two strides crossed the small space separating them, and faced up to the major. "Me it not make laugh at all," he said.

The major grimaced, his face blanching as he heard the man's insolence. He didn't remember asking this tall foreigner for his opinion. Had anybody asked for an opinion from anyone? And before he had a chance to translate what he meant for this insolent man, his hand had dropped to his belt, drawn a Beretta 22 mm pistol and stuck its short steel barrel to Joe's Adam's apple.

The touch of the hollow metal was surprising: cold and round and very, very close. Joe sensed the skinny finger tightening on the trigger and the hammer rising over the primer. He swallowed the little saliva he had in his mouth, his pupils dilated and he starting sweating.

The Englishman pushed the pistol barrel into his throat and spoke quietly.

"This isn't your country, young man," he hissed through his large teeth, "so move your arse out of here and don't interfere. Am I clear?"

Joe wriggled out of the major's grasp, tripped backwards over a pail and the filthy water spilled over his shoes and wetted the legs of his pants. The subaltern giggled.

The black prisoner slowed and cautiously raised his eyes.

Nobody noticed him. From the belt holding up his sweat-soaked pants hung a short piece of string, and when he tugged it a small switchblade emerged from his pants leg. He palmed it with callused fingers, then he bent down, lifted the thirty-first barrel onto his glistening neck and carried on walking. From somewhere on a nearby street a dog barked and a woman shouted at her children or husband, and for him, this was the right moment.

Joe saw him running from the direction of the bridge and saw the turbid green of the sea as it washed below him, and the flash of the blade as it was raised in the muscled black hand and brought down powerfully onto the officer's shoulder; he didn't aim for the heart, the head or the belly, he went for the epaulette, the major's insignia.

For one long frozen moment he saw him, muscular, his face contorted, moving with unbelievable speed, as if all at once he had shed the prisoner's gray uniform and become the angry youngster he once was. His black eyes shone and his shiny, coal-black features twisted into a triumphant smile. Then he heard two shots.

All at once there was a godawful commotion. Coughs and barks and shouts and a volley of shots into the air, and not only into the air. Almost choking from the terrible stench of the formaldehyde gushing from the bullet holes in the barrel, hardly able to stand, Joe staggered to the rail, lowered his streaming eyes to the sea, and saw the last thing he wanted to see: the black prisoner's body floating in the gently swirling water, facedown to the deep.

But he didn't tell them a word of this on the shore leave he'd had afterwards. He had a secret pocket in his memory for that final scene, a zipped pocket that was never opened. He didn't even have the words for it, it was his personal nightmare.

It's not hard to die, he'd thought then, when the *Netanya* left port and began making its way back to Israel, but evidently dying isn't everything. The trick is dying right.

Translated by Anthony Berris and Margalit Rodgers

Ayelet Shamir:

"*I didn't want to write about family—none of the characters have a family—or about love either, I didn't want to write a book with a corny, "feminine" kind of sweetness to it. I wanted to enter male territory in every respect.*

These characters need to fight over their place and their selves, and this struggle amounts to an inevitable conflict between locals and outsiders, the strong and the weak, between the men and then between the men and women.

The paradox is that only by virtue of this other, which I eliminate with my gaze, do I become aware of my own existence. When someone eliminates you, he also gives you strength. His mere existence defines something about you. The transparent person has meaning, he says something about the person looking at him without being able to see him.

My book arouses no sympathy or an urge to hug, but simply puts a mirror before the reader's eyes, one which offers no comfort. The book has no catharsis; justice is not reinstated. Man is indeed evil by nature and I didn't want to produce a sense of righteousness that could cleanse one's conscience.

Within this inner unresolved ambivalence, violence trickles into the bloodstream and into the mental space. This cramming together of opposite forces creates an infection. The book tries to drain the pus, explore the margins—not of insanity and madness, but of our own human endurance.

(From an interview with Omri Herzog)

SHOSHI BREINER was born in Haifa in 1952. She studied literature and art at Haifa University and Ben Gurion University of the Negev. Later, she lived for several years in Amsterdam where she taught art and worked as an artist. Her work has been exhibited in private collections in Amsterdam and Israel. Breiner has also worked as a teacher and editor. *Hebrew Love* is her second book.

The novella *Girls* follows the lives of three women who experience a crisis in their marriage around the age of forty. As the three friends attempt to escape their bourgeois lives, each one explores a different way of coping, according to her personality and experience. And as each of them weighs her need for personal freedom against other considerations, Breiner brings out the wonderful friendship that binds these women together.

A collection of stories filled with understanding and humor.

Hebrew Love

Tel Aviv, Am Oved, 2006. 233 pp.
novellas & stories

Shoshi Breiner

Hebrew Love

An excerpt from Girls

Meanwhile, Shulamit and Olaf took advantage of their day off between the end of the workshop and their flights back home to see York. On a guided tour of the huge cathedral, they thought that the height was most fitting to the aura that enveloped them. They felt no reverence, only the desire to break away from the imprisoning substance of the body and soar together to a place that had neither borders nor laws. Shulamit knew that the woman who'd landed at Heathrow eight days earlier was not the same woman who'd board the plane now. All her channels of energy were wide open and tuned in. In Yorkshire, the fragrance of the narcissi in the market square on Saturday made her cry. The green of the grass dazzled her and chamomile tea intoxicated her. In her dance workshop, she danced with the women in her group to the light of the moon, and unconsciously broke into the center of the circle, moving faster and faster until the force acted on her and the women swore she was floating.

Even though the earth meridians were swollen, she and Olaf did not have sex, out of respect for their earthly guides and the heavenly ones, who joined in the request to store that pure energy. Olaf admitted to her that he'd had an erotic dream about her that ended in ejaculation, but since it was a dream, he was sure that the heavenly guides had sent it to him, so he didn't think it would deplete his store of energy.

When Dov opened the door for her at home, he saw that she was thinner, her eyes were greener and her cheeks were pink and glowing. He told her he'd missed her, the house had been empty without her. She looked at him and told him quietly that it had been very interesting, she'd learned an awful lot about herself and a few things about them. Her cheeks began to blaze and her voice began to rise.

"For example, my channeling guides showed me what happens in your clinic. Not that I didn't know in some way myself, and not that I didn't get an anonymous call that gave me the details, but I didn't want to go there because I felt I wasn't enough for you."

Dov said, "Nothing happens in my clinic that isn't completely professional. I know what I'm doing."

Shulamit blushed and was silent, but a long moment later, she said, "I was with someone else there, and even though we didn't have sex, we had something that's made me want to be with him and not you."

Dov said, "Shulamit, that hurts, but it's really such crap. Do you think I'd let you throw away what we have together because of some passing fling?"

"What actually do we have together?" she asked. "Why haven't I been able to give it a name for years now? How come your understanding of women doesn't include me? No, don't answer, I already have answers. Now I have to go with my own truth. I'm not living in the same room with you anymore."

She took her suitcase to the guest room, where she began sorting the laundry that had accumulated during the workshop.

Dov said, "I canceled today's appointments because I was hoping we'd do something nice together." When she didn't reply, he added, "Come on, Shulamit, let it go. We can talk about anything."

And Shulamit replied, "We can't talk about anything. You've already disappointed me in previous reincarnations, and every time

I connected to you, I should have learned a lesson, but I didn't. Well, I've finally learned it now."

Dov said, "When you talk like that, I stop knowing who you are."

"That's exactly it," she replied. "You have no idea who I am and you're not interested in finding out either."

From that night on, Dov found the guest room door locked and Shulamit entrenched behind it. Their daughter, Adi, was in the army and their younger son, Yoni, was sleeping in a commune with a girl he met there, now his girlfriend, who was three years older than him. So they were spared the embarrassment of explaining their new sleeping arrangements to the children. The first two nights, Dov slept alone in their bed. On the third and fourth nights, he slept in a sleeping bag in front of her locked door, and on the fifth night, he charged the door, kicking it violently. That scared Shulamit, so she called Hemda and Danny, who came over after midnight to calm things down. Dov, who was all riled up, yelled that this was no time for a visit. He kept pounding the door while Shulamit cried inside. Danny hugged him hard and said, "Stop it, Dubik, that's enough, let's talk. We'll calm down a little and see what's going on here and what we can do about it. Force won't solve anything." Dov kicked the door one more time, and it suddenly swung open, leaving the lock dangling from the frame like a pulled tooth.

He saw Shulamit curled up on the bed with her hands over her ears, her face pale with terror. The anger drained out of him all at once and he saw the neighbors' daughter, a somewhat dreamy, somewhat helpless girl who, devotedly and loyally, had allowed him take care of her all those years. He let Danny take him into the kitchen, while Hemda went into the guest room and sat on the edge of Shulamit's bed.

Danny filled the electric kettle and made everyone verbena tea. Dov said, "Tonight, I'd drink something stronger," and Danny looked at Dov, whose dark hair was being infringed upon by gray areas. Deep, slightly angry furrows already stretched from the sides of his aquiline nose to his mouth. He was unshaven, and in his T-shirt and flip-flops, he looked a bit shabby.

Danny asked hesitantly, "Do you want to talk to me?" Even after so many years of friendship, he didn't feel close enough to push his way into that shadowy crack.

Dov said, "I know I'm no saint, but I'm really afraid she's gone off the deep end. That spiritualism business doesn't leave any room for our life here and now. She's mad at me not only because of where I stick my fingers in the clinic, but also because of things I did in previous reincarnations. How can I justify what I did before I was born? I can barely remember myself before the army. But I can tell you that I've been thinking hard these last few days and I know that I want what's best for her. It's not just competition with another man, even though if I ever get my hands on him, I'll kill him on the spot. I really believe I'm good for her, and I'm ready to work harder. It wouldn't hurt her to take a good look at herself either, and I mean in *this* reincarnation, and ask herself how much passion she brings to our life together."

Danny asked, "What do you suggest?"

"What's the difference," Dov said, "she won't listen to a word I say."

"I'm going to Germany tomorrow for a week," Danny said. "Maybe Shulamit should stay at our place for a few days until you iron this out."

Shulamit told Hemda that she was crazy with missing Olaf, that he called her cell phone five times a day. That he'd be coming to Israel on Independence Day. That she was planning to go to Eilat with him for five days.

They met in the hotel lobby. He'd come on a direct flight from Norway. He was wearing a suit with a lined raincoat over it, and after he got off the plane and walked to the small terminal, he felt the heat scorch his nostrils and then his lungs. By the time he reached the hotel, he'd taken the taxi driver's advice and removed the raincoat, but when he hugged Shulamit, his cheeks were still bright red and he still smelled strongly of the sweat that was coming through his undershirt, his shirt and his suit jacket. Shulamit didn't remember him being so light-skinned or so heavy.

He said, "I'm so happy to see you," and wiped the beads of sweat from above his upper lip before he kissed her on each cheek. She told him to take off his jacket and tie immediately and drink a bottle of water. Again, she had the strange, frightening feeling that she was in a reincarnation, the native girl welcoming him, a foreigner from a distant land. But the pleasant, air conditioned room diffused the tension a little and she hugged him tightly and whispered to the man who'd called her so frequently that she'd missed him terribly too.

He said he had to shower and take a short nap because he'd been awake for thirty-two hours. The image of them falling onto the bed and peeling off their clothes as they felt each other all over, curious and excited after eight days of restraint followed by two weeks of expectation, shrank into what felt like a bitter, black olive shoved into her larynx. With the thoroughness of a doctor packing a first-aid kit, he chose what to take to the bathroom with him, not even forgetting the Q-tips. Smiling at her, he closed the door behind him. The sound of water and gargling came from the bathroom, reminding her that she was with a man who had a long history she had no part in, a man with habits acquired from his mother, his country's climate, his lovers, his wife and his genetic tendencies. All of that made her vaguely afraid, but she pushed the fear away, telling herself that when it came to the deeper things, they weren't strangers at all.

Olaf came out of the bathroom wrapped in a bathrobe, lay down on the bed and told her, "Come my dear, rest here," pointing to the triangle he'd made for her between his arm and his body, which was padded with turquoise terrycloth. He turned and kissed her softly on the lips, then smiled at her with his blue, slightly red eyes. He asked her to wake him in an hour, then turned over and immediately fell asleep. Shulamit paced the room with growing restlessness, trying to think about a book she was supposed to design a jacket for. A few times in the past, after meditating, with all her senses alert, she'd managed to summon up images easily. But now she couldn't meditate, and the only image that entered her mind was an obelisk. When an hour had passed, Olaf was sleeping so soundly that she couldn't bring herself to wake him. He woke up three hours later and found her watching a mute television.

He sat up in bed, his whitening hair sticking up in all directions, and said, "What a shame you didn't wake me." She said to herself, stop feeling offended, nothing here was done to hurt you, and she went over and hugged him. He pulled her to him and kissed the hollow of her neck. "I've been dreaming about this moment for two weeks," he whispered to the hollow. "Touch me," he said suddenly with Viking imperiousness and opened his robe. His prick lay dozing on his heavy testicles like a chick in a nest. She reached for it apprehensively. If it hadn't risen by now, who knew if her hand would be able to raise it. For a moment, she felt it stretching a bit, and Olaf cupped her breasts. But he abruptly turned away from her and said, "I have to put on a condom." The robe fell exposing his large, pale, freckle-covered rear end to her as he muttered angry Norwegian words to the recalcitrant condom. Then, red with the effort, he turned around and said, "It's not working."

"Why do you need it?" Shulamit asked. And he looked at her in surprise.

"What else can we do without taking a blood test?"

It was already dark outside, and Olaf said, "Let's go eat something, take a walk in the fresh air." Shulamit got up, and without a word, went into the bathroom. She filled the tub with water and the aromatic bubble bath supplied by the hotel, and got into it. She tried to empty her head of all thoughts. She imagined that a black bag full of garbage was lying on her heart. She raised it high, towards her neck and began coughing again. Then she gave it a hard shove and tossed it out of her mouth into the air. For a moment, she thought she'd freed herself of it, a black plastic bag of smelly garbage, right before cleansing herself completely, but then she realized that another bag had taken its place. She decided to stay put until she was cleaned out.

A long time later, a knocking began at the door, hesitant at first and accompanied with words: "Is everything okay?" But when she didn't reply, the knocking became louder and the words more probing: "What's wrong, don't you feel well? Do you need help?" And then: "Are you angry? I'm sorry. I'm really sorry, I have no control over it." Shulamit squeezed her eyes shut and tried to ask her guides what lesson she was supposed to be learning from the fact that time after time, she's impelled to barricade herself behind locked doors that the men in her life bang on, either angrily or timidly.

In York, she thought she knew so much about him, about the skinny boy who had to show his nails before every meal, who sat across from his mother and grandmother with a mouth full of gruel he couldn't swallow.

But what can she do with that, Shulamit asked herself in the bathtub. How can she save a fifty-two-year-old man with a mild hatred of women and an eating disorder that makes him overweight and constricts his blood vessels, which in turn conspire to work against the delicate, fragile mechanism that activates his penis?

Olaf knocked at the door again. "Enough, Indo, your actions only work against us. I don't know what you want. Do you want me to start feeling anxious? What's wrong with you, darling, I just have a physiological problem. I'd already taken half a Viagra, but you woke me too late. Next time will be fine, you'll see."

She has to break away, she has to enter a state of total calm, she has to talk to her spiritual guides. What should she do?

Shame. Shame was the word her guides sent her. His shame and hers, that's what she had to come face to face with here. Her shame for not being attractive enough, restrained enough, forgiving enough, shame for not being able to escape from the demanding energy of the body and be a soul. She sat up straight in the tub and said aloud, "I'll be right out." Wrapped in a towel, she said to him, "I'm terribly sorry. What happened brought a lot of demons out of me. I'm cleansed now and I love you."

Darkness brought no relief from the heat, and outside, a blast-furnace wind was blowing. They walked quickly toward the little fish restaurant across the street. Olaf ordered draft beer and wrapped the hot, white bread around the salads the way Shulamit showed him. By the time the fish finally came, he'd ordered another liter and dunked the bread in the remains of the spicy salad. Shulamit vaguely recalled something she'd read about those miracle pills that restore potency—that they shouldn't be mixed with rich food and alcohol—but said to herself, he's a doctor, he must know. Olaf ordered them Crème

Bavaria for dessert and sang to her in Norwegian. His nose was red and he fondled her knee under the table, saying, "Oh, Indo, I want to go back to the room with you." On the short walk back to the hotel, he said he wished he had sunglasses because the passing cars were blinding him.

She helped him undress and put him into bed, lay down next to him and stroked his forehead until he stopped mumbling and fell asleep. Then she went down to the hotel beach and sat cross-legged on the sand close to the water, raised her forearms to the sides of her body, touched index fingers to thumbs, closed her eyes and made the inside of her mouth vibrate with "oom"—but her brain refused to empty out.

She heard the ebb and flow of the water and tried to match the rhythm of her breathing to the movement of the sea, to be one with the Absolute One, to feel the joy and serenity of self-negation that reminds you that you are nothing, a grain of sand, and yet as eternal as nature. But the smell of the salty sea released the tears of this particular Shulamit, whose knees were touching the sand now, the Shulamit whose third eye saw herself through the darkness standing at the hotel reception desk buying a plane ticket to Tel Aviv on the first morning flight.

Translated by Sondra Silverston

TAMAR GELBETZ was born in Tel Aviv in 1957 and studied cinema and English literature at Tel Aviv University. She worked for many years as a journalist at *Haaretz* and *Ha'Ir* newspapers, writing mainly on culture and entertainment. Gelbetz has also worked as editor and TV reviewer for the daily *Maariv*, and as scriptwriter and editor for Channel 2 TV. She published her first novel in 2004. Gelbetz received a special citation in the *Haaretz* Short Story Competition (2004), and the Prime Minister's Prize (2008).

Folding chronicles a woman's separation from her husband after twenty years of marriage, from the day her husband leaves till the day she removes her wedding ring. But what makes the novel unique is the way it confronts conventional stories of break-up with its rambunctious language, its perceptive insights and self-directed humor, which turn it into a droll nightmare that one cannot put down.

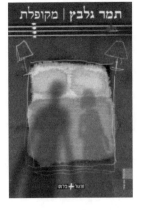

Folding

Tel Aviv, Xargol, 2006. 187 pp.

Tamar Gelbetz

Folding

I decide to go back to the moment when I realized that my *An excerpt from the novel*

marriage was over. I try to immerse my head in it for a second, to flood my entire self with that moment so that it encompasses me, spins me and fills me completely the way a slim test tube or a jug or a narrow-hipped vase is filled up, to the lip and a little more. So that it even overflows a little. As if it's lots and lots of water. Too much. But I'm not sure I can. I want it to rise and flow. But it doesn't. I think it was right then that I ambushed that moment and darkened it and covered it with a blanket and bound it tightly with rope and kicked it aside. Exactly the way you do with abuse in early childhood: you put it aside, very deep inside, and forge ahead as if nothing had happened. I do remember the first candid, penetrating talk. The one when I asked and didn't even understand what I was asking: Tell me, don't you love me anymore, and he refused to answer. Except that the blood drained from my face and it became as gray as cement that had dried and started to crack. We were sitting in the study that we both used, and now is only mine. In our permanent positions, he in the swivel chair by the desk and me on the futon facing him. Both of us stunned. Not by what is happening but by what is about to happen. I try to remember what happened beforehand. And I don't remember a thing. Most of all I don't remember what happened before the beforehand. Really before, when we were still a real husband and wife. It's hard for me to remember now how we really were before, so I try my luck with the photograph album. I leaf, leaf and leaf and stop. Leaf, leaf and stop. And I stop at a square, not a square, a rectangle. And there I see a man and woman. Normal. They are bending their heads towards each other. The woman looks sweet to me. Compliant. And sure of herself. But with loose edges. Unraveled fringes of disquiet. I try to see if I know her. If I know him. She isn't familiar at all, but he is. I suddenly remember this familiar man with gum in his mouth and sunglasses. He looks handsome. A real head-turner. I smell the spearmint of the gum wafting from him. I think I know who he is. I've no idea who she is. Six months he hasn't been here. A year since he came and said he was going. The album stops about two years ago. There's no evidence of the death of our marriage. He stopped taking photographs at some point. At some point I stopped saying, Don't forget to take the camera with us. This photograph is really old. Two and a half years. Maybe three. My birthday, maybe a wedding anniversary. Something from the great autumn days in our family. I don't remember who photographed us or where our daughter was at the time. I don't remember a thing about it. We don't look particularly festive. Ordinary. Daylight. I'm wrapped in a black vest and he's wearing a white T-shirt. Both of us have the pale remnants of a tan from the neck down. It evidently *was* autumn. We're not smiling. We never smile in photographs. Neither him nor me. But we still look cute. Cute but not buttering up to whoever photographed us. And not to one another either. For a moment I want to drown in the cuteness and flattery that existed between us but isn't evident in the picture. To dissolve in it like a cube of brown sugar in tea. To change the way I am. Evaporate into sweetness. Slowly turn into a trail of sugar. Become granule after granule of nostalgia. I want to pinch my heart and make it skip a tiny beat. But it doesn't work. So I close the album on the two faces, an ordinary unsmiling man and a woman, wondering how I can imprison them one inside the other in everlasting disgrace, and put the album back in its place on top of the hallway cupboard, high above, deep inside.

At which point in time, precisely in which tiny hole in the net of events did he decide to leave me. When did it hit him? Did he decide to cut himself away from me with the hiss of a sword stroke? Or did the idea of running away from the house mature slowly, then wrinkle and rot like a purple passion fruit? When did it happen? When did he say I've got to get the hell out of here and rent me a brand new apartment with shiny smooth spotless tiles, without a single *pitta* crumb or tangerine juice stain or anything, just square after square as smooth as the harmony of a block of white chocolate? When did he decide to throw me the hell out? The sequence of events. That's what will wake me up and give me life. If I can understand the meaning of the sequence of events. If I can understand what exactly happened, and when. When he decided to leave.

I'm unhappy, that's what he said. Those two words, right out of the blue. I'm unhappy. And you can say it in one word too. Imunhappy. Each syllable on its own, splendid and melodious, their togetherness sounding like an egg slipping from the plastic tray in the fridge and smashing onto the floor. Not noisily, not angrily, but completely apart. I'm unhappy. And then I'm unhappy with you as well, I'm unhappy at home, I want to go, I need to go, I've got to go, it wasn't planned but it hasn't just happened, I've got to think things over, I'm confused, I'm scared, I need time. And again that "I'm unhappy," and I've been unhappy for a long time, it's not that I don't love you and it's not that I won't go on being with the child but I owe it to myself, I've got to try and think things over quietly on my own. And from that single "I'm unhappy" that oozed like an egg white onto the floor and the yellow that broke and blended with the white and got scrambled like a wet omelet on the tiles, it was just a technicality. Who'll go here and who'll go there afterwards, who'll go and who'll come and who'll bring and who'll take and who'll give. And that's how it's been since he uttered his first "I'm unhappy" in a feeble voice with a thin flow of air from his mouth: I drive our daughter to him and he takes, he brings and I take, he returns, I bring.

The night before my husband packed his Imunhappy in his Adidas bag and left home, it was quiet. Even the security system of the villa opposite, the one that gets carried away with flashing circuits, claps of thunder, bolts of lightning and electric shocks three or four times a night, was as silent as a good, well-groomed little girl. The man with the dogs that bark like crazy wasn't being dragged after their entangled leashes on the square of lawn under the house. The TV sets weren't echoing and churning out opinions. The neighbors' baby wasn't crying or coughing its thickly wet asthmatic coughs. Our daughter was sleeping like the dead, not a snore, not a peep. Twice I kissed her as she slept and she didn't even raise her warm hand in a mosquito-swatting movement the way she usually does. Nothing. What quiet. In the morning he'll get up like every day, we'll each spend the night wrapped in the shrouds of our summer quilts, darkness and silence on the face of the deep. Why is this night no more special than other nights, how is it that he's leaving and the sky isn't dripping blood or oozing pus or bird shit onto the shutters of our apartment? Why aren't horrifying balls of fire rolling around the sky where the shadows of the two huge buildings going up floor by floor are standing like a pair of upright draftsman's rulers against the heavens? What's this indifferent, callous nothingness?

It all began in Crete. And ended. I'm pretty sure of that. Let's gain altitude for a moment and look at the aerial photo, a bird's eye view of a beautiful, small hotel veranda with wooden beams embracing it strongly from the outside, while in the room there's a small excited Israeli family. Our Passover, their Easter. Our daughter arrived in this paradise running a fever of a hundred and three. We dragged her, burning and gasping, from her strep-throat bed in Tel Aviv and set out, mainly so we wouldn't waste the charter flight tickets and vacation plans. She more or less held up during the flight, but when we collapsed there she started boiling like a pancake on a hot griddle, her whole body fever blisters, and at five in the afternoon she fell asleep snoring like a fuel tanker driver. Our plans for dinner at the authentic taverna in the fishing village next to the hotel went out the window. No stuffed and tart vine leaves, no huge warm beans in tiny dishes, no ivory feta cheese like smooth marble, no ouzo, no white wine, no nothing. A hotel room. So the openly disappointed husband and me disappointed inside started plowing through the room service menu, each of us balled up in separate corners of the double bed leafing through a copy, and came back to each other with an alternative plan. We'll order a bit of this and a bit of that, just small bite-sized portions, not lamb with pine nuts, not lamb chops and tarragon, nothing fancy or heavy, and we'll eat in the room, no problem. Carpaccio on a bed of aragula with with slivers of Parmesan, cold roast beef on dried tomatoes with olive oil, eggplant slices in sheep yogurt, baby spinach and truffles. It'll be okay. And white wine. Chilled. Cool. From local grapes.

The husband dialed room service, read from the plastic-encased Biblical menu in stumbling English, replaced the receiver, and we gawked at CNN while we waited, tense and silent. And all the while, our daughter snored and burbled in the single bed by the veranda door. Fifty minutes later the hi-tech doorbell rang, not a loud ring, more like a subdued trill. The husband threw on a vest and ran to open the door. The rest was all modern dance, Pina Bausch no less. Two starched waiters. A room service cart. Pristine serviettes with emerald rings hugging their hips, gleaming dinner plates with ancient clay rims, silverware, a small arrangement of water lilies, thin-stemmed wineglasses whose tinkling caresses our four ears and causes the snorer to shudder in her sleep, a blue-fringed linen tablecloth. The sun goes down, making its anguished farewell to the turquoise sky over the Crusader monastery opposite, the pools below flashing joyfully like diamond earrings, the water jug with the curved spout and sliced limes in the middle of the table. The two starched shirts exchange murmurs in the language of the gods, their mustaches synchronized as they bend over our pleasure trove, the table of love on the veranda, the altar on which our love of many years will be sacrificed. They arrange the place settings, with skillful fingers they smooth first the tablecloth, then the serviettes, and then they place the huge silver salvers covered with domes, perfect half circles, like lighting domes in wedding halls, under which our wonderful lustful food resides. Steaming and ready to be devoured. The truffles, carpaccio, Parmesan, moist and dried tomatoes; the olive oils, cheeses, spinach and aragula leaves; the Thassos olives, the rolls in glittering black dresses trimmed with black caraway lace, a bottle of semi-sweet wine from the vines of the neighboring village, the one whose lights twinkle at us like lanterns, one going out and another being lit as if in a game of Morse signals in the scouts, now that the sun is down, evening not yet here, and the bluish light shines palely, heightening the heartbeat.

We drag chairs over and carefully sit down. It's been a long time since we had a romantic evening in the sleazy Channel Two sense of the word. An evening on a veranda on a Greek island with wine, real silverware, candles, a flower arrangement, fruit and herbs, and the low hissing of the waves. It so forces us. Our pulses race. Inside, the little one mumbles in her sleep but we ignore her, voluptuaries dying of hunger, longing to tear off a piece of warm bread and dip it into warm virgin olive oil, to bite into the fleshy black olives, stick horny fingers into the crispy eggplant, suck the sour, milky, come-like droplets of yogurt. We want to gorge ourselves. Together. Quickly but in moderation. Both. With four hands, two hearts and twenty eager fingers. We attack. Until breathless, we reached the ripe yellow pears, the blushing figs whose stalks had been brutally cut off in the bowels of the kitchen, and the purple grapes of wrath with droplets of water still dripping from them. Then a cigarette. Shared. And another. The island opposite has disappeared into the blanket of darkness, the church bell clappers have begun striking heavily, the Christian festival is at its height and we are one small Jewish family gathered on a veranda, drinking and gorging on happiness as Jesus suffers agony on the cross. We are so focused on ourselves as we drag on the third cigarette and search the bottom of the glass to trap a last drop of sweet wine, our daughter sweating out her fever onto the 100% cotton sheets of the Greek Orthodox, that it seems we will never know another night as romantic and profound as this.

We are both conscious of this moment in time, forcing ourselves to fall asleep and awakening to the siren of our daughter at six thirty in the morning. She is completely dry, cool and crisp and she wants to go to the beach. The silver domes on the veranda table, round and heavy as flying saucers, are the only and positively the last witnesses to our love story. From there everything would go downhill, wane, drop a gear and another and yet another, the husband with his tortured soul and me with mine. Very soon, if we go back to the bird's eye view we'll see how our ways parted, our paths irretrievably split, or more precisely he parts from me while I stick to my restless sleep, my ever-oilier hair, and my lust for vengeance that floods me till I'm drowning in it, swallowing mouthfuls of salt water and choking and puking over and over. The cloud of olive oil, the truffles and sweet or semi-sweet white wine, leaden and heavily perfumed, will hover over both of us forever. With the Crusader monastery opposite, that night when the very depths of my body moved to his touch and our cries, that rose heavenwards in supplication, met and clashed in millions of shining stars—since then we have been completely silent. A month of total silence. A month of back to front. A month of pleading and two weeks of begging. Tell me what's the matter, tell me what's happening to you, tell me why, tell me, why is it like this, tell me what I've done, what you want me to do, tell me what I've done wrong, tell me.

Translated by Anthony Berris and Margalit Rodgers

photo © Dan Porges

MARINA GROSLERNER was born in Russia in 1967 and came to Israel in 1973, at the time of the Yom Kippur War. She studied philosophy and linguistics at Tel Aviv University and works as a translator and editor. Groslerner currently lives in Tel Aviv and Barcelona. *Lalya*, her first novel, has been published in German.

A group of abandoned youngsters take over a deserted construction site in south Tel Aviv and make themselves a ramshackle home, which they name Beita ("home" in Aramaic). Soon enough, it becomes a microcosm of their conflicted minds and an imaginary realm that they create to protect themselves from the outside world and the past. But when the city decides to demolish Beita, their demons take over and they give their all to maintain the fantasy.

Motherwolf

Tel Aviv, Yedioth Ahronoth, 2007. 348 pp.

Marina Groslerner

Motherwolf

ho is it?" Noa asks. *An excerpt from the novel*

The sounds of munching stop. The muncher is listening to the night.

"Who is it?" Noa demands once again.

"It's me," Orit's voice replies.

The munching sounds resume.

"Why are you sitting by yourself in the dark?" Noa asks.

She turns on the light but Orit immediately shouts "Turn it off!" and Noa quickly presses the switch again. In the short flash of light she manages to see Orit's face, yellow and sickly. At first they thought it was natural to vomit like that during the first trimester of pregnancy, even to lose some weight. But Orit didn't lose a little weight, she became skinny with alarming speed.

Noa feels her way in the dark and sits on the bench opposite Orit. Only now, in the weak light of the street lamp, does she see that Orit's hand is holding a large grilled turkey thigh that Hanan had brought that same day from the market just for her. Orit casts a guilty, frightened glance at her, and pushes aside orange peels and cigarette butts with her fingers, clearing a white triangle of space on the plate and carefully placing the meat on it. A minute later, as in an afterthought, she tears up the orange peels in the plate. But not, Noa notes, the cigarette butts.

"Why are you sitting here by yourself in the dark?" she asks again.

Instead of answering, Orit points to her belly and says, "She eats too much."

"Who?" Noa asks.

Orit places her greasy hands on her belly. Her fingers curl as though she wants to pull the tiny creature out from there.

"That's natural," Noa says. "You're pregnant. You're hungry."

Orit doesn't answer. The world outside is unnaturally silent, like during a siege, or a war. They feel a sense of relief when they hear a police van screeching in the distance. They sit there and listen to the van until it's far away.

"We should probably get more meat and fish for you," says Noa. "Maybe that's what you're missing—protein."

She wants to take advantage of the opportunity to try and convince Orit to go to the doctor. She already tried to do so, but Orit kept refusing. She even refuses to go to the clinic for foreign workers, where they don't ask any unnecessary questions. She isn't even willing to talk about it, and not only with Noa. She barely talks to Hanan and Maia. For weeks she's been sleeping by herself, curled up in her corner, and when they try to approach her, she hurls abuses at them and screams at them to leave her in peace. Hanan and Maia observe her with concern but don't dare to argue with her. A short time later they are once again at her side, pleading, begging, bringing her offerings of food, vitamins and books about pregnancy and birth, but Orit rejects them all, and Maia reads the books instead of her, as though she could relieve her distress that way.

Noa looks at Orit's face. No, she decides, she won't urge her. Let her advance at her own pace.

She places her elbows on the table and waits. Her eyes become accustomed to the darkness and she sees how sunken Orit's face has become. It looks gaunt and bitter. She once used to wear wide black T-shirts, but now, in the cool night, she is wearing a revealing hot-pink bustier. Her breasts look like balloons with the air gone out of them.

Noa waits for a long time. Finally she spreads her arm on the table between them and tentatively touches Orit's hand.

"Orit," she says. "Orit, what's happening to you?"

For a moment Orit doesn't seem to hear. Her eyes are vacant and empty.

"She doesn't care about anything," she says finally, her lips barely moving. "She doesn't care about me at all. All she wants is to eat my flesh and to get fatter and fatter." Her voice is cracked, sizzling with hatred.

"Why do you think it's a she?" Noa asks. It's a stupid question, but she doesn't have a smarter one.

"Because I can feel what a pig she is," Orit spits out.

"Orit!" Noa protests. "She's not too big. You heard yourself what Amina said. If anything, she's too small for the third month."

Amina is a friend of Yonatan's, a Senegalese woman who worked as a nurse in her country. A week ago Yonatan brought her to Beita as an emergency measure. She examined Orit, determined that she was approximately at the end of her third month, and that the baby was alive. Then she shook her head. Orit must see a doctor, she said. Orit pushed her away with angry screams and refused to see her again.

"For God's sake, Orit," Noa pleads, "Eat as much as you need."

But Orit no longer answers, she only breathes heavily. Another of the worrisome signs, this heavy breathing, as though the tiny creature, whose existence is barely noticeable, is stealing all the air out of her. She gets up, collects her plate, crosses the kitchen and throws its contents into the garbage bin. Afterwards, next to the garbage bin, she lights herself a cigarette.

"She just eats and eats," she says in her new, hoarse voice, sending Noa a mischievous glance that looks terrible on her sunken face. "But I pulled one over on her, didn't I?" she gestures with the cigarette towards the garbage bin.

Noa gets up and approaches her. "Orit, Oriti." She tries to catch her glance but Orit's eyes are now hidden among the shadows and she can't see them. "Orit, I don't know much about it, but I think that it's not too late to have an abortion. You don't have to give birth if you don't want to. You're still terribly young. Maybe it's too early. I'm sure we can manage to get money together for you to have an abortion."

She gathers Orit's large body in her arms—it is as flaccid as a rag doll. Orit tries to put her head on Noa's shoulder but she's much taller. So she just turns her head aside and lets Noa embrace her. Her large body trembles with terrible spasms of weeping. Between the sobs Noa hears her saying, "Hanan and Maia would never forgive me!"

"Nonsense!" cries Noa. For a moment she moves Orit's body away from her with her two hands in order to see her face better. "Hanan and Maia love you, not the unborn baby. And maybe a baby now is not the best thing for you." But even she doesn't believe it. Again and again she is alarmed by Hanan and Maia's fervor. It's more than happiness. There's a spark of madness in their enthusiasm. They sit together for days on end discussing the sex of the fetus, choosing a name for it, planning for it one future after another, each more glorious than the last, and all that time they apparently don't notice Orit, who is steadily shrinking in the fervor of their enthusiasm.

Orit's body continues to tremble.

"Shh, shh, shh," Noa murmurs, helplessly caressing her back.

She is still murmuring when suddenly, she is pushed backwards. She wasn't expecting that. Even in her weakness Orit is much stronger than her. The corner of the table stabs her cruelly in the back and a moan of pain escapes her, but Orit apparently doesn't notice, because she continues to stare at her wildly. "So now you want to turn me into a murderess too?" she cries in fury, fleeing from the kitchen.

In the darkness Noa sees the snakes of her hair flying around her head like Liliths smuggled from their lair.

*

Now of all times, Yonatan thinks. To lose the job, now of all times, when they need the money so badly. Five weeks have passed and he still hasn't found work. Neither has Noa, who worked all summer for the woman from the Nahalat Binyamin pedestrian mall, but now it's winter, and there are no customers.

Again you're sighing, he says to himself. Lately you sigh all the time like an old man. But he can't stop himself when he thinks about Shlomit, who broke her leg two weeks ago, and about Petro, who doesn't stop coughing.

They are lucky that Hanan is still working. Double shifts, works for all of them.

For the first time he asks himself if they'll stay in Beita forever, Beita, the abandoned house where they have taken refuge, now looks to him like a dark, demanding entity with a will of its own. Will they stay there even after the child is born? And when they're thirty years old? And forty? And fifty? And a hundred? Will they never leave Beita? He tries to imagine Shlomit at fifty. Will she be still able to float among the high ceilings? He laughs to himself bitterly, and sighs agian.

*

Now of all times, Noa thinks.

Already right at the start it was clear that this winter wouldn't be like the previous one. First the toaster oven broke. Hanan promised to fix it but every evening, when he came back from work exhausted, he put off the repair for the next day. Orit's large and efficient hands stopped doing any work. In an attack of optimism, one sunny day, Noa took the toaster oven to an electrician on Levinsky Street, but he decided, after glancing at it, that the repair was more expensive than buying a new one. She brought the broken toaster oven back home and waited for a burst of initiative, but it didn't come.

Afterwards, as though the toaster oven had spread a mysterious virus, all the electrical appliances stopped working one after the other. Almost every day bulbs burned out, handles fell off burning hot pots, windows refused to close, gas burners spit out flames to the skies, greenish damp stains grew on the walls, faucets gurgled, coughed, and spit out their rust-eaten lungs into the glasses, the water froze, drainpipes exploded and the electricity was repeatedly cut off.

99

Beita, which had always been a safe haven, suddenly gave up. The vegetable garden died of cold or perhaps an illness. Doors barked at one another with rhythmic slamming, mattresses got wet in the interminable rain that penetrated the cracks whose existence they hadn't noticed previously. Even in the yard, which had always grown by itself, there were suddenly ugly bald spots between the bushes, as though invisible fires burned there at night.

*

When Yonatan returns home, Beita greets him with evil growls and he senses the despair spreading within him.

Their eyes are big, their faces are pale—it's as though Beita's walls exude a poison that is infiltrating their bloodstream. When he sees them like that he turns his back and flees into the rainy streets, but there too he can't stop thinking about their glances. These glances hurt him. Mainly Noa's. A few days ago he dared to say to her: Let's leave everything, let's escape from here, we'll disappear, we'll rent a little apartment, we'll study at the university. She looked at him, and he knew that like him she wanted to escape, but he also knew she would refuse.

"We can't leave now," she said after some thought. "Not in this situation. Not with Orit."

And again he's here, in the rainy streets, thinking.

He lifts his gaze to the sky and feels how the fingers of rain are sobering him up, dissolving his little fantasy about a student life, a fantasy that now seems to him complacent and tasteless. He thinks about Orit, and about Hanan. And about Maia and Petro and Shlomit. He thinks about Noa. He tries to imagine how his life would have looked had he not met them. He would probably have become a different person, but he can't imagine that person.

"You'll have to live this story to the end," he says to himself, or to the rain. "To the very end."

Translated by Miriam Schlusselberg

ERAN BAR-GIL was born in Holon, Israel, in 1969. He studied
psychology and comparative literature at Bar Ilan University, and is
also a musician. Bar-Gil writes for the Israeli press. He has published
a book of short stories, two collections of poetry, two novels and the
first part of a literary-musical trilogy. He has spent the last few years
between Israel and Africa. Bar-Gil has been awarded the Bernstein
Prize (2006), and the Johanna Prenner Award for the script of his
forthcoming film and book, *Iron Squared*. His first novel, *Horseshoe
and Violin*, is forthcoming in German.

In this story of inner growth, Haim Palach goes to Angola to supervise
the construction of a bridge and escape from his empty life. Some
thirty years ago, his son Asaf went into a coma, and his family fell
apart: his wife left him and his youngest son drifted away. In Africa,

the walls of his despair start to crumble,
mainly through his friendship with his
interpreter, Ariel. Through Haim and Ariel,
the reader meets various African characters, including Armanda, Ariel's moving
girlfriend.

The Bridge

Jerusalem, Keter, 2007. 272 pp.

Eran Bar-Gil

The Bridge

An excerpt from the novel

I really didn't love him then. He attracted me, intrigued me and interested me, but my heart didn't open up to him like my body. I didn't give anyone at home cause to talk about me, I shared the work with everyone, even when I stayed with him all night and only came home in the morning, tired and light-headed. I liked the house in Catumbela-Nomoro. There are only nine houses there on the hill, and the neighbors are good people, all of them well-off with jobs, and the houses are surrounded by yards, not stuck together like in our neighborhood. He lives in this huge house alone with Palach, the engineer who's building the bridge, who when I first met him seemed even stranger to me than Ario, but when I got to know him I quite liked him, because he is a man with a good heart. When we traveled to Bahia Azul together, they came to pick us up at home for the first time; Ma peeked at them through the window, and when she saw Palach she calmed down a bit, she was even glad that we were taking Bella's children with us, because it was their first time at Bahia Azul. On the beach Palach looked at Do, and Ario kept pushing her onto him, and afterwards, when we swam in the water together, he embraced me and tried to come inside me without a condom; I was a little angry with him, but when we came home we took a shower together and afterwards we went to bed and it was a pleasure. Ario made sex with his eyes closed, but I like looking at our contrasting colors mingling, and also at his face because when it strains the eye-lids begin to tremble. Whenever I went to Benguela to learn about the computer from Do, I would pass the bridge that he and Palach are building, and the more I saw it progressing the more it bothered me. Ario said it would take them two years to build the bridge, and he didn't know what would happen afterwards, if he would stay or not, so even though I know a lot of things can happen in two years, I guarded my heart from him, although it didn't look that way from outside, because I would jump on every phone call of his, and on the days when we didn't meet I felt something missing and I was a little impatient. Then he got sick with malaria, and something changed, in both of us.

I'm not stupid. I knew that Ario only came here for two years, and we didn't owe each other anything, and I was fine with it. We had interesting conversations, and sweet moments, and a strong attraction, but the wall that stood between us because of the limited time hanging over us collapsed when he got sick; suddenly I met him all over again when he was vulnerable and weak, and my heart was taken by him, and his by me.

When the doctor told him it was malaria, I felt a wonderful relief, because malaria has a cure. I watched over him on the days of delirium, until the drugs bring down the fever and the person returns to being who he was. When his fever went up he spoke his language from Israel, which sounds like nuts being cracked, and when he woke up I would feed him tea like a baby, and wipe the sweat from his face. Ario is a funny guy, but on the days of the malaria the sad man inside him came out, and he held my hand, and he didn't let go even when he got better. Instead of talking about Angola and Israel, we talked about Ario and Armanda. In the darkness of the room he told me that sometimes he feels the world doesn't make sense, and he's afraid something bad will happen to his body, and sometimes he

takes drugs against this feeling, which started when he was a soldier in
the Israeli army, and sometimes he feels that he isn't doing anything
with his life, that it's just passing without any purpose, day after day,
like I sometimes feel too, and this feeling makes him sink even further into his idleness. I didn't tell these things to Do, or other things
either, which I told Ario during the wonderful days of the malaria.
Do noticed the change immediately, she told me to be careful because
it was clear he had entered my heart. But it was too late. I had fallen
in love with him, and he confessed that he had fallen in love with me
long ago. He promised to pay for my studies next year, he even said
that he'd take me for a visit to Israel, and dreams began to blossom
in my head, and the more I think about it the harder I cry, and my
whole body fills with nerves because of his lie.

Do comes into our room and finds me crying under the pillow. She
sits down on the edge of the bed, strokes my back and whispers, "Stop
it, Armanda, nobody is worth your tears." I try to calm down, but
the tears go on coming, and I surrender and let them flow. All day
I had a terrible feeling. Yesterday I didn't stay to sleep at Ario's but
came home instead; I was a bit surprised that he didn't call me like
he always does in the morning when we don't wake up together, but
I didn't attach too much importance to it, and I made the children
breakfast, and sent them to school, each with his little plastic chair
and his bag with toast and fruit for lunch. Afterwards I went to the
hairdresser and had the hairdo that's being ruined now under the
pillow, and then I took a kandongero and rode to Benguela to sit at
the computer with Do, and when I passed the bridge and didn't see
their pickup there, I tried to call Ario but the telephone was disconnected, and an uneasy feeling began to develop in my stomach, and
I went on trying to call every hour, but I couldn't concentrate at all
when I sat at the computer with Do; and when we went home in the
afternoon and again I didn't see their pickup next to the bridge I said
to Do I had a feeling that something had happened. And when we
passed the hill of Catumbela-Nomoro, I peeped though the window
of the kandongero at their corner house, but I couldn't see anything,
and when we reached Lobito I said to Do that I had to go back

there to see what was going on, even though I knew that if I went to Catumbela and back I would be late for making supper and bathing the children. Do suggested that I go there later, in the evening, but I couldn't wait. I took a scooter-taxi and all the way I held my head with my hand, so my hairdo wouldn't be ruined.

Little by little I calm down, and Do takes the pillow off my head and makes my neck feel good with her hands. "Enough, it's over," I say to her still lying down, and she says, "Good, then get up and let's see that pretty face smiling," and I say quietly, "I didn't mean the crying, I meant Ario," and Do asks, "What, you split up?" and I say, "No, he just ran away," and I sit down on the bed, and Do opens her eyes wide at me and asks, "What does that mean, ran away, ran away where?" and I say, "How should I know where, he's simply not here;" suddenly Yola opens the door and says, "Armanda, Ma wants to talk to you;" "Tell her I'm bathing," I say, and I quickly take clean panties out of the closet and the bag with things for bathing, and Yola, still standing in the doorway, asks, "Why did you cry, Armanda," and I put my hand on her head while peeking into the passage to see if the way is clear, and say to her, "It's to do with love, Yola," and she says, "If it's love then why are you crying," and I reply, "That's how it is, Yola, tell Ma I'm coming in a minute." Then I slip away from her to the bathroom, lock the door behind me, look in the mirror, and feel glad I didn't go out like this to Ma.

I take off the tank-top, the trousers and panties, and throw them into the laundry basket, then I wash out the tub from the little ones' dirt, fill a whole pail and get in and sit on the cold enamel. I sink the blue jug into the pail, remove it heavy and dripping, and pour the water slowly over my body. After three jugs I stand up to soap myself, and I scrub myself all over, careful of the ruined hairdo, then I sit down again to rinse off the soap without getting the whole bathroom wet. Bella knocks on the door and says, "Get a move on, Armanda, other people have to shower too," and I shout back at her, "I've only been in here for five minutes, why are you pestering me already," and she goes away. I dry myself thoroughly and stand naked in front of the mirror, wash my face and start smearing on the face cream Ario bought me. He was always bringing me little gifts, he almost always knew exactly what I needed, and sometimes I would give him a hint too. My time with him was like a bubble outside the time here, at home, in Lobito, and he said that for him I was like a refuge from the world. I can't say that I really fell in love with him with all my heart and soul, because I still couldn't rely on him being something permanent and not passing, but I saw him as an option, a dreamy kind of option, with a man as soft as him. He always exaggerated everything, and from every little thing he knew how to make something big, and maybe his illogical attitude towards me is part of his exaggerations. What didn't he say to me? "I love you," "I'm your captive," "I want to take care of you," and all kinds of other things that seeped right into me until they got stuck there, like a potbelly. I smear his cream on my face, and I feel it sinking in, cooling my cheeks and soothing my forehead. If he'd cheated on me with some other girl, I could have forgiven him, but like this, without saying anything, after letting me believe? And for what? I would have stayed with him even if I knew he was going to leave so quickly, maybe it would have been less confusing like that, but why did he have to say all the things he said to make me believe I had entered his heart, and then vanish without a word?

I got this hairdo today for him, and now I try to fix it in front of the mirror and freshen up the hair, although there's nothing left from the bottles in it. I stretch the extensions a little and try to curl them round my finger, and this puts a bit of life back into the hairdo, but it doesn't gleam like when I walked out of the hairdresser this morning, and afterwards I put on my panties, wrap the towel around me, and go to the room to get dressed.

Do is waiting for me here, sitting on her bed, leaning against the wall and writing to someone on her cell phone. I drop the towel and put on a white bra, and Do asks, "Well, so what happened there, Armanda?" "Where?" I ask, and she says, "In Ario's house," and I say, "I found Kandido, who works for them there; he told me that they left this morning, with their suitcases and everything." "And he didn't say anything to you?" she asks, and I say, "Not a word, not even a hint." "What a coward," she says, and I thread myself into my purple skirt, fasten the zipper that goes from the waist to the thigh and say, "At least he could have called to say goodbye," then I take the embroidered blouse off its hanger, put it on and turn to Do to lace me up at the back, and while she ties the laces, she says, "Why don't we go out today?" and her little fingers tickle my back. I say casually, "Francisco was here before," and Do pinches me behind my back and says, "What did he want all of a sudden?" and I say, "He must have smelled something, all it needed was for someone to see them leaving in the pickup with the suitcases and you can be sure it reached his ears." "There you are, you're all laced up," she says, and we sit down on our beds and I say, "It's like getting a slap in the face," and Do says, "Perhaps it's better this way, Armanda," but I can't get over my anger. And we begin to chew it all over again, and suddenly my cell phone rings, and we both freeze. An unfamiliar number appears on the screen, and when I hear Francisco's voice on the other end I cover the mouthpiece and say to Do, "It's Francisco." "Ask him how he knows," she says, and I say, "Are you crazy? I don't want him to know that it matters to me at all," and I talk for a minute to Francisco, who says he's just stepped out of the bar on his way to the discotheque, so if I intend coming to meet him I should know that he's there; and I tell him that if I want to meet him I can call him up and ask him to pick me up when I'm ready and take me wherever I feel like going; Do claps her hands in the air, and grabs her mouth so he won't hear her laughing, then Ma knocks on the door and opens it, and I hang up.

Mamma holds onto the door frame and looks at us sitting on the beds, sniffing the air, as if words have a smell. "Should I put Papa to bed?" I ask for the sake of asking, and Mamma says, "Papa is still sitting outside, Armanda, and I'm waiting for you in the kitchen;" Do asks, "Is the bathroom free?" and Mamma says, "Bella's there, you can go in after her," and she beckons me to follow her.

When we're sitting in the kitchen she bores holes in me with her eyes, waiting to hear what I have to say, until I give in. "What do you want to know?" I ask, and she says, "I spoke to Linda's mother, you really were in church today." "Right," I say, "I already told you." "And what were you doing in church?" she asks, and I say, "What do you mean? I go there sometimes," and she says, "Since you've been with that white man of yours you haven't been there once, what made you go today?" And I say, "I felt like it today." She keeps quiet for a moment and her eyes wander round the room as if she's looking for something she's forgotten, then they come to rest on me, and she says, "So you're not going to tell me, Armanda?" I still try to avoid the issue so I ask, "Tell you what?" and she says, "Tell me why your face is like that," and I understand that I no longer have a choice so I say, "He left." "That I already know," Ma says, "Asli's sister's son works at the airport, he saw your white man on his way to Luanda today." I stare at her and ask quietly, "Did he say anything else to you?" "What else could he tell me, Armanda?" Ma asks, and I say, "How long have they gone for?" Again her eyes glide around the room, and I ask, "What, Ma, did he say anything to you?" and she says, "I see you've made up your mind." "Made up my mind to what?" I say, and she replies, "Made up your mind to hide from me the fact that you're pregnant." "I'm not pregnant, Ma, I swear to you," I say to her. "So why did he run away from you all of a sudden?" she asks, and I say, "I don't know why, Ma," and the tears well up in my eyes again. Ma grabs hold of my wrist and says, "Armanda, swear to me," and I say, "I swear to you by all that's dear to me, Ma, I'm not pregnant," then she gets up from her chair, puts her arms around me and says, "Enough, Armanda, enough crying for him. As long as you're not pregnant, nothing's happened. Pull him out of your heart like a thorn and forget him. I knew from the start that he wasn't a good man for you." "He was a good man for me, you just don't like him because he's white," I say, and Ma answers, "White or black, it makes no difference, a good man is a man who also stays with you," and we extricate ourselves from the embrace, and Bella shouts from the passage, "The bathroom's free." Then she comes into the kitchen with the towel wrapped around her, all smelling of soap, and goes out to the yard on her way to her room. Ma says to me, "It's time you found yourself a job, otherwise you'll be dependent on your man like your sister," and I say, "I'll start looking tomorrow," and Ma says, "Let Do help you with her connections at the warehouses, you already know how to work on the computer," and I say, "Yes, I've already learnt most of it from her." Then Ma grips my wrist tightly, shakes it and says, "You have a good head. You can get ahead, you hear me, Armanda," and I say, "I know, I'm still young." "It would be a good thing if you started going to church again too," Ma continues, and I say, "First I'll find work," and Do shouts from the passage, "I'm going in." A minute later Yola bursts out of her room and shouts, "I'm next," and Ma shouts back to them, "Be quieter, girls," and she signals to me that I can go, but before I leave the kitchen she says to me, "A stone has been lifted from my heart, Armanda, I really thought you'd gotten yourself into trouble with him." I return to the room, sit down on the bed, and wait for Do to come out of the shower; we'll make ourselves up and go out to the discotheque, and I think about how Ario left the opposite of a pregnancy in me. He left a void in me.

Translated by Dalya Bilu

BEN VERED was born in Azur, Israel, in 1978. He studied law at the Hebrew University of Jerusalem, and is at present doing his legal internship at the Rishon le Zion Court. Vered was also the editor of the Hebrew University students' magazine. He won First Prize in the IDF Literary Competition (1999) during his military service, and *Makor Rishon*'s Short Story Competition (2005). *Summer Dogs* is his first novel.

Three lonely people are trying to escape their dull lives and their memories. Skarzisko, an eccentric, lonely old man needs someone to clean up his yard. Fourteen-year-old Henrietta, feeling deserted by her mother, and in conflict with her father, answers his advertisement, and a unique relationship develops between them. The narrative also takes us into the inner world of her mother, Kahina, who is hospitalized in a psychiatric facility, and explores how her delusion of being the Queen of the Berbers comes from her childhood as an orphan in the Atlas mountains of Morocco.

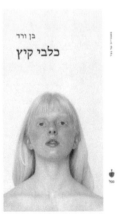

Summer Dogs

Tel Aviv, Babel, 2006, 320 pp.

Ben Vered

Summer Dogs

I
An excerpt from the novel

n the mountains, she was wide open to the light.

"You, go fetch water," the old women would say to her because Kahina's legs were as sturdy as the cedars sticking up in the valley. From the moutaintop the cedars looked like nails stuck into the ground and in the dark you could see green demons gliding among them. She delighted in the way down to the pool, the empty leather bags on her tail, skipping and getting full of dust like blind moles. Her long black hair was tied with a green cord, and when the village disappeared behind the rocks she would untie the knot and it would pour down her back like a cascade of water. On her way down she would long for the Father-of-a-hundred-days to come back with his bags full. A father coming home, like most of the men in the village, at the end of three months work in the towns. She liked to see him in his thin cloth shoes, sitting on top of the goods piled on the big truck, all around him frightened chickens with one leg tied to a stone, dropping their excrement in all directions, soiling the brightly colored textiles, the wool and the silk ribbons. After the truck was unloaded, she would walk proudly by his side, so that everyone would know that she too had a father and she had not been abandoned to their mercies. At home he would sit with the newspaper in his hands, from time to time he would read her what was written there and show her pictures from faraway places. When nobody was looking she too would hold the soft paper in her hands, look at the rounded letters, rows and rows of them, dancing like little ants, and stroke them wonderingly with her fingers. She envied the men: if only she could, she too would have left the village which was swarming with evil instincts and dark suspicions. And perhaps it was the same for everyone who lost their mother when they were so young they couldn't even remember her face, their roots were short, their grip was loose, and a light wind could carry them away. The earth was not a person's motherland, it never had been, there was no such thing as mother earth, there was no land flowing with milk and honey. The only motherland was a mother flowing with milk and flesh and blood.

And in the meantime, until her stepfather returned, she would run to the pools and waterfalls, raising clouds of yellow-brown dust, long and convoluted, hoping for the thrill that would carry her far away, or at least relieve the boredom. And when the leather sandals tautened on her feet, the lizards and the agamas, the snakes and the birds fled in all directions, they all knew, Kahina was charging. Her thoughts wandered to the old folks' stories about Adam and Eve who were created from the dark rain-drenched earth, to their naked limbs clutching each other, to the games of approach and withdrawal which only came in order to unite them. The story of creation fired her imagination, it had struggle, sensuousness, desire and even love, and it also had playing with mud. She wanted to know where Adam and Eve came from and what happened after them, but the old people couldn't tell her.

It was autumn and the soft sun called her to go out to the rocks. The village was empty of men, distilled and steeped in melancholy, and their place was taken by the mountains, silent and commanding. When winter came the women were tucked into their houses like peas in a pod. The domestic animals too obeyed the sentence, submitted to the sign of order and wandered idly through the rooms without dreaming of running away, and only the old people and the babies stuck out their heads to the light, pleading for a sunbeam, toothless and hairless, buried in thick blankets so as not to catch a chill, looking at each other and laughing.

Ever since she was born Kahina had found it difficult to grasp the world. This difficulty appeared in speech and in understanding what was happening around her. Life decided to make her up of opposites. Even though she was hard of understanding and heavy of thought, she showed a natural curiosity and possessed an insatiable thirst for knowledge. She was very late in saying her first words, and in the first years of her life everyone thought that she was dumb. She was like one of the domestic animals wandering in and out and they sometimes found her wallowing among the beasts with her clothes filthy. Even when they put shoes on her she would come back with her feet dirty because she gave her sandals to strangers or threw them from the cliff, and watched them falling into the valley. When they sent her to feed the rabbits, she would forget to close the cages, and the rabbits would scamper about, left to their own devices. The eggs she gathered from the broody hens she would absent-mindedly leave by the roadside, a prey for wild animals, and in the evening she would be found wandering round the village, as if she had not been sent to collect the eggs, wild flowers in her hair, immersed in her inner world which had nothing to do with the world surrounding her. Sometimes she could be seen chasing a chicken with a stick in her hand, intending to kill it, terrified by the bird that flapped its wings but could not fly. Tasks that required more attention, like taking care of the elderly and the babies, and cleaning the house, were beyond her. Everyone regarded her with indifference and spared her their pity. An orphan seeking a kinsman to depend on, a parent to follow, a kind soul who would answer the questions welling up in her about the world. But in the little village in the mountains, there was no guiding hand to be found, and the many hands that were held out to her were hands that meant her harm and found their way to pinch and slap her cheeks, her arms and her buttocks. Children with no parents and family are free game, unprotected. For the most part she didn't understand why she was being beaten, and nevertheless her pride did not allow her to cry, and since she did not cry she was only taken for more of a fool and the blows increased. When the boys approached her, flushed and panting in the sunlight, she had the strength to fight back and repulse them. At night things were different. The blood flooded their eyes and the fire burned in their loins, she had no choice but to bite her hair and part her legs until the passion was spent.

Against all the odds she found a life to cling to in the village and established herself as the owner of a good pair of hands. Sewing, patching, and even weaving turned into works of art in her hands. Delicate handicraft, demanding concentration and dexterity, imagination, patience and good taste, was a talent she was born with and it served as an escape from the harshness of the life assailing her from every quarter. Rags and tatters were conjured by her racing fingers into little coin purses, an impressive sheath, or a splendid ornament. With her two hands she succeeded in saving old dresses, cloaks that had gone to the dogs, shirts and bandanas doomed to extinction, and giving them new life. A picked apart bed cover turned into light summer blouses, a righteous man's robe turned into a bridal gown, a torn bandana into a wall decoration, a pair of old trousers she succeeded in patching into three bags, and a tattered carpet was transformed by her fingers into a magnificent saddle. A woman who doesn't know how to weave, said the village women, isn't a woman at all.

But most of the time she was a stranger to everyone, and everyone was a stranger to her. Who are these people around me? she would ask, seeking an answer from the mysterious force hiding in the reservoir waters. Why are they persecuting me? she asked the force riding on the winter winds. What do the green demons want of me, what are these mountains surrounding me? The hidden force was everywhere, that she knew. It was enough to look at the people of the village rolling their eyes to heaven and talking to it. She wanted to do as they did, but she felt it wasn't proper. Although the force was all around her at all times, it couldn't be addressed in all places at all times, but only in its own place, and only in solitude. She kept her leisure moments only for it, and devoted herself to its big toys, the pools and waterfalls. She would drop the leather gourds into the cold water, kick off her sandals and jump in in her clothes, disappearing into the depths, hidden from the village and the mountains. In her imagination threads of many colors were woven into mats and carpets. Patterns of animals and flowers, palaces and princesses floated before her eyes.

One day she lay fainting from the heat on a wet rock whose dampness came from the pool water, her body drinking in the sunshine, her garments slowly drying, and she sighed with pleasure. Deaf to the noise of the waterfall, her body grew heavier until she fell asleep, with her leather sandals blazing next to her head. She opened her eyes and groped with her fingers before she looked, and saw a slender shadow on the other side of the pool. She sat up, covering her half naked body with her dress, adjusting her sight to the glare. A strange boy, short of stature, wearing a colorful striped tunic, looked at her. His mule waited below, with bundles of firewood on its back. He stared at her legs, shapely from climbing the mountains, at the cloth bodice sticking to her chest. Even after being caught he did not take his eyes off her and he smiled at her with a mouth full of sun. She clenched her fists and waved them at him, but the boy was not so quickly frightened off.

As evening fell she hurried home—the mountains were dangerous, at night everyone huddled together. Now windows opened in the eyes of the women and the little village sank into twilight and repose. The women lit fires, brewed tea, and filled the air with a pungent smell. The old people gathered slowly, moving like prehistoric animals towards the big square, casting a long shadow. The children skipped like lambs and there were flames in their eyes. That night a strange man arrived carrying a big string instrument, which he set on his knee and began to play. Kahina brought the man food and he stopped playing and thanked her.

"What's that?" she asked him pointing at the music-making marvel. But the stranger chewed hungrily and did not answer her. "Why did you put it on your knees?" she went on questioning him, ignoring his hunger and his silence.

"That's how it's played," he said with his mouth full of food.

"Are you from down below?"

"What do you mean from down below?"

"From down below, under the mountains."

"I'm from the desert."

"I've never been to the desert."

"In the desert I lost my father and my mother."

"How were they lost?" she went on weaving her questions, squatting with her knees bent, resting on the soles of her feet, her open arms leaning in front of her. "They were lost, in other words they died, the king killed them, the desert covered their bones, swallowed them up. Now they are part of the Sahara." He went on chewing while he told the story, as if it had nothing to do with him. "I had parents too, they were also lost," she said eagerly, she had found what they had in common, already she saw them as good friends. "That's very bad," he said, "and who looks after you?"

"Another father. But he's down below," she pointed her hand, "in the cities."

The man examined her from top to toe, there was no flaw in her. "Teach me to play. If I know how to play I can go from town to town."

"I won't teach you."

"If you teach me I'll sew you a new cloak, better than the miserable one you're wearing."

"I won't teach you."

"Why?"

"Because you're a woman," he said simply. She stood up and looked at him with terrible eyes, spat at him and kicked the leather case he made haste to catch in his hands as if it contained a hidden treasure. She ran past him, absorbing his curses in her back. The next day, still upset, she took the leather gourds and dragged them noisily to the waterfall, sending up clouds of dust behind her. When she got there, she saw the boy again, standing on the distant bank, his body neatly encased in the colorful tunic. "Hey, you," she addressed him in an angry shout. He smiled at her but she didn't smile back. "Are you from the desert, did you come from there?" she shouted and pointed past his shoulder, "I'm talking to you, answer me."

"Why are you shouting at me?"

"Answer me," she said and came closer to the water, not noticing that he wasn't speaking her language, the language of the Mahgreb, the language of the Berbers.

"Don't come near me, I don't want an angry woman," but Kahina didn't care, she was used to rude men, "if you come near, I'll hit you." Determined to win him over she advanced towards him, skipping lightly over the rocks peeping out of the water.

"You're from the desert, you know how to play. You have to teach me."

"What do you want of me, go away," he pushed her away. She pushed him back and and he hit her with his fists and felled her to the ground. Blood oozed from her head, covered her eyes, streamed onto her dress. But Kahina did not give in, she pulled him down to the ground, wrestled him with all her strength. And a minute later they were already rolling between the rocks, covered with dirt and mud. He was smaller than her but his agile hands beat like hammers and gripped like a vice, for every blow she gave him, he gave her two. In the end she retreated with him on her tail. "By God, I'll kill you," he cried, "I'll drown you in the water and throw you off the mountain." Her legs were longer and faster than his and soon she disappeared from his sight and found herself among silent crags, her fists clenched and furious tears on her face, which was colored like red soil by the blood. She wandered round until she found another pool, dived into it and disappeared in its waters, the hidden force calmed her and wiped away her tears with sweet water, the leather gourds drank the water greedily, swelling like horses' bellies. She put them on her back and climbed up to the village.

At the end of autumn the men started to come back, returning to their familiar homes, which opened to welcome them one by one. The Father-of-a-hundred-days arrived with roar of engines, shaking the quiet earth, forging ahead like a giant through the crags and dirt roads. The house filled with treasures from the big city. "See what beautiful colors," she called to the women unpacking the hairy sacks and smiling at her graciously in the presence of her stepfather.

She waved the linen and woollen fabrics in the air, strummed her fingers on the skeins of wool that turned into fat balls of color in the women's hands.

"Did you take care of the house when I wasn't here?" She nodded. "I'm hungry."

"The food will be ready in a minute," she turned round and stopped, "Father, were you in the desert?"

"No, in the city."

"And in the desert?" she insisted.

"No," he chuckled. "And I have no intention of being there either," he spread a sheet of paper over his knees and began to read. She stared at him admiringly, she didn't know exactly what it was that lit the fire in her, she felt that the art of reading had something sacred about it, and the hidden force was woven into it warp and woof. "I'll be there," she hid a smile, in love with the thought, turned her gaze back to the wool and fabrics in her hands, roused herself and went to heat up the food. In winter, the cedars in the valley looked like upside-down icicles growing out of the ground. The green demons were only waiting for credulous souls to come to them, and Kahina was very careful and did all she could not to annoy them. Nevertheless, whenever she was beaten by the women or one of the little boys who had grown up came onto her with his body, she knew that the demons were behind it. The first snowflakes were dry and heavy. "This year a lot of snow will fall," said one of the old men, tightening the woolen blanket around him and blinking at the gathering clouds. Afterwards he laughed a broad, generous laugh, exposing a toothless mouth, and his eyes laughed with him. His words echoed in Kahina's head, the old men knew how to predict the weather with great accuracy. She raised her head and scanned the grey-black horizon, and out of the corner of her eye she saw that he was looking at her. "Why are you looking at me like that?" she asked him. His irises were as bright as if the years had not touched them. "How?" he answered her with naked gums.

"Like that, following me with your eyes, old man."

"I'm looking at our dear queen," he answered her sweetly.

"I'm not a queen, I'm an orphan."

"You're Kahina the Jewess, the Queen of the Berbers." She knew that he was laughing at her, for being a stranger among them. "Keep away from me, you hear?" she said and went to gather wood for the fire.

"Kahina the Jewess," the old men would call her when they were in a good mood, patting her head with their gnarled hands, "the Queen of the Berbers." But she didn't understand, she would repudiate them and their laughter, sure that they were mocking her for being an orphan.

She appealed to her father, "Why do they call me a Jewess and the Queen of the Berbers?"

"Your parents were Jews."

"And what is a Jew?"

"The people of the book," he replied and sorted out the hairy sacks, folding the torn ones and putting them on one side and the good ones on the other side, preparing for more days outside the village. At the sound of the name her imagination caught fire, she belonged to the people of the book. "What book is that?"

"I don't know."

"What, are you leaving again?" she asked and her voice trembled.

"Yes."

"Can I come with you?"

"No."

"Why?"

"You're a child, you have to stay here."

"And when I grow up?"

"Then too." He stood up and turned to other occupations.

She went up to the old men sitting in the fading light and asked them about her Jewishness. They told her that the Jews had a book which they read every day and guarded with the utmost care. They hid it from all eyes and would not allow anyone to see it. They were stubborn and brought destruction upon themselves. About Kahina they said that she was their beloved queen. And where is this Kahina, she wanted to know, but they could not tell her and they began to argue among themselves as to whether she was a queen or a princess, or maybe it was a king, whether it was a true story or a fiction, and how come every year the winter grew harder. One of the old men said that all the Jews were stupid and deaf, they wouldn't listen to anyone, and Kahina was nothing but a fairytale they invented to win respect.

"And this child is unclean," he said and spat at her feet, "and deserves a beating. If she would only disappear, the whole village would be blessed." The old men nodded their heads and Kahina went away.

Translated by Dalya Bilu

From the Classics

LEA GOLDBERG (1911–1970) was born in Königsberg, East Prussia (now Russia). After completing her Ph.D in semitic languages at Bonn University, she immigrated to pre-state Israel in 1935.

Goldberg was a member of the Shlonsky group of modern poets. She was also a successful children's author, a theater critic, translator and editor. In 1952, she established the Department of Comparative Literature at the Hebrew University of Jerusalem, which she chaired until her death. Goldberg published 10 books of poetry and two novels, as well as plays, essays, and children's books. She was awarded many prizes, including the Israel Prize for Literature (1970). Her work has been published in 27 languages.

Lea Goldberg's first novel is a series of letters written by Ruth during her

tour of Europe in 1934. Whether this journey is real or imagined is unclear, but it brings out the writer's deepest thoughts about European culture in the years leading up to World War II, as well as her sensitivity to evil portents. On the personal level, Ruth's letters to Emanuel reveal a sad, unrequited love, leading to a double farewell – to Emanuel and to Europe.

Letters from an Imaginary Journey

1937; Tel Aviv, Hakibbutz Hameuchad/ Sifriat Poalim, 2007. 180 pp.

Lea Goldberg

Letters from an Imaginary Journey

An excerpt from the novel

*E**vening in the room was as familiar and as inexplicable as a pet dog laying his head in his master's lap. Ruth flicked through some foreign-language poems and marvelled at the fact that she hadn't written them. There was the grief of distant cities in the poems, and the human faces in them flickered and passed on—pale and lofty—like the tops of towers floating in train windows. She remembered the train windows... She wrote:*

Berlin, 21.10.34
Hotel Bamberger-Hof

Dear Emanuel,

A sensation long since familiar: the train is approaching Berlin and I am once again the fifteen-year-old schoolgirl hurrying for the first time to an interview. When the train reaches Schlesicher Bahnhof and races on towards Alexanderplatz, and I know, know so well, that on the way to the Zoological Garden it passes by the green carpet of the Tiergarten, and I interpret the expectations of the roof-tops crowding around me—I can't help thinking, this is the city whose streets my feet loved so much. A strange sentimentality assailed me: I'm not in the habit of weeping out of emotion, but I resemble a person moved to tears.

From the train window I see one of those nights that have not yet happened here—and think: the city will meet me at Zoo Station. It received me there once before.

But the city didn't come out to greet me. There was the stark light of flickering electric lamps, a few station employees, bare rails yearning to leave this city. No one was waiting for me. No one was waiting for the others. Only two or three got down from the train. On the other side of the tracks the municipal train stopped, almost empty on its last trip for this Monday night. The little clown who was riding on my heart and kicking the wall of my chest with his long legs, scoffed: "You could recite the funeral prayer over this city!" but there was sadness in that too.

At the hotel they knew I was coming, but I felt no inclination to hurry towards that unknown building. I left my suitcases at the station and set out on foot. The short and familiar distance between the station and Bambergerstrasse was a pleasant enough walk.

But the streets were strange to me. The big store windows, half-lit and empty, were like the blind eyes of a princess from a fairytale. Only in one of them, under an ice-cream advertisement, a red and black swastika was revolving.

When I came out into Tauenzienstrasse the darkness was astonishing—perhaps this wasn't darkness, perhaps it was emptiness. At this hour, which wasn't late at all, I was pursued by lines from Kastner's poem:

> *At night the streets are so empty*
> *Just now and then*
> *One car symbolizes traffic…*

And I'm livid. Like Jonah, I have spared this gourd on which I have not labored, which my forefathers did not plant.

I loved you once, Berlin. I loved the foppery and the ostentation here in these streets and the dark looks in the Wedding district, the gleam in the storefront windows of K.D.W.—Kaufhaus des Westens—the smell of salt in Alexanderplatz, your varied form, incomprehensible as the mind of a kinsman. And before me now is a strange and unfamiliar city.

It could be that a few years from now we will meet this way, El. My train will rave and whoop as it approaches you, but you won't be at the station. And when I come out to you, I shall find a look with all its buttons fastened, a cold hand bearing me only a little hatred. And that will be you.

In K.D.W. the windows were still lit; big and desperate they looked out into the street. And for some reason the building gave the impression of a mountain hovering in the center of the city. This was the way I used to return home from the theater or from visiting friends. At night, by the windows of the department store, smartly turned-out whores used to circulate, wrapped in furs and shod in high-heeled boots up to the knee. Red, yellow or black. I remember how astonishing it was to my nineteen-year-old brain when I discovered that the color of the boots signalled a different "class" of whore. Black—for sadists; yellow—for masochists, and red—for those with "conventional" taste. This classification followed me like a personal reproach. There weren't many things I could forgive mankind. Now, this business would not astonish me, although, to my eternal bemusement, I still belong to the category of people capable of being shocked and ashamed. My inner self has not yet become a foundry for the manufacture of skeptical smiles over every woe that may or may not transpire. But things like these…In the north of the city and on Nollendorfplatz, groomed and preening boys are strolling, waiting for customers. They could still be listening to their mothers telling them the fable of the goat and the wolf and the goat's revenge, and believing that in the real world virtuous, victorious goats exist. They could be sitting on a school bench reading an introduction to anarchism…In crowded taverns in the east of the city, little girls are weeping, chastised by their loved ones for "neglect of duty" during the night; drinking beer and weeping, weeping and drinking beer— one way or the other, which is worse?

Here, at the corner of two streets, Tauenzien and Passauer, there was always a blonde girl walking to and fro, wearing black fur and high red boots. About seventeen, perhaps only sixteen. On cold and rainy nights she used to stand here, and her face—only slightly embellished—was very cheerful. My face, when passing her, was gloomy, but she would smile and look at me with a kind of unfathomable friendship. Sometimes it seemed she wanted to make my acquaintance, and I couldn't forgive her for not hating me. I was ashamed that I came from the theater, that I had spent the day at the university, that if anyone should dare to approach me in this dark street, I would pass him by with a look of contempt blended with fear, go up to my room, insulated from all the world, and sleep. Because she will go to the doctor a few years from now and hear, with hatred, his confirmation of everything that her fears have promised her; a few years further on, having had no treatment at all, faded and ugly, she will stand in Bellevue Square and be "cheap," the place of the red boots will be taken by a huge leather wallet; and in one of the banks perhaps an account will grow and prosper, but there will no longer be any need to return to Ernst or Otto, on whose behalf the "business" once began, because Otto will have two children and a petulant wife, a past life as an experienced waiter and an unemployment certificate in his pocket, nor will there be the inclination or the energy to rent a small apartment and live quietly, without strangers, without men, according to the idealistic scheme of the times; there will be no one to whom the sum deposited in the bank can be bequeathed, not a small sum by any means (the rates on Tauenzienstrasse were quite reasonable). As for me—I shall never have a bank account. I shall follow my course from frugality to frugality, from loneliness to loneliness, but, to paraphrase Ecclesiastes, "My garments will be always white and my head will not lack for oil." And I was ashamed in front of her with the searing shame of my nineteen years. Don't mock, El, this was long ago…Now I'm ashamed of being ashamed.

I wanted to see her again, and there on the other side of the house I caught a glimpse of red boots, but the autumn raincoat was old and worn, and the head above it was aging and ugly. Morals haven't changed under the National Socialist regime—they have been devalued.

Bambergerstrasse was always empty at these times, but the few passers-by were sociable people who enjoyed a joke. I remember one evening when I was returning home at a vigorous pace, and my shoes were pounding the pavement like the beat of a drum, an elderly German chased me for ten minutes just so he could say to me, in a barely comprehensible dialect: "Oha! She's walking like a girl who knows what she's doing!"

And today this is the haunt of lonely shadows, wandering without pleasure.

The door. My hotel. The building hasn't changed. The landlady, a Jewess from eastern Europe. The hotel dates from about 1919 and I am astonished to find it still standing today. It has undergone all the troubles of every era, yet it stands and survives. When Berlin was the center of Russian migration, Andrei Bieli lived here. He used to envy the fish for the happiness that the Creator gave them in the depths of the sea, and day after day he would sing the praises of his father, Professor Bugayev, promising that of all the dances there was a future only for the "non-stop quadrille" (he used to dance Number 8 on the floor), and he disappeared from here one fine day, when no one expected it. In times of inflation, millions were born and died here, billions and trillions. In times of unemployment, apprentice barbers and stenographers wept here in their rooms over those who had driven them from their jobs, then they left without paying their bills and were lost among the crowds at the municipal fair, four million strong. Now, everyone here is confused, pale and whispering—the frying pans whisper in the kitchen, landlady and chambermaid whisper in the corridor, residents whisper in their rooms. It all gives the impression of a conspiratorial cell, preparing weapons for a revolution, but no revolutions will be born here.

The window of my room overlooks the street. And after a whole day of running hither and thither, attending to my affairs, I am tired but don't want to sleep. From time to time the tram stops outside my window, and I know: no one will get off here, no one will direct his steps towards my room. All my friends left long ago. And yet despite this, tomorrow I have a rendez-vous with two loved ones from days gone by (if only you were capable of envying me a little!), with two who never change, who in the midst of this unfamiliar Berlin, among the swastikas and the brown shirts, have preserved their precious and profound individuality—one with an engaging smile, the other with grief strong enough to shake the very foundations of existence: "The Young Master" of Botticelli and Ribera's "Saint Sebastian."

The night sleeps outside my window.

At night the streets are so empty…

Have a peaceful night, El. Don't see me in your dreams tonight. I'm not coming back to you.

Ruth

XV

Paris, 10.11.34

My dear boy, our Emanuel,

When I woke up this morning it was cold in the room and through the window I saw the first flakes of snow dancing in the air. No one was expecting it and it came as a small miracle, like a strange and unexpected memory. The street isn't white yet, just patches of lightness here and there, like those anemones in Heidelberg. Soon they too will melt and there will be muck in the street. But for the moment snow is falling, real snow. And at the corner of the street the dark-skinned woman, wearing an overcoat and a gigantic grandma bonnet, has lit a small brazier and is standing there now, shouting: "Marrons!"—chestnuts. In the midst of the whiteness and the swirling dust of the street—a reddish flame. And the few people passing by my window look very cold indeed.

A workman approaches the woman and buys from her a portion of "marrons." I see through the window that he's joking and shivering and warming his hands over the fire. It may be that an hour from now, when I leave the house, I'll meet him on the bridge and he'll say to me with a mocking contraction of his eyes, his teeth chattering from the cold: "Voulez-vous un apéritif, mademoiselle?" He'll whistle cheekily while I pass by him with head bowed, making no reply. And I shall know that he's cold, and that all the same he too is stimulated, for some reason, by this rare whiteness—the snow.

The street is almost empty. I have never seen it so empty, quiet and strange. And I remember in spite of myself a very distant winter morning in a small town in central Russia. Sunday, bells ringing and the street very quiet. Just a few people on their way to church, and I sitting by the window feeling a powerful urge to join them. Even as a child I was a little saddened by other people's festivals. And here too—three tall women, straight-backed, dressed in black like figures from an antique woodcut—long wax candles in their hands. A gift to the church? Atonement for sins? But as they come closer I see that what looked to me from a distance like candles are in fact quite simply—long white loaves of Parisian bread, which always remind me of candles—my Catholicism is somewhat flimsy!

And anyway, anyway the snow in this long, gray street with its tall houses crammed together is not the snow of those childhood expanses. It isn't the snow of those barren steppes, stretching from horizon to horizon, with only the iron of the tracks crossing them, like an incision in the flesh of that hapless victim, the earth. And it's impossible to believe that a train passes this way, that the foot of man treads these plains; when the snow envelops them, they grow even bigger, and as sad as the tables abandoned in a house after *havdala*, when the white cloths on them still preserve a glimmer of the sabbath, and the emptiness all around them knows it is a secular day. No, the snow here isn't the snow of those little towns, with the huge onion-shaped towers of the churches, the snow-covered crosses and screeching ravens flying about them, with the silvery gleam of frost on the branches of poplars, over which the teacher in school recited the innocent poem by Fett, and the legend of ice on the windows, painted by that genius of the homeland—Chirlionis.

The snow here has a special language of its own, and for that reason I can't think today as I look out of the window, in the words of Bialik:

"Chill of the morning, screech of the raven…"

That is why I think of this snow in its own language, a language that was so alien to me—in the French lyrics of Francis Jamme:

A few days from now, it will snow
I remember last year
I remember my unhappiness…

There is no brightness in the snow and it does indeed remind me of the griefs of yesteryear—sadness soft as the white anemones falling from the sky. There was a lot of it. There were very bright days of snow and for some reason I always interpreted days such as these as liable to bring the greatest despair. Was I right? I don't know, when did the greatest pain and despair come upon me—winter days or other days? Perhaps they were always with me.

And the snow is falling, my first snow of this winter, the last gift of Europe. Apparently, I shall not see this white dance again for many years. It seems to me the city is bidding me farewell with a little sorrow.

Where will I be, when skies capable of embracing clouds of snow are no longer stretched out above me? Where will you be?

Ruth

Translated by Philip Simpson

A Story

YEHUDIT HENDEL was born into a rabbinic family in Warsaw, Poland, and immigrated to Haifa as a child in 1930. A well-known author, Hendel has published six novels, four collections of short stories and a book of essays. Many of her works have been adapted for stage, screen, radio and TV. Among other awards, Hendel has received the Jerusalem Prize, the Bialik Prize (1996), and the Israel Prize for Lifetime Achievement (2003). Her work has been published abroad in 14 languages.

This powerful collection of stories gives us a rare look at the loneliness of old people and the emptiness that both surrounds and lies ahead of them. Yet the obsessive characters that Hendel depicts here, and the ones that most fire the imagination, are the most realistic she has ever created.

The Empty Place

Tel Aviv, Hakibbutz Hameuchad/Siman Kriah, 2007. 114 pp.

Yehudit Hendel

The Dancer

I used to meet him sometimes in the street or in the park opposite my house. Over the years we became friends in a way, and he would nod to me as old friends do, and perhaps we were old friends, because he apparently had lived here for years, like me. And over the years he also told me that his name was Haim-Shmuel. His name was really Shmuel, but he had been very sick and added the name Haim (life), in order to recover and have a long life.

Recently I met him in the park. I sat on a bench in the shade of the tall treetops, and he asked whether he could sit next to me.

Certainly, gladly, I said.

I'm glad to meet you too, he said, after all, we've known each other for years.

Gladly, I replied.

Suddenly he stood up and began to dance.

He dances like a monkey, said the children in the park laughing.

He stood under a tree as though confronting a storm. It seemed to me that the treetop bent over, as though bowing down to him and trying to protect him, and he jumped and hid behind the tree, standing there for a long time, hugging the trunk with his two hands and pressing himself against it hard. It seemed to me that it was a lone tree in the park, and he hugged it hard, waiting.

The children suddenly stopped laughing and didn't open their mouths.

He's not a monkey, he's a human being, I said.

It's all from God, he said, life, fate, and it's all a mystery, me, you, dancing, life.

But he dances like a monkey, the children said again laughing.

I said again, he's not a monkey, he's a human being.

He's a human being who dances like a monkey, laughed the children. But he appeared from behind the tree and resumed dancing in the park.

Is that what you do at home too? I asked.

Yes, I dance, he said while dancing, I dance all the time, as long as I dance I'm alive, because life is one big dance, you go around and around and get dizzy. And don't you dance? he asked.

No, I said.

So what do you do all day?

I try to write, and it's almost hard labor.

I understand, he said. Try to dance, release your hands and your feet, it will be easier for you, believe me.

I'll try, I said.

Excellent, he said, a broad smile spreading over his face, and still he danced. You'll feel better, believe me.

I believe, I said.

In God too? he asked.

I don't know, I don't have an answer to that, I said.

I believe in God because life is hard, he said.

Very hard, I said.

That's it, he said, and only God knows why, because that's how he wants it, the One who sits on high and rules the world and determines our lives and fate, and it's all one big mystery. My dance, me, you, life, everything, in general.

A wind began to blow in the park, causing the treetops to dance.

Yes, God created the wind too, believe me, and it's also a big mystery.

He continued to dance silently.

What can you do, he started talking again, that's how God created the world, and it's all one long darkness.

Perhaps, I said.

He laughed.

But the dear God has abandoned me he said, stopping helplessly.

A moment later he resumed dancing.

Sometimes I think about the force that ties a person to life, but in an old man this force disappears.

Now he stood as though a huge hole had opened up beneath him.

I ask too many questions, he said, but people think that there's order in the world, and I think there's chaos.

No, God forbid, I said.

He looked frightened now.

The worst thing is uncertainty, he said, looking around him as though a fire had broken out in the park.

And do you eat at home? I asked.

He laughed.

I like olives and fruit and a plate of soup.

You're a lion, I said.

He looked at me, annoyed.

And perhaps nevertheless I'll still enjoy God's graces, he said.

Amen, I said, and I envy you, I would also like to dance.

That's good, it does a person good, he said, starting to dance again.

Yes, yes, I said, looking at the man dancing in front of me in the park, twisting his body and waving his arms.

His face shone.

So that's what you do at home all day, I said.

Of course, thanks to this force I'm alive, and I'm an old man.

But you dance like a young man, I said.

Because that's how God wants it, he said.

This man is a strange bird, I said to myself. An old man dances in the park and he has a God.

Dancing is my life, he continued. If I stop dancing I'll die, and I still want to live, as long as I dance I'm alive.

I see, I said.

That's it, he said, I still want to live, I'm still dancing.

I'm happy, I said, and I see that you're also happy when you dance.

Of course. As long as I dance, I know that I'm alive.

So please, I said, the entire park is yours, the entire street, the entire world.

I hope so, he said.

The gleeful children had already begun to jump around him and imitate his movements.

That's not funny, I told them, it's his life, you can see that.

But they continued to shout with glee around him, and he continued to dance, and continued even after they tired and returned to their game.

And do you really dance all day long without a break? I asked.

Of course, because I don't want to die, after all, death is man's real enemy.

God save us, I said, you won't die because you dance.

I hope, I hope, he repeated, and looked to the right, and to the left, as though bells were ringing in his head.

I understand that you're afraid, I said.

Every person is afraid, he said. Everyone wants to live and is afraid to die, and death is at the door, a terrible black angel.

Everyone has his own black angel, I said, he waits at the door for everyone.

Yes, it's terrible, he said, but that's how God created the world, he didn't want us to live forever, he wanted everyone to die, everyone, and it's impossible to get a reprieve from death.

Even though he smiled a small smile, his face was gloomy, and with a gloomy face he sat down next to me on the bench.

Maybe it's good in the ground, at least it's warm there, he said, do you think there's no life in the ground? The ground is full of life. And here in the garden there are lots of ravens and bats, and the bats see at night, and what does a person see? He doesn't see even himself, he doesn't know even himself, as though he were a stranger.

They're all strangers, I said.

Strangers even to themselves, he said.

There was a long silence.

I've been walking around for years already with my face in the ground, he said.

Yes, yes, strangers even to themselves, I repeated, that's how it is in the world, and it's cold in the world.

And even in the summer it's cold inside, he said, but where will salvation come from?

He turned to me, waiting for an answer.

When he saw that I was silent he continued, what can we do, but that's how God wanted it, he created the world and the seas and the oceans, the plants and the animals, and he made human beings strange creatures.

Perhaps, I said.

He wants to win me over, I said to myself, he wants us to be friends, but we're actually strangers.

Each to himself, I said aloud.

Each to his own body, he said. You don't know what betrayal by one's body means, only old people like me know that, and betrayal by the body is a terrible thing, and every night, every night, I think about my grave, that's why I can't sleep at night, and I lie awake and think and think; the night is very long, and there's no end to thoughts, and thoughts are a cruel thing, they don't give you a moment's peace, they don't give a moment's quiet, every night I'm pierced by my thoughts until I bleed, and all in all, every person has an area the size of a grave, think about it.

And I thought, who knows about him? Who even knows of his existence? About the forces he expends on dancing in order to live. Maybe there's even heroism in that. But what heroism? After all, that's all nonsense, I said to myself. It's as though by dancing he takes his revenge against life, against fate. But maybe it only *seems* to me that that's what I thought. After all, thoughts are one great mystery, always, and great distress, I've learned that first hand.

He continued: Sometimes I tell myself that maybe I was born to dance, as though there were some relief in that thought, but that's also nonsense, believe me, and an old man lives in darkness even in daylight.

He got up from his place and started dancing again like someone drugged, trying to dance high, as high as possible.

I watched him.

Only now did I see that he was dancing with large exposed feet. He looked pale, and in the sun his glasses looked like gold, and it seemed to me he was dancing in the sun as though dancing in the dark, in conflict with himself, as though some curtain had come down on him.

And still I watched him.

You know, he said standing in front of me, I once dealt in diamonds, and I thought then that diamonds are the stars in the sky, but I discovered that they bring only a curse, so I left the diamonds and began to dance. Would you believe it?

That's your good fortune, I said, the fact is that you dance and it makes you happy.

A person is never happy, he said, he is always imprisoned in the splint of life, and at my age he already knows that everyone has an area the size of a grave, and there's no escaping that, and every night, every night I say to myself that there's the line of death and the line of life, and I'm still somehow on the line of life, but every night I'm abandoned to the line of death, and death is a black plague. They say that there's a white cat and a black cat, but next to me at night lies only a black cat, and every day I get up in the morning and think, am I still alive? Am I still here?

My body is tired at night, but my mind works, he said, and it doesn't let an old man sleep at night.

He spoke about the power of death, but I looked at him and thought about the power of life.

You'll live for many more years, I said, and you're strong, because you dance.

Because it gives me strength, and with that strength I live. At my age people already die. All my friends have died, all of them. Sometimes I think, where are my dear friends, but only empty houses remain, and I'm left alone in the world. You always remain alone and live alone, even young people, I said.

Do you think so? Do you really think so? He said.

Of course, I said, otherwise I wouldn't be brave enough to say these words.

He gave me a strange, silent look.

And do you believe in the World to Come? I asked.

Of course, he said, otherwise how would I be able to dance? I believe that I'll dance in the World to Come too, if God helps me a little.

Do you watch television? he asked suddenly.

I said I was addicted to television.

He laughed. And when he saw that I was getting up and wanted to go back home, he said, I hope we'll meet again in the park, but an old man is not allowed to say I'll be seeing you, and he resumed dancing, dancing several centimeters above the ground.

Translated by Miriam Schlusselberg

Essays

Savyon Liebrecht

Women in Israel: The Stated Truth and the Hidden Truth

I was about ten years old and already short-sighted because of bad genes and too much reading, when the teacher, a woman, sat me down on the chair nearest the blackboard.

Israel was then my age, a ten-year-old state; most of its inhabitants had immigrated from the four corners of the world, and our teacher seemed to think her most urgent task was to give us a sense of belonging and national identity. So she hung large pieces of cardboard on the classroom walls. At the top, the word "Israel" was written in large letters, and photos cut out of magazines and albums were glued onto them. One of these cardboard panels hung on the wall facing my chair, so that for many hours, in fact for the whole of that year I gazed at the profiles of men and women, secular and religious, light and dark—a large and heterogeneous group.

From all these photos, I remember three women. It is probably not accidental that we cherish a certain memory and archive another. From the top of the cardboard panel an Orthodox Jewish woman covered in a lace veil looked at me with soft eyes; she sat in a room furnished with heavy furniture and her arms were folded on her bosom. Later in life I saw similar pictures in art albums and sometimes they were called The Rabbi's Daughter. Next to it, a female kibbutznik looked at me. She stood with her legs apart, wearing work clothes and heavy boots, and holding a hoe. The beautiful girl soldier next to her looked to the side, pointing a machine gun at a target that was hidden from view.

From a distance of more than four decades, I want to examine those three mythological figures that the young teacher in a young state wanted to engrave into the minds of her pupils, and uncover the fate of those myths when they encountered reality. I do not have intimate knowledge of the Orthodox Jewish woman or the world she lives in, but it seems to me that I know the other two pretty well: I lived on a kibbutz for a year and I served in the Israeli army. If we place the three photos side by side, both the differences and the similarities immediately become apparent. The first difference is that we are talking about one Orthodox and two secular women. In Israel, their ways of life are so different that on the whole they do not meet. The Orthodox woman would not be a guest in a secular home and would not eat from the dishes or cutlery of a secular kitchen. This Orthodox woman does not watch television and does not go to see most of the plays and films that the secular woman goes to. The three women also differ in their approach to child-rearing, education, the way they dress, and the way they relate to their professional world. In the photos, all three wear modest outfits, with long sleeves buttoned up to the neck. But while the rabbi's daughter is modest and feminine, the other two are modest and masculine. Instead of the light lace blouse with pearl buttons, we have a masculine shirt made of rough material; in the picture of the soldier, the color of the uniform and the ranks on the shoulder have been added, and delicate shoes have been replaced by work or military boots.

The second difference is found in what, in the world of theater, one would call the "accessories." The Orthodox woman sits with her hands clasped, resting on her bosom. In contrast to these empty, gentle hands, the kibbutznik's hands hold a hoe, and those of the soldier, a gun.

The third difference can found in the setting. The Orthodox woman is sitting in a closed room; the other two are outside in the open air. The former knows her humble place between kitchen and bedroom; the latter have broken out of the domestic sphere into the public sphere, which used to be a male domain—the field and the military base.

However, as in life itself, what one sees is not always what is happening behind the scene. And reality has turned the picture that my teacher tried to give her young pupils upside down.

There is an interesting change going on in Israel today among religious women. Without declarations, without feminist protests, without noise or bells ringing, they are going through a quiet revolution. Many religious women are acquiring computer skills because this type of work can be done from home, and many of them prefer not to work outside the home. They have established study environments that did not exist before in the religious world. They have managed to penetrate the religious courts, the only authority that deals with divorce in Israel (also for secular Israeli Jews). In the past, these courts were male territory and therefore became known for discriminating against women. And today, women serve as pleaders facing the rabbis and usually representing and serving as watchdogs for the rights of women requesting divorce.

What we see about the female kibbutznik and the girl soldier is an illusion as well. Actually, they are much less liberated than the photos and the myth suggest.

Women in Israel do compulsory military service at the age of eighteen, immediately after graduating from high school. The length of their service changes periodically but it is about two years. During the first weeks, a girl does basic training during which she receives a large dose of "militarism"—line-ups, familiarity with different types of weapons, long marches, wake-ups in the middle of the night and target exercises. Generally, when basic training is over, she waves good-bye to her rifle for good; kitchen dishes and office equipment will replace it. She is most likely to become a secretary and make coffee for her commander and his guests.

I spent the second year of my military service as secretary to a colonel who was in a combat unit during the Six Day War, and the number of cups of coffee I made that year is far greater than during all of the following ten years.

To be fair, I should make it clear that women soldiers' jobs have changed in the decades since I served in the army. Young female soldiers have succeeded in penetrating previously all-male precincts, but most of them still serve coffee like the girls of my generation. In some places, the inclusion of women was a natural process, but in others the courts had to intervene.

In this connection, there have been two interesting court cases. About six years ago, a female soldier sued commanders in the Israel Defence Forces because they didn't allow her to test for a pilots' training course. Her case went all the way to the Supreme Court and she won. The judges instructed the Air Force to allow her to do the test. She passed and was accepted into the course as the only woman. All the other candidates were men. Like many of them, she did not complete the whole course, so she herself did not become a combat pilot, but she paved the way for other women. The second trial took place in 2007. A female soldier asked the court to release her from the duty of serving coffee to her commander, and the judge took her side.

For the first year of my military service, I was on a kibbutz. All I wanted to do then was to write, and the army allowed female soldiers to serve on kibbutzim close to the border. This was within a civil framework where female soldiers were not required to wear uniforms, but had to work eight hours a day along with the other kibbutz members. Most female soldiers had traditional women's jobs in the kibbutz kitchen, taking care of the children or sewing and ironing in the sewing workshop.

I was promised a room of my own and I believed that here I would find the conditions for writing. In fact, I wrote my very first novel there. At the kibbutz, I was an eighteen-year-old guest and I examined my new environment with curiosity. Two myths crashed for me that year—the myth of equality among the various members of the kibbutz, and the myth of equality between men and women. To my astonishment I discovered that behind the ideal, the kibbutz actually retained the mentality of a tribal society. There was a very clear hierarchy with higher and lower ranking families. However, it was a huge disappointment to discover the status of the women within their own community. She who, according to our history lessons, paved the roads shoulder to shoulder with the men, whom I saw for a whole year leaning on her hoe in the open field, found herself right back in the traditional women's places: the kitchen, the sewing workshop, and the children's rooms.

And this is how I learned an important lesson about the gap between the stated truth and the one hidden behind the myth. The Orthodox woman now walks the path of feminism without knowing its discourse, sometimes not even knowing the word "feminism." For the female kibbutz member and the woman soldier, however, the male outfit, the uniform, the ranks, the hoe and the rifle are merely "accessories," like decorations that serve every lady at a fancy-dress ball. There you have the reality of Israel.

And what—I am often asked during my visits abroad—is the role of creativity in general and of women's creativity in particular within this reality? Until about twenty years ago, women were on the margins in most areas of artistic expression. Because Israel has been in a state of war from the day it was born, and its existence is fragile, the male world was the center of life's intensity and the heart of artistic expression. In the first four decades of Israel's existence most of the artists in the fields of literature, poetry, the visual arts (painting, sculpture), cinema and theater—were men.

When Israel entered its fifth decade, about twenty years ago, a quiet revolution began, and today—maybe because women have broken through the walls of the male citadel and demanded a new, original way of thinking—women can be found at the forefront of all artistic fields. In literature, maybe more than in other areas, the voice of the Israeli woman writer (if one can make such a generalization) is fresh, clear and determined. Women write about the emotional and sexual life of women with a courage and sometimes a bluntness that men's writing does not seem to be familiar with.

The old myth of women crossing boundaries, which in the past had no place in real life, is becoming a reality today through art.

Rochelle Furstenberg

Recent Women's Writing

The 1980s witnessed a turning point in Hebrew literature. Young Israelis, weary of constant involvement with nation-building, yearned for works about personal relationships. And women's writing, reflecting sensitive psychological situations, emerged amidst great celebration. Where has this celebration of women's writing led? Almost monthly, new works by Israeli women find their way to the bestseller lists, many of them fulfilling the promise of realistic narratives about personal relationships, stories of romance, marriages, single mothers. There's been an outpouring of popular literature portraying educated women struggling to find a balance between autonomy and commitment, heightened sexual expectations and the everyday companionship of marriage. Some of these works are thin, realistic pieces lacking the multilayered suggestiveness of Israeli literature of earlier generations. This is equally true of much fiction of the younger generation of Israeli men, who also seem to be setting their sights on the bestseller list rather than on creating nuanced language and characterization. At the same time, it must be said that the realistic Israeli women's writing of the last decade has given us some fine psychological works by writers such as Zeruya Shalev, Alona Kimhi and

Avirama Golan. And most recently, a whole new batch of younger women's voices has erupted.

As a critical mass of women's fiction develops, new directions and motifs—including a fresh comic tone—can be discerned. The high-pitched sense of humor in some recent women's novels might be traced to the self-mocking tone of Orly Castel-Bloom's earlier expressionistic work, *Where Am I?*

Traces of this absurd, self-mocking tone can be found in Tamar Gelbetz's novel, *Folding* (2006) about a woman whose husband gets up one day and declares "I'm unhappy." And that is his name from then on—Imen Happy. The protagonist herself remains nameless. She's "the woman," an upper middle-class North Tel Aviv type, with one child and no economic worries. With much playfulness of language, Gelbetz transforms this common theme, the painful breakdown of a marriage into a funny-bitter, ironic depiction of the situation. As many recent Israeli women novelists, she sees herself as an outsider, in her case because she has been banished from the mainstream of domestic Israeli life. She feels a sense of shame, imagining people pointing to her and saying, "There's the one whose husband threw her out of bed and left." From this alienated point of observation, she describes everything around her in the most minute detail, creating a vision of the bourgeois life she has lost. She describes the smell of chicken soup in the hallway as people prepare Shabbat dinner, even in this secular Israeli enclave, and her sense of exclusion from the cozy, domestic world she describes so well. Inadvertently, these descriptions offer a wonderful picture of Israeli society and all its accoutrements. Objects take on a life of their own, and reflect back on their owners' emotional state—she talks, for example, about the "open, hungry mouth of the washing machine."

Gelbetz most animated descriptions are reserved for body parts. "And when I'm left alone with my "Tzuptzik," I ask him with an intimacy known only to us, 'How was it sweetheart?' And he nods, 'Pleasant, pleasant,' but begs for some respite. Until next time." It is interesting that contemporary Israeli women's fiction is not shy about graphically describing sexual experience, and often, as in Gelbetz's novel, it's achieved with much humor. That doesn't mean to say that there are not abundant descriptions of depression and sleep, and even thoughts of suicide, but humor wins out and the heroine realizes that it would be difficult to throw herself off a Tel Aviv roof as they have all become penthouses with potted plants.

In a similar Tel Aviv tone of irony and humor, Shoshi Breiner's *Hebrew Love* (2006) includes stories and a novella about the bored, empty lives of married women at mid-life, who begin seeking new sexual partners. Breiner's irony is particularly targeted to men and women adopting New Age practices, the latest Tel Aviv trend. Dina, the protagonist of the story "Buildings" is an architectural photographer who ends up becoming a vegetarian and living an ascetic life, making a pilgrimage to the Taj Mahal to devote herself to an architecture of love-mausoleums. Breiner captures the lack of vitality and the absurdity of upper middle-class Israelis today. In her novella, *Girls*, she details perceptively the moments when marriages begin to sour, the women's pent-up anger, and the eventual realization of the limitations of their new lovers.

The novella *Hebrew Love*, the title work of this collection, is of another mode entirely, and emotionally deeper. It is about a second generation writer invited to Paris to lecture on her work, the story of a girl growing up in the home of survivors, where her "parents lived their lives as a type of punishment." Aunt Dora, her mother's sister, presents an alternative free-spirited, but ultimately self-destructive model. Breiner's writer, the protagonist Chana, juxtaposes these survivor stories with an imaginary one. She creates the life she would have liked to have as Dafna, a daughter of "real Israelis," whose father is an Israeli military attaché in France, where Daf-Daf, as she's affectionately called, takes ballet lessons and has beautiful clothes and toys. But Chana's imaginary character fails her. Her life is far from ideal. Dafna's parents divorce. And Dafna, no less than Chana, takes on her parents' burden, albeit of a different kind. She relives her mother's affair when she too comes with her husband to Paris. Breiner has some interesting things to say about survivor parents, although they sometimes feel tacked onto the narrative via the writer-protagonist's lecture.

Nurit Zarchi, a veteran novelist as well as poet and writer of children's books was writing whimsical works before the flowering of women's writing in the 1980s, when Orly Castel-Bloom came on the scene. Her recently published collection of stories, *The Sad Ambitious Girls Of The Province* (2007) reflects a different type of whimsy and playfulness—not Castel-Bloom's brilliantly zany tone, nor Gelbetz's sardonic humor, or Breiner's detached irony, but one of a magical world of limitless possibilities, that is nevertheless permeated by existential sadness and loneliness.

In "The Misty Kingdom," two sisters try to raise their father from the dead. The sense of crossing borders between life and death is playfully done. In her story "Café K, Afula," a young girl meets Kafka's eponymous character, who sends her on a mission to the library to find out if his friend Max Brod really burnt his manuscripts as Kafka had requested before his death.

But Zarchi's stories can also exhibit a sad realism. In the title story, "The Sad Ambitious Girls of the Province," Bella, a married woman with two children, finds a job in a newspaper archive during wartime. In addition to providing pictures for newspaper articles, parents of missing soldiers fall on newspaper pictures to prove to themselves that their sons are still alive. "See, this is the watch I bought him for his birthday," one woman declares. With the painful suggestiveness of a Solomonic judgment, two mothers fight over the same picture, each claiming that it's a picture of her son.

With the emergence of women's writing, the topic of motherhood—women's attitudes to being a mother, as well as to mother-daughter relationships—surfaced in Israeli literature. In the pre-state period and during the first decades of the state, Israeli writers, who were canonically male, struggled with the issue of fathers and sons, of how sons lived up to their fathers' pioneering ideal, and how to create a new Jewish man. When women writers came to the fore, they began to confront the overprotective "Jewish mother" within themselves. They began examining Israeli obsessiveness with motherhood and family.

Orly Castel-Bloom's brilliantly zany, expressionist *Dolly City*, published in 1992, revealed how the existential depths of a mother's anxiety for her child can be transformed into its sadistic opposite.

In the novel, Dolly, who has studied medicine in Katmandu, wreaks havoc on her son's body—because of motherly overconcern.

More recently, *The Ravens* (2004), journalist Avirama Golan's first novel, grapples with the Jewish mother. It is a tour de force depiction of a ravished, destructive Jewish mother. Genya, a bitter, paranoiac eighty-two-year-old woman, is originally from a shtetl on the Polish-Ukrainian border, and talks and thinks in a rich Hebrew-Yiddish medium. As in the case of the stereotypical American-Jewish mother, she projects all her hopes and aspirations onto her son, who is tragically killed in a navy operation. Although Genya mourns the death of her son she perceives it self-centeredly: "Why has it happened to me?"

Genya, an extreme figure, becomes the yardstick for neurotic motherhood. But the novel also offers variations on the theme of motherhood. Didi, a young TV researcher, struggles with her resentment towards her kibbutz mother who, she feels, was devoted to the "communal cause" above all. In reaction, Didi initially stifles her own daughter, but slowly gains greater self-awareness as a mother and woman.

The family is never far from Israeli consciousness. But recent novels also suggest alternative types of family. This is perhaps a throwback to the collective kibbutz family in earlier pioneering times, a suppressed aspect of the collective consciousness rising to the surface.

The army, as a society unto itself, is portrayed in Michal Zamir's book, *A Ship of Girls* (2005), dealing with the sexual exploitation of young women in the Israeli army. There have been books written by male writers such as Yitzhak Laor, Yehoshua Kenaz and Haim Be'er exposing the hard, often cruel relations in the army hierarchy. But the voice of women's experience of the army is just beginning to appear in Hebrew literature.

In *A Ship of Girls*, a young unnamed protagonist depicts this macho society, where young women surrender to the pressures of their officers for "easy sex." The protagonist replaces Michaela, who commits suicide after becoming pregnant by an older officer, a serial seducer. Alma, on the other hand, decides not to abort the fetus as most of the young women soldiers do. She opts to go through with the pregnancy and keep the baby. But she won't give the name of the father. "The army is its father," she declares, and this image captures the imagination of the other young women soldiers. The child that Alma expects is seen as everyone's child, just as children in the early kibbutzim were seen as children of the whole kibbutz society, and not just the biological family: "A family feeling grows among us, the seventy soldiers in the regular army. As if we were gently disconnected from our own family, and had established a new one, here on the base. A great love suddenly connects us."

The new young women writers have no romantic illusions, no sentimentality. As Gelbetz and Breiner bring a cynical eye to marriage relationships in Israel today, Zamir shows the shabbiness of the officers' attitude to women soldiers. They slept with them not because they cared for them, but because "they were there." Ultimately, the protagonist finishes her army service, and tries to put the chapter with its six abortions behind her. She sees herself as part of an anti-macho-establishment underground.

The sense of anti-establishment alienation from Israeli society is nowhere as evident in recent women's writing as it is in Marina Groslerner's novel, *Motherwolf* (2007). A group of homeless young people, pariahs from society, inadvertently meet in Clore Park on the Tel Aviv beach near Jaffa. They find an abandoned factory near the old Tel Aviv bus station which they fix up and call "Beita," the Aramaic for home. The Russian-born Marina Groslerner—she came to Israel when she was seven—creates a Dosteovsky-like underground world of young people struggling with their demons. Orit, a large, ungainly seventeen-year-old whose brown "snakelike hair almost covers her face," is unloved by her drug addict mother. Maya, a fourteen-year-old Ethiopian girl, has no family and runs away from a dormitory with Orit whom she sees as a mother and lover. Noa, the most mainstream Israeli among them, hides her burden, while Jonathan who becomes her boyfriend, carries the secret of family insanity, embracing it in a self-fulfilling prophecy rather than living in dread of its onset. Petro, a bitter, mean-spirited fourteen-year-old asthmatic from the former USSR, has seen his mother die of overwork. His hate of the establishment makes him scheming and demonic. Hanan, a religious settler, feels guilty for having survived while companions in arms were killed. Shlomit, a strange agile monkey-like woman, tattooed and earringed, with a turquoise Mohican haircut, comes from a good Jerusalem family. But she sees herself as "born to the wrong family, an orphan in her own home." This surrealistic family supports itself by finding jobs in the Carmel shuk or as dishwashers in restaurants. The sense of family is reinforced when Orit becomes pregnant by Hanan, with Maya portrayed as a mystical partner to the conception. But woven into this new family are legends of demons and of child sacrifice that eventually dominate their subjects, a mad psychological underside that eventually overcomes the innocence of the community. Paranoia percolates in the deep anti-establishment thrust of the group, and takes over when word gets out that the factory building which has become their home is to be leveled for a new mall. They gather arms and grenades, mining the area around them to oppose the real estate takeover. In a drug-or-madness induced trance, Petro imagines the signal has come to oppose the establishment, and throws a grenade which blows him up and starts a fire that engulfs the building. The group with the newborn baby escape, hopefully to a new, more sane beginning.

Groslerner has written a surrealistic novel that points to the seething violence beneath the surface in Israel, even among groups ostensibly seeking to create a new more ideal community. It is, perhaps, not coincidental that Hanan has brought arms from the territories, and that the group is reminiscent of the extremist "hilltop youth" in the territories of the West Bank.

The novels discussed above indicate that contemporary Israeli women writers are beginning to take on large societal subjects in their narratives, as did Orly Castel-Bloom in her novel, *Human Parts* (2004) about the Intifada and the terrible social gap in Israel. But the woman novelist who is most profound about Israel's situation today is Michal Govrin. Her novel *Snapshots* (2002) depicts the attempt of a left-wing intellectual to create a more universalist paradigm in opposition to the Zionist vision of the father she adores. Govrin's rich language and symbolic thinking is in many ways closer to the sensibility of writers such as A.B. Yehoshua and Amos Oz than the personal narratives of contemporary women writers. At the same time, she paints a portrait of a headstrong, free-spirited woman, Ilana Tsuriel, an Israeli-born architect who, determined not to be harnessed to the dreams of her father's generation, goes to Paris to fulfil her own universal ideals. She joins a team of socially aware, radical architects building projects for immigrants, refugees and the homeless, and marries Alain, a Holocaust-survivor scholar alienated from Israel, which he sees as a place where Jews are gathering for another Holocaust. Moving, for professional reasons, between Paris and New York, New Jersey and Jerusalem, Ilana celebrates the Wandering Jew in herself. She photographs and magnificently describes the gritty specifics of each place.

Ilana has proposed a peace monument on the Hill of Evil Counsel in Jerusalem, which is not to be a grandiose monument, but a sukkah, a temporary dwelling, and a series of huts for different groups to occupy, which will be the joint work of Palestinians and Israelis. A Palestinian theater group is to participate in the opening of the monument, and Ilana becomes passionately involved with its director, Sayyid Ashabi. Examining Jewish concepts like the sukkah and the sabbatical, she emphasizes the tentativeness of possession. "The people get the land, only to know how to let go of it," she preaches. And when she relates this to her father on his death bed, he reminds her that "you can only let go of what you love." Ilana realizes that she must renew her connection to her birthplace. And she returns to Israel, ostensibly to work on the project, in spite of the threat of the first Gulf War. The description of the war, of protecting her children, running with them with the gas masks, is emotionally riveting. But her reconnection to Israel emerges primarily through simple people, her neighbors who help her through this difficult period. Her hopes for a Palestinian-Israeli *détente* are aborted for the moment. But upon returning to Paris and her husband, she resumes her efforts for Mount Sabbatical. Again she becomes the Wandering Jew, driving from Paris to Munich for a conference, to lecture on the peace monument. And she chooses to drive rather than take a train "because she wants to feel Europe in her body." It turns out to be a tragic decision, for she is killed in an automobile accident. Her writings, drawings and sketches are collected by her husband to be made into a book.

Govrin is one of the few Israeli writers today whose work encompasses large conceptual frameworks. There is a density of thought and image that can sometimes be overwhelming, but her materials are driven by a strong dramatic narrative. And in Ilana Tsuriel she has created a protagonist that captures many of the conflicting emotions that characterize Israelis today.

To close: it may be said that Israeli women's literature today is truly "normal." After introducing "light" normal literature in the 80s with Batya Gur's detective stories, it has for the last decade produced many personal, psychological bestsellers for which Israelis once yearned. But contemporary women's fiction, as that of Israeli men, can be credited with a variety of modes, a large sweep of interests. It is a fiction that is engaged by public, historical, and ideological issues as well as by psychological and personal ones, and as Michal Govrin and Marina Groslerner's works indicate, it often embraces both. The tone of women's fiction today can be wonderfully comic and ironic, as well as realistic, symbolic and surrealistic. Although many works are characterized by a flat "street language," there are also novels that are richly stylized. And in a period when widespread ignorance of the Bible is lamented, it is quite surprising how often biblical and religious references are transformed into contemporary, and even humorous, context. Finally, women's writing is "normal" today because it reflects the broader, more complex Israeli reality, and is no longer perceived as only personal and domestic, although there is plenty of that too.

Amalia Kahana-Carmon, a fine philosophical novelist of the 1948 generation, complained that, whatever they write, Israeli women writers are ghettoized into the personal and domestic modes, just as they are designated for the women's section of the synagogue. Thankfully, recent women's writing indicates that they can now choose where they want to place themselves.

New Novels of Note

YORAM KANIUK, one of Israel's leading writers, was born in Tel Aviv in 1930. After being wounded in the 1948 War of Independence, he moved to New York for 10 years. A novelist, painter and journalist, Kaniuk has published 17 novels, a memoir, seven collections of stories, two books of essays and five books for children and youth. He has been awarded many literary prizes, including the Prix des Droits de l'Homme (France, 1997), the President's Prize (1998), the Bialik Prize (1999), the prestigious Prix Méditerranée Etranger (2000), the Book Publishers Association's Gold Book Prize (2005), and the Newman Prize (2006). His books have been published abroad in 25 languages.

In his literary testament, Kaniuk describes the four months he spent in a Tel Aviv hospital, hovering unconscious between the living and the dead. It is also an attempt to penetrate his lost consciousness and understand what led him to hang on to life with such desperate stubbornness. Writ-

ten in his unique style and rich language, his narrative moves through the way stations of his life, shifting between memory and illusion, imagination and testimony, through which events and people—some real and some not—blend into a vast fresco.

Between Life and Death

Tel Aviv, Yedioth Ahronoth, 2007. 207 pp. an autobiographical novel

Yoram Kaniuk

Between Life and Death

An excerpt from the novel

After these things—after disease and after death and after pain and after laughter and after betrayal and after old age and after grace and love and after a foolish son the heaviness of his mother and a woman of valor who stayed with me in beauty in the abyss—after all that I woke up into a half sleep and stayed there four months. And it was bad and it was good and it was sad and it was lost and it was a miracle and it was what it was and it wasn't what it wasn't and it could have been and I recalled it was night. A night sealed up in its night. I spent it in bad dreams and woke up dazed with sleep, I was healthy, in my house at 13 Bilu Street, and suddenly I recalled that at night I'd dreamed of screwdrivers. I had no need of a screwdriver and so I didn't search and I didn't find it, but in the place where the screwdriver could have been if there had been one, I found an old map of Tel Aviv, and since the map was already there, I left it and went to drink coffee and I ate a croissant they call "corasson" here and returned home, to the map, and thought of looking for the street where I lived. I spread the map on the table and wandered around with my finger until it landed, but not on Bilu Street where I live and not on the nearby corner of Balfour and Rothschild Boulevard where I lived my first three years, but on Arlozorov corner of Edward Bernstein, near the place where I really grew up. Naturally, I had no choice but to go to the corner of Arlozorov and Bernstein, where, except for the days when I walked in the sands, I passed by for eight years, ten months a year, almost every morning, walking from my parents' house to the Model School and back—a distance in which I could, if I wanted, get to the moon.

At the street corner, which was ugly even back then, stood the wretched house where Agu lived. He was two years younger but older than I, and was taciturn, scorned, solitary and full of hate. I think he stayed in third grade for three years, or maybe that was somebody else, and he had sparkling brown eyes and he was killed in the war in a battle for Neve Samuel soon after he ran into me in the dining hall of Kibbutz Kiryat Anavim, when he recalled who I was even before I reminded him where we knew each other from. We were then digging pits before the battles, and all you had to do was return from the battle and bury, and since only I knew who Agu was I was asked to write his name in a florid hand, but I didn't know his real name only his nickname, Agu, and I didn't know if, when he was born, he even had a name, and in fact I have no idea if he was even born, and I recall him as somebody who had been here forever, maybe because the Moslem grave garden flowing down to his house on the corner of Arlozorov Street was so close.

Agu's father had a bicycle repair shop on the corner of Jabotinsky, which was called Ingathering-of-the-Exiles Street back then. The exiles didn't manage to be gathered in, but they've already forgiven Jabotinsky and changed the name of the street to his name, and that's how the names changed. His dog, Topsy, would run to the Tribes of Israel Street from the other side of Jewish National Fund Boulevard to attack the composer von Sternberg, whom he loathed. The composer would walk around dressed even on weekdays in a German hunter's outfit and would brandish a bamboo walking stick and look frightened with his eyes shut and was married to Genia, a beautiful woman who was my first love and who brought up her son and became a nun in Lebanon. Sternberg the putz wrote a work that three people in the city could listen to without killing themselves and called it "Twelve Tribes of Israel," after the name of his street, and Moshe my father said we were lucky he didn't live in Meah Shearim with its hundred gates.

I used to play with the dog Topsy on the way to school, and Agu was mad at his dog for wagging his tail at me and he was jealous of me and yelled at Topsy, but Topsy was fond of me and sensed that I liked him and waited for me every morning with his tail wagging, until one day Agu got upset and jealous and sicced Topsy on me and yelled at him to bite me. Topsy, who loved me but belonged to Agu, tried to bite him in panic but then was kicked and his tail drooped, and his eyes raged and he whined horribly and approached me, and Agu shrieked again and Topsy didn't know where his greater obligation was and bit me because he had no choice. Poor Topsy was taken to the veterinary department for tests and I had to get twenty shots in my stomach. I went with Sarah my mother to the Strauss Clinic on Balfour Street and they'd give me a shot every week with a giant needle and after my portion of torments, we'd leave there, go down to Allenby Street and Sarah my mother would buy me an ice cream at Shnir's and call it "some consolation" for what I had gone through.

Agu's father has been gone a long time. Not only him. All of them have gone with the wind. Even the watchmaker Yashka Silberman, who taught Stalin Yiddish, has gone, and Goldbaum, the licensed barber from Warsaw for men and women, whose wife ran away from him wearing a corset and he was afraid to run after her because of the Italian planes that were bombing and because he was wearing a gas mask and couldn't get it off, he's gone too, and the shoemaker Joshua, who taught me to cut soles and spit nails in an arc into a sole, is gone, and the limping upholsterer Yashke Weisman, who was killed in an accident and his wife married her lover, and Mr. Polishuk, who dreamed of a furrier's shop but sold falafel on the corner of Lasalle Street, and the upholsterer Zuska Shlinov, who was found dead in a small room at the Jordan Hotel on Ben-Yehuda at the corner of Jewish National Fund Street with lipstick smeared on his lips, he's gone too. So many people I knew have died, more dead than living are left, Bill died, Danny died—who didn't die? Sarah my mother, Moshe my father, Ruth Olitski, Shalom Yakir and Rina Helfand whom I loved in fifth grade died and the aunts and uncles died, the disease of death came down from the sky and swallowed most of the people I knew and nothing is left. The sands of the sea that came as far as Ben-Yehuda, were shifted back because the city leaders thought they were superfluous, and the lowly huts of the Mahlul neighborhood, which looked like the Bedouin women from Jaffa who used to come sell fish their husbands caught, and the tarpaper shacks mounted on limestone hills at the edge of the sea and smelled of saltwater and the waves lapped them and hit them, they've disappeared too. The tanning factory on Hayarkon Street, that dripped black water and reeked, is gone. The Moslem grave garden was wiped out and became a national park of the Jews with the Hilton Hotel as an upside-down statement.

And here am I hemorrhaging in my head and returning from what isn't, but before that really happened and when like an idiot I searched for a screwdriver and found a map, rain in its season fell on me, and I stood shaking from the wind blowing from the sea and I was excited, but I don't remember why. Maybe because I grew up woven into that sea and the melody was in me. I'd sit in the dark on the veranda, back then we called it a porch, and like most of the residents of our city I'd peep in the windows of the neighbors to see how they were creating the Hebrew soldiers of the future. Years ago, long before I got sick and before I was transferred a little to the other side, years when I dreamed of growing old and dying by the sea, with the strong wind and the taste of salt in my mouth, because that was what was always here, the surest future was the sea. I thought that if I got sick, and back then I wasn't really sick, and if I lay dying at the sea and I listened to the singing of the wind, I would love my death.

I stood at the corner of Edward Bernstein Street and looked up. The veranda we had, the small panorama to the sea, was hidden long ago by tall buildings and the sea was hidden by big, indescribably ugly buildings. But I can still picture the veranda next to ours, where even now you can see a little bit of sea, the poor Lichtman maiden, may-she-rest-in-peace, standing strong and weeping like a captain on the bridge of a sinking ship, and even though she died years ago, she's still holding the telescope she was sold by the black market egg seller, Mr. Bein, who carried the eggs in a small splendid suitcase, always dressed in a suit and tie he said he'd brought, in his words, from Berlin—and she stands and looks out sadly at Germany, and sees those who were her parents in Berlin, and tells us, foolish children that we were, who at the age of eight were already training to establish a Jewish state that was impossible but essential in hostile regions, and getting ready to take revenge on the Nazis with slingshots and sticks—she tells us she saw what was there before they made soap of them, and every hour she takes the shaver and the razor blades out of the case and shaves, and between one shave and another you can see her beard sprouting, bursting from her cheeks like flowers after the first rain, and she'd search for her father even in the fuse box and explain that he had to be someplace, so why not there, and she'd say that it was all from the Holocaust, and she missed Germany so much that she'd sing sweet *Lieder* to the sea, though she had no voice at all, so that it would take her back, and I told my friend Amos who would come see her beard grow, I told him that she wanted to swim to Berlin, but she stayed to die in Palestine the Land of Israel; clinging like a leech to stormy regrets. For regrets gave her sweet pain, and I would cuddle up to her pain which I almost understood, and draw it into me and it stayed in me like a guest who stays forever.

I remember the sight of the ships on the way to the port of Tel Aviv. I loved them, like rocking nutshells during a storm, and I loved the whistle of the strong wind. Now I'm old and without a screwdriver, unneeded guys like me are called seniors, and I walk on Edward Bernstein Street whose houses, gazed for years from our veranda at 129 Ben-Yehuda and Strauss, next to the veranda of the maiden Lichtman may-she-rest-in-peace, have already sprouted storeys and new-fangled Israeli architectural decorations that turned the ruins into something to wish for.

The opera singer Giulini also died, the father of the outcast, who surprised me years later, and before he was killed in the war he saved Agu who ended up killed himself but who wasn't killed back then; all of us killed and were killed, and Agu and the outcast, whose name I've forgotten, we buried on the kibbutz at Kiryat Anavim, and Giulini, father of the outcast, no longer practices the melody of the late Dr. Mazeh Imber's poem, "The Shofar," and Jacob Avinoam, who called himself Blood and Fire no longer recites Jacob Cohen's poem, "in blood and fire Judah fell in blood and fire will Judah rise," as an awful flow of tears pours onto his cheeks, and our other teacher, who called himself Pure and Simple, and whose previous name was Yasha Levotinvitch, must be dead too.

Orange trees, once the pride of Zionism, have all been cut down in the neighborhood, except for one lemon tree and one chicken coop that remained for a while and were the glory of Ashael's yard, and Ashael disappeared along with the concrete cases his father would build in the yard next to the lemon tree for no visible reason, because nothing was packed in them and for years they piled up on top of one another and broke, but they continued to be piled up because he continued to build them until they reached the top of the lemon tree and then he cut down the lemon tree, which served as a lesson to Ashael and so when the war of liberation broke out in 1947, he ran off to America and a few years later was called to the US army to fight in Korea, and his mother, who said that Ashael was both her son and a substitute for her idiotic husband who had spent all his days building concrete boxes that looked like coffins for dwarfs, flew to New York in an aeroplane, today we call it a plane, and flying was a rare thing back then, and bought somebody important from city hall with the money of Ashael's father which she smuggled in in her gigantic bra, and that somebody arranged papers for Ashael and released him from the war.

Near the house, right across from the calm hidden beauty where I searched for a rain pipe to play me the lullabies of my childhood, a little bit of sea is still open. Moshe my father would swim in it every day at exactly five in the afternoon, after most of the swimmers had already gone home, because he loved the sea all to himself. In the spring and fall, the sea was sparkling and smooth and soft, and sometimes in the morning, on the way to school, we'd walk barefoot in the sand along the shore, and under the hewn limestone wall, we'd take off our shoes, hang them by the laces on our shoulders, put our schoolbags on our heads like the Arab women who carry ewers of water and bundles of wood to the ovens, and we'd walk in the shallow water teeming with seashells, some were broken and cut our little feet, until we came to the sand dune across from the Model School.

At that same time, Moshe my father would lead his bike in the sand to the road, look at the sea sadly because on its other side was still Europe, and then ride his bike to the museum, but not before pinching the bottoms of his trousers with clothespins so they wouldn't get dirty. He always dressed properly even when he rode his bike, dressed according to the German season, tie, a lot of pockets for pipes and tobacco and the beret of a bohemian. I thought of him when I saw the rain pelting down here at the corner of Edward Bernstein and Arlozorov. I loved the smell of the rain but those devils have killed most of the gutters for me, and not far from what was the school for workers' children—Moshe my father said their parents were born apparatchiks and didn't work a day in their lives and at most would be photographed with a hoe in a kibbutz whose name I've forgotten—suddenly came the death I'm trying to tell about here, since I saw a procession of black ants moving together like a swaying snake.

I don't know today where in fact I was when everything I've written here happened or didn't happen, I only remember that at the corner of Edward Bernstein and Arlozorov, I bent over to find out what the ants were carrying on their back and I saw that they weren't carrying anything but were escorting a most splendid ant bearing a small canopy of dry grass, and under the canopy I saw a tiny tumor, snug as a king bug. Meanwhile the sky cleared and the clouds went off. At the sea, the secret bays and the natural pool weren't yet murdered, and above the pool cut in the limestone was the secret cave with the canned goods and the rusks that we hid in case Rommel won in Egypt and the Nazis conquered the Land of Israel and we'd make Massada in the cave, and we said that as in the poem, which the teacher Blich would recite excitedly and tearfully, we would build Jerusalem on the hill like those who mount the scaffold.

The son of the teacher Blood and Fire Trumpeldor, who was said to be the most beautiful boy in our school, and who certainly joined or didn't join—I don't remember anymore—the group of "Massada rebels on the limestone" as we were called back then, stood proud, beautiful and well built on the rock in the natural pool, and Zilpha S., who was already wearing a bra, and we knew she was wearing a bra because we'd hit the girls on the back to know and with her we felt the buttons, and there was even some slander that she once kissed and even danced ballroom dances, Zilpha S. said that Blood and Fire Trumpeldor looked like Tarzan on the rock, and I annoyed her when I laughed at what she said, because what little girl, even if she did wear a bra, understands Tarzan from seeing him at the community center at eleven cents a movie. Afterward, I was sorry and I said he looked like a hero to me. Trumpeldor, we called him Trumpel, spread his hands, leaned forward a little like Nimrod the mighty hunter, and everybody stood amazed and applauded him. He waved his hands and waved us away with a certain contempt and raised his head and looked at me and laughed because I always made him laugh with who I was, and he shouted as always, "To Yoram who will conquer a cloud," and then he added of course "To Life and to Death" and stretched his hands forward and then leaned a bit more, and all of a sudden a frozen silence reigned over the face of the water and he roared like Zilpha S.'s Tarzan, and rose on tiptoe and jumped head first into the shallow water and I saw his beautiful head touch the water, hit a rock, and I heard the sharp crack and the water turned red and pieces of head were in it.

The tumor in the ants' cradle looked nervous but detached, maybe it was searching for victims with indifference. I sensed that tumors, microbes and ants love each other and I thought there was some justice in that, in a world where everyone swallows everyone else. The ants were escorting the tumor under the canopy in splendid formation, and they looked as if they were part of an expedition of divine adulation. Maybe ultimately some microbe died that had clung to the tumor's body, and the ants were the only ones in this country that really maintained the friendship of the poem and were holding a proper funeral for the microbe, and so the tumor apparently came and attended his dear one's funeral. I thought that I do know tumors. I'm eaten by them. But I didn't hate them and I looked on impressed and didn't think about the procession anymore. The next evening, I went to meet the intended bride of Rebecca's son who always walked around with an enormous rifle and found the smallest Australian woman on the continent and was about to start a family with her and the two of them together, head to head, were maybe seven and a half feet tall. At the end of the evening, I went back to my house on Bilu, and on my way there I came to Marmorek Street. From the corner of Ibn Gabirol stretched a line of cars toward the parking may-it-rest-in-peace of the concert hall.

I'm lying now in the miracle of my life that has passed and thinking of the miracle. Of the procession of the tumor. Now I remember that I don't know where and why, how in 1945, we all went to Massada to shout "We won't forget you, Exile" and one guide who was in the Palmach shot a bullet from a gun he had hidden on him and I marched on the crest, it was Hanukkah and cold and dark, and I looked out and in that whole landscape there were lights like a giant Christmas because the blackout of the great war was lifted and I thought that what I was seeing was the Garden of Eden sparkling and beautiful, but I felt shocked and I heard a stone falling into an abyss, and I walked behind with a kind of skip and I understood that I was standing on the edge of Massada and in a little while I would become a stone at the foot of the mountain, and I thought that when Jews stand on the edge, they see the Garden of Eden, and vice-versa.

And I thought, despite the death that was lurking for me twice yesterday and seemed determined to harm me, I was quite a healthy man. Old age had indeed leaped on me as it leaps on all of us, and age isn't something that showers favors and not a big holiday either, and my blood pressure is quite high, and I've got back problems and migraines, and I had a prostate operation, and once I had herpes like Golda, which was an affliction, that is both of them, the herpes and Golda, and I thought, what's so bad about living a little longer?

Translated by Barbara Harshav

photo © Dan Porges

A.B. YEHOSHUA was born in Jerusalem in 1936, a fifth generation
Jerusalemite. After studying at the Hebrew University, he taught in Paris
for a few years. He is now Professor of literature at Haifa University.
Yehoshua has published many novels, stories, plays and essays and is
one of Israel's best known authors abroad. Among his many literary
prizes: the Bialik Prize (1989), England's "Best Novel of the Year" for
Mr Mani (1992), the National Jewish Book Award, the Israel Prize (1995),
the Giovanni Boccaccio Prize (Italy, 2005) and the Viareggio Prize (Italy,
2005). His work has been published abroad in 28 languages.

Friendly Fire is the literary "duet" of a long-married couple, who are
spending a week apart. Daniella is in to East Africa mourning the
death of her older sister with her brother-in-law Yirmiyahu. Alternating
between Africa and Israel, the story follows her husband Amotz as he

juggles the daily needs of his elderly father,
his children and grandchildren, and the
unfolding confrontation between his wife
and the anguished 70-year-old Yirmiyahu,
whose soldier son was killed six years earlier
in the West Bank by the "friendly fire" of
his comrades.

Friendly Fire

Tel Aviv, Hakibbutz Hameuchad, 2007.
375 pp.

A.B. Yehoshua

Friendly Fire

An excerpt from the novel

Just before midnight, the women arrive at the base camp of the scientific mission, located at a colonial farm built at the beginning of the last century. Following Tanzanian independence, the farm was confiscated from its European owners and turned into an elite training camp for army officers and public officials favored by the government. But tribal conflicts, and violent regime changes, did not permit officers and officials to maintain domestic tranquility within a single locale, and it was abandoned and forgotten for many years, until two African anthropologists discovered the place and approached UNESCO with a request for help in renovating it as a service facility for new excavations.

A generator thumps. In the darkness, the outline of the farm house seems a ghost of the colonial past. But a light is burning on the ground floor. That is the kitchen, where he is no doubt waiting for you, says Sijjin Kuang to the passenger, who suddenly feels too weak to lift her small suitcase. After the Sudanese woman collects a package from the back seat, she leads the visitor toward the light.

If her sister only knew how far she had traveled alone, to rekindle her memory, she would have been pleased, and perhaps even proud of her, but surely also fearful, as she is now, of her encounter with the widower left behind.

"Here he is," points the nurse to a tall silhouette in the doorway.

Instead of running to his sister-in-law to embrace her and help wheel her suitcase, Yirmiyahu remains distant, waiting at the entrance for the two women to come to him. And only then does he hug Daniella tight, and fondly pat the shoulder of the black nurse who brought her.

"What happened?" he asks in English, "I thought that you maybe changed your mind and canceled at the last minute."

"Why? Did you want me to change my mind?"

"No, I did not want anything."

He insists on continuing in English, on account of Sijjin Kuang, who stands still as a statue beside him, carrying the package in her arms like someone offering a sacrifice. And as if feeling sorry for his sister-in-law, who made the long journey all by herself, he hugs her again, and takes the handle of her rolling suitcase, and she senses that his body has a new, pungent smell.

"The water is heated," he says, sticking to his English, which sounds a bit rusty. "But if you wish to drink a glass of tea before sleep, first let's go into the kitchen."

The three enter a large hall containing an enormous refrigerator and stoves for cooking and baking, and also what seems to be an ancient boiler to heat water for washing. The huge pots and frying pans, the ladles and spoons, graters and knives, testify to generous cooking for a good many people. A pile of firewood stands in the corner and dozens of empty plastic boxes are arranged on tables. While the newcomer looks around with wonder, the host relieves the Sudanese nurse of the bundle in her arms, thanks her for her trouble, and bids her good night.

"I asked her to buy you new sheets, so you'll feel safe and sound in your bed."

Daniella blushes. She ought to say, "Why? Really, no need," but she can't deny his display of sensitivity. He knows well that in strange lodgings she requires, like her sister, a pristine bed.

As he sets a kettle on the fire, she studies him. His white hair, which she remembers from their last meeting, has fallen out, and his bald skull, resembling the fashionably shaved heads of young men, slightly arouses her anxiety.

"I brought you a bunch of newspapers from Israel."

"Newspapers?"

"Also magazines and supplements. The stewardess collected them on the plane and filled you a whole bag, you can pick what interests you."

An ironic smile crosses his lips. His eyes flash with a fresh spark.

"Where are they?"

Despite her fatigue, she bends over the suitcase and extracts the bulging bag. For a moment he seems loath to touch it, as if she were handing him a slimy reptile. Then he grabs it and rushes to the boiler, opens a small door revealing tongues of bluish flame, and without delay shoves the entire bag into the fire and quickly shuts the door.

"Wait," she cries, "stop…"

"This is where they belong," he smiles darkly at the visitor, with a measure of satisfaction.

Her face goes pale. But she keeps her composure, as always.

"Perhaps for you it's where they belong. But before you start burning things, you could warn me."

"Why?"

"Because there was lipstick in there too, which I bought at the airport for my cleaning lady."

"Too late," he says quietly, without remorse. "The fire is very hot."

Now she regards him with hostility and resentment. In her parents' house, he was the one who had devoured every old newspaper. But he returns her look with affection.

"Don't be angry. It's no big deal, just newspapers, which get thrown out anyway. So instead of the trash I threw them in the fire. You'll compensate your cleaning lady with another present. I hope you haven't brought me any more gifts like these."

"Not a thing," she winces, "that was it. Nothing else. Maybe only...Hanukkah candles..."

"Candles? Why Hanukkah candles?"

"It's Hanukkah now, did you forget? I was thinking, maybe we would light them this week, together...It's one of my favorite holidays..."

"It's Hanukkah? I really didn't know. For some time now I've been cut off from the Jewish calendar. Tonight, for instance, how many candles?"

"It started yesterday, so tonight is the second candle."

"Second candle?" he seems amused that his sister-in-law thought to bring Hanukkah candles to Africa. "Where are they? Let's see them."

For a moment she hesitates, but then takes out the box of candles and hands it to him, in the odd hope that he might agree to light here, in the middle of the night, Hanukkah candles that could ease her sudden longing for her husband and children. But he, with the same quick, slightly maniacal movements, again opens the little door and adds the Hanukkah candles to the smoldering Israeli newspapers.

"What's wrong with you?" She stands up angrily, but still maintains her cool, as with a student in her class who has done something idiotic.

"Nothing. Don't get angry, Daniella. But I've decided to take a rest here from all of that."

"A rest from what?"

"From the whole messy stew, Jewish and Israeli...Please, don't spoil my rest. After all, you've only come to grieve."

"In what way spoil it?" She speaks with him calmly, without rancor, feeling pity for this big man with the pink bald head.

"You'll find out soon enough what I mean. I want quiet. I don't want to know anything, I want to be disconnected, I don't even want to know the name of the prime minister."

"But you do know."

"I don't, and don't tell me. I don't want to know, just like you don't know the name of the prime minister here in Tanzania, or in China. Spare me all that. Come to think of it, maybe it's too bad I didn't insist that Amotz come with you. I'm afraid you'll get bored here with me on such a long visit."

Now, for the first time, she is insulted.

"I won't be bored, don't worry about me. The visit isn't long, and if it gets hard for you having me here, I'll cut it short and leave earlier. Do what you need to do. I brought a book, and don't you dare throw it in any fire."

"If the book is for you, I won't touch it."

"The nurse you sent to get me already warned me...By the way, is she really still a pagan?"

"Why still?"

"You mean, she believes in spirits?"

"What's wrong with that?"

"Nothing wrong. A very impressive young woman...Elegant..."

"You can't remember, but before you were born, before the State was established, on street corners in Jerusalem there stood Sudanese like her, very tall and black, wrapped in robes, roasting these wonderful, delicious peanuts on little burners, and selling them in cones made of newspaper. But you weren't born yet."

"I wasn't born..."

"Her whole family was murdered in the civil war in southern Sudan, and she grew up to become a woman of great tenderness and humanity."

"Yes. And she said that you didn't come to meet me because you were afraid to run into Israelis. Why would there be Israelis on the plane?"

"On every plane between two points in the world there is at least one Israeli."

"But not on the plane that brought me here."

"Are you sure?"

"I'm sure."

"And a Jew?"

"A Jew?"

"Maybe there was some Jew on the plane?"

"How would I know?"

"Then imagine that I didn't want to run into him either."

"That bad?"

"That bad."

"Why? You're angry at—"

"No, not angry at all, but I want a rest. I'm seventy years old, and I'm allowed to disconnect a bit, and if it's not a final break, then a temporary break, or let's call it a time out. Simply a time out from my people, Jews in general and Israelis in particular."

"And from me too?"

"From you?" He regards his sister-in-law with fondness, pours boiling water into her teacup, puts a flaming match to the cigarette she clenches between her lips, absolutely her last one of the day. "With you I have no choice, you'll always be my little sister, as I told you when you were ten. And if you came all the way to Africa to bond with Shuli's memory and mourn her together with me, it's your perfect right, since I know as well as anyone how much you loved her and she loved you. But that's all. I warn you in advance, grieve, but don't preach."

Translated by Stuart Schoffman

HAIM BE'ER was born in Jerusalem in 1945 and was raised in an
Orthodox home. He teaches Hebrew literature and creative writing at
Ben-Gurion University of the Negev, and is on the editorial board of
Am Oved Publishing House. Be'er has published a collection of poetry,
four novels and a biography. Among his awards for poetry and fiction:
the Bernstein Prize, the Bialik Prize (2002) and the ACUM Prize for
Lifetime Achievement (2005). His novel, *Feathers*, is included among
"The Greatest Works of Modern Jewish Literature" (2001). His work has
been published abroad in nine languages.

This novel centers around the Jewish book—acquired, transmitted,
destroyed, restored. And connected to it, a number of fascinating
characters: the millionaire Zussman, a cruel philanthropist who, since

his daughter's death, seeks to understand
the secrets of existence; old Shlomo Rap-
poport, a businessman and book collector
who wants to restore the library of his
father, murdered by the Nazis; Katrina, a
conflicted young German woman; and the
author himself. Significantly, it is modern
Berlin, caught between past and present,
that brings these characters together.

In that Place

Tel Aviv, Am Oved, 2007. 298 pp.

Haim Be'er

In that Place

An excerpt from the novel

Too bad he isn't younger," Katrina said, and after a slight hesitation she added, "and that you're not available." The two of us, she continued, unlike most of the men she knows, don't make any effort to hide our love for children. And she herself is just dying to have a child. It wasn't only by chance that she'd replied cordially to the invitation received from Patricia Reimann, my German publisher, to present my novel, *The Pure Element of Time* at that literary evening in Berlin, where we first met. The figure of the mother as she emerges from the novel—"Tell me your mother's name. Why did you avoid mentioning her name even once in the story?"—is always with her. When her heart stirs and burns within her, she goes back to reread the pages where this woman is described, this woman whose life was shattered by the death of her two children and her husband's betrayal, who goes up to the roofs of Jerusalem over and over in order to throw herself off, until she discovers that she's gotten her period and becomes convinced of the hope that a new life will be woven in her womb. From the time she'd hit puberty, the young woman said, her monthly cycle always troubled her but she never thought it was also a sign the body sent a woman of the life forces stored within her.

Katrina spoke softly to me while her hands waved a cell phone without ever putting it down, as if she was trying to rock a baby to sleep. And yet, you could tell that she hadn't just arrived at these formulations on the spur of the moment but had been waiting some time for the right opportunity to share them with someone else.

The feeling is new to her. Especially since she was never one of those children who spent a lot of time taking care of their dolls or looking after a younger sibling, a little mommy preparing herself for the future. She always detested the idea that one of these days she would have to clean the shit of needy newborns and dip their tiny, wrinkled, red bodies in bathtubs without forgetting to check the temperature of the water first, and this detest was mixed with anxiety at the constant responsibility for the welfare of the creature you've brought into the world. "You should know, Katrina, that a child is not some fashionable jacket you wear one day and donate to one of those churchyard charities the next," was the fear instilled in her by one of her acquaintances who, together with her boyfriend, had adopted twins whose parents had been slaughtered in Kosovo, "a child is a project you take on for life, and many times it even extends beyond it."

The sudden change came as a surprise even to her. It was towards the end of the summer that preceded my arrival in Berlin. She had turned twenty-eight. The morning after the celebration she sat in her room surrounded by bunches of flowers, birthday cards, scarves and books that she had received from her friends, and in the midst of a rare bluish orchid, shaped like a bee, that she had been given by her boyfriend at the time, an introverted, silent guy who worked in high-tech and had to travel to Singapore at dawn, she sat and contemplated what the future held for her. The expected telephone call from her mother, who had moved away to Arnberg the year before to her best friend's apartment, finally came. From a distance her mother sang her that song she loved, the shepherd's tune that her mother used to wake her with when she was a child, and she sent her little daughter hugs and kisses.

"Now I'm exactly as old as you were when you gave birth to me," Katrina said to her, in an outburst of closeness, "and now I also want to become a mother."

Her mother cleared her throat out of embarrassment and then said something about the connection between various dates in the lives of parents and children. In her case, as an example, she began to become aware of her approaching death only when she reached the age at which her own mother, Grandma Helga, had left this world.

The words, which typified her mother's lack of sensitivity, effectively concluded the happy-birthday conversation between the two of them. She sat alone in the sun-washed room that looks out on the roofs of the Miete district, and wept bitterly; but once again, not even this insult was enough to kill the new craving that had awoken within her.

Rather than wandering among the bookstores, she began to spend more and more time in stores where they sold maternity clothing or toddler supplies; she began staring at every convex belly, and more than once, as she sat in the neighborhood café, she was facinated by the sight of a young mother nursing her infant or playing with the child on her lap.

"Perhaps it's impolite or even unwise of me to burden you with a women's conversation of this sort and to involve you in the most intimate matters in my life," the young woman crossed her arms like a student who has just presented the thesis that she labored over for many days. "But this kind of miracle occurs only rarely, the miracle of spiritual proximity between reader and author, your words crossed time zones and borders, surmounted language barriers and cultural differences and pierced my heart like an arrow."

It was, without a doubt, the most emotional meeting I had ever had with one of my readers. I wanted to caress her and hold her close, but I couldn't find the courage in my heart.

"Motherhood lies hidden within me like this bee," Katrina pulled from her black shirt collar the amber stone that nestled between her breasts, "and I'm waiting for someone to come along and set her free." She closed her eyes, and in the cry that rose from her very depths she said, "above all I want my child to be Jewish." Then she opened her eyes, adding with a smile, "Don't worry, sweetheart, I don't plan on seducing you, at least, not this time."

When she came back from the bathroom her lips had been coated with lipstick, her face looked refreshed, the stone pendant was back hiding in her bosom, and only her green eyes, which were speckled with golden dots, revealed the emotional storm that had just raged within her.

"Your story about Holgar hasn't given me a moment's rest since I heard it this morning at the meal," she said and called the waiter. She ordered two servings of passion fruit ice cream and asked if we continued to meet after that unbelievable visit to his father's basement.

The day after the trip to Stauffen, I told her, Holgar called and apologized that he had to make an urgent business trip. When he returned, in two weeks at the latest, he would call and we would renew our meetings. One evening, when I returned from my daily walk in the forest near Lake Titisee, Mr Isele was waiting for me. He handed me a little gift box and said the gentleman with the silver "Mercedes" had stopped by about an hour before, apologized that he hadn't found me in and asked Mr Isele to give me his warm regards and this package.

It was a copper case for a writer's quill, the type that clerks and court scribes of past generations carried in their belts when they went traveling. An inkwell, also adorned with arabesques, was soldered to its base. Connoisseurs to whom I showed Holgar's gift were all of the opinion that it was late-eighteenth century work from Damascus. In the space for the quill, Holgar had placed a strip of light blue paper on which was written, in a hand that he'd struggled to make legible, "An emergency kit for when all the other writing implements betray you. Yours, H."

"And did you call to thank him for the gift?"

I reminded her that our contact had never given me a telephone number or address for Holgar, and that I never dared to ask Holgar himself for the information after he had avoided answering even the most innocent questions, like where he lived and where his mysterious company's headquarters were located.

A few hours after my return to Israel, my friend the "Mossad agent" called.

"How is he?" he asked after I'd locked myself away in my office.

"Great," I answered laconically.

"Fine. You've received what you were supposed to receive from him. Now cut off all contact. And don't go looking for him. Ever. Is that clear?"

"Yes, sir," I said and the call was disconnected. Fortunately, I didn't mention the quill case from Damascus, because he would have probably confiscated it by orders of the "Mossad."

Later, during our meeting at Café Olga, next to Kikar Ha'medina, my friend told me which details I ought to conceal when I tell of my meetings with Holgar, both orally and, most definitely, in writing.

"And that included the number of the submarine that his father commanded." I could see the teeth of hidden gears spinning incessantly in Katrina's vigilant eyes. "And of course you changed his name too?"

I smiled and bit my tongue.

"I guess the whole Stauffen story also never happened," she said, and added that at breakfast that morning in Wannsee, it became clear to her that an artist's imagination works overtime. "You couldn't stand the temptation, my author friend, but placing the story in Stauffen was just too symbolic and therefore the whole thing is baseless from the ground up." She also advised me that in my next book I ought to place the father of Holgar—or Volker, or whatever his real name was—in a city with fewer literary and cultural associations.

I smiled again and said, it's true that sometimes the imagination outstrips reality. She's right, of course, and in fact Holgar's father didn't really live there. But on our way to his house in a nearby village, the agent turned from the road and drove into Stauffen to give our trip a little added value and let me see the place where, according to local tradition, Dr. Faustus sold his soul to Mephistopheles.

"Let's drop it for now," Katrina raised her ice cream cone in a toast to Holgar's life and the lives of his experts who, just as we spoke, were maybe installing a state-of-the-art air conditioning system in the younger Assad's office or in Bin Laden's cave. She said that if, in our eyes, Holgar's father had sold his soul to the Nazis, well then the Arabs, if they found out about that, would claim that his beloved son had sold his soul to the Zionist devil. And, as she licked the remaining ice cream with obvious pleasure, she wondered if I'd received a sign of life from him since.

I said no and added that although many years had passed, my friend's commandment still had a hold over me—my friend who, in the meantime, had left the service, and, as far as I could tell from the newspapers, had either become an international arms dealer or a supplier of security systems for South American dictators on the run from their enemies—and that I'd avoided tracking Holgar down.

"If you had the courage to tell me his real name, I could locate him for you dead or alive," she said. "Here, in this country where order is a disease, nobody can disappear just like that."

But through the obscure workings of fate, Holgar returned and invaded my life. On July 29, 2006, the sabbath of "The Prophecy," the Literary Colloquium of Berlin hosted a wide-ranging cultural event in its garden. Under the banner "Small Publishers in Greater Wannsee," the owners of small but respected Berlin publishing houses set up their stalls on the lawns surrounding the building, and spread out a selection of their books on the tables. Next to the stalls, benches had been arranged in a semi-circle and young artists, most of them in their thirties and forties, read from their work. In the shade of the old plane tree in the corner of the building a young writer who had caught my attention because his family name was the same as Holgar's had drawn about twenty-five listeners and was reading them a chapter from his new book. At the end of the reading, which lasted about twenty minutes, one of the heads of the LCB led me over to the young writer, who was mopping his brow, and introduced me to him.

"Meet our dear guest, Mr Be'er, a writer from Israel."

"Haim, I presume?" the young man asked me, much the way Stanley turned to Dr Livingstone.

"And you, of course, must be Holgar's son."

"I see the two of you are getting along just fine without me," crowed the best man, and he ran back with renewed energy to pair up other couples among the participants of the Colloquium.

When he was first starting out as a writer, my conversational partner said, his father told him all about me: how I would jot down bits of information and travel logs in my notebook; how I would enter into the minutest details; how I grilled him about local foods, drinks, place names, and above all cloaked myself in a mantle of innocence to hide the extent of my curiosity. "That's how a writer has to work." His father turned me into a model to be imitated and told him about the episode of our joint trips to Hirschsprung, to the ancient Jewish cemetery in Worms, and above all about our trip to Stauffen, and in the end he even revealed the story of our descent into his grandfather's secret cellar.

"Is the old man still alive?"

"He died exactly three years ago, may Allah have mercy on his soul."

"You speak Arabic?"

"Dad didn't tell you that for five years we lived alternately in Baghdad and Damascus?" He was surprised.

Since the young man had chosen writing as his path in life and rejected outright his father's recommendation to study air conditioning technology and follow in his footsteps, Holgar had decided to sell his share of the company and retire. Now he'd moved his operation to South America and worked as an engineering consultant. "He has an Israeli partner, a retired 'Mossad' agent," the young writer revealed. "Maybe you happen to know him, his name is Boaz Livnat."

"Yes, I know Boaz pretty well," and for the first time I dared to pronounce the name of my friend the secret service agent out loud. "It's thanks to him that I met your father."

Holgar's son apologized that he couldn't talk longer, but he had to run after his publisher and, in particular, to flirt with the woman who ran the publisher's public relations, but before we parted he wanted to give me a copy of his new book as a gift, even though he knew that I wouldn't be able to read it. On the cover page the young man wrote me a rather cordial dedication and added a business card where he included his parents' home telephone number. "Dad will be back home, in Berlin, at the beginning of September. Call him. He'll definitely be happy to renew the relationship between you."

"As far as I'm concerned, you should forget about Holgar already," Katrina concluded this chapter of our conversation and told me that not long after our first meeting in Berlin she'd won a scholarship from the Rockefeller Foundation and had gone to study Hebrew at Brandeis University for a year. I didn't know if she was trying to change the topic or if this was about to become another variation on the subject of relations between parents and children, which had held her attention from the moment Rappaport had left us alone.

"Our Hebrew teacher was a Jew from Vilna who spoke English, Hebrew, Russian and some half-dozen other languages, all with a thick Yiddish accent," she said, as she casually played with the sugar packets. "In one of the classes, he wrote the following biblical passage on the board: "the fathers ate unripe fruit but the teeth of the children are blunted." He explained what the Hebrew words for unripe fruit and blunted meant, and said that what most touched his heart about the passage was its uncertainty. Let me tell you, young people, the old Jew spoke decidedly, unable to restrain the sadness in his voice, there's always a cloud of uncertainty hanging over children's entanglement with their parents—it's tricky sort of weather, that changes again and again without warning, from cold to hot, overcast to sunny, arid to humid, a sudden storm and then peace and tranquility.

On the table at the bistro the sugar packets were piling up, and the waiter, who was standing in a corner, sent a pleading glance our way, but of course didn't say a word. Katrina closed her eyes and asked if I dreaded the day when one of my own children would muster the courage to write a book about me, the same way I had written a book about my mother and father in *The Pure Element of Time*.

"The main thing is that they should write," I said with resignation. "I guarantee you that whatever they write will be received with love."

"You're deceiving yourself, sweetheart. You think you're open to criticism. After all, in your eyes you're such a severe judge of yourself that nobody could possibly surprise you with things you hadn't already accused yourself of. But of course, you're wrong. Like all of us, you make endless concessions and compromises with yourself. No one can see all their own weaknesses, especially the ones you can't change. And children, who have a uniquely sophisticated intelligence for anything concerning their parents, excel at touching the most painful and sensitive spots."

Katrina separated the packets of sugar into two camps, brown sugar in one camp and white sugar in the other, and said that pure logic was trying to subdue her craving for a child. "Why bring a being into the world who will just torture me the way that I torture my mother?" she whispered.

She apologized in advance for what she was about to say. In her opinion, the unfinished business that she and all her generation have with their parents concerning the repressed past, the hidden past, the oppressive past, or to put it another way, concerning the Nazi filth that was never cleaned up, is the mirror image of the grudge that the second generation in Israel hold against their parents who survived the Holocaust. "But I never forget for a moment that our unfinished business is with the executioner, and your unfinished business is with the condemned—with who was lowered from the scaffold at the last moment still sporting the signs of the rope on his neck. To say nothing of the fact that you and your writers are much stricter with yourselves, and many times more candid and decent than we and our writers are."

The packets were gradually being gathered up and returned to the ceramic holder, to the obvious relief of the waiter, who had stopped nervously clicking his ballpoint pen, and Katrina asked if my next novel was also going to deal with the entangled relations between children and parents.

"If you'll let me give you some advice," Katrina took hold of my hands, which were moving nervously across the table, "the time has come for you to stop writing about a little boy who looks up at his father and mother from below. Enough. You're already a parent yourself. Your children are grown up. You're even a grandfather. After all, you dedicated *The Pure Element of Time* to your granddaughters. Stop it. Grow up. Start writing from another point of view. Write honestly and lovingly about your loves. True, it's much more difficult, much more complicated, but it's also more interesting and courageous than writing all the time about men and women who died a while ago."

I admitted to her that a respected literary scholar had said something similar, quite excitedly, during the summer we'd spent at Yarnton, outside Oxford, when I was trying to revive the novel I'd begun writing in the Black Forest.

"Who is authorized to tell writers what to write anyway," Katrina changed her tone and hinted to the waiter to bring her the check. "Don't listen to anyone, do only what your heart tells you. Afterwards the critics can write whatever they want, and the readers will either read it or not, but you'll have the book that you dreamed of."

A noisy group of young boys and girls, art students from the look of it, entered the inner room where we were sitting and began talking up a storm, but we both sat lost in thought, looking at each other.

"No, don't start telling me what your new novel is about," Katrina said. "A book, like wine, has to age in sealed casks."

After she took care of the bill, she passed her finger over my lips that had cracked from the cold. "You can use my lip gloss," she said and asked if I'd made use of the book that she'd given me when we parted the evening after our first meeting in Berlin, standing awkwardly, full of emotion, at the entrance to the U-Bahn. "Now, too, I feel like giving you a story as a parting gift. Maybe this story will actually be of some benefit to you."

"We're not saying goodbye yet," I added hurriedly. "We're meeting tomorrow before lunch at the Colloquium."

"Tomorrow the whole gang will be there and we won't be able to exchange a single sentence."

Katrina took her coat and hat from the waiter and said that a colleague of hers, a folk art scholar who was studying Mizrahi synagogues, told her that in the ancient Aram-Zova synagogue in Aleppo, she'd seen ostrich eggs hung before the holy ark. The old caretaker who'd opened the place told her that according to local legend, the female ostrich does not sit on her eggs like other birds, but warms them with her gaze until they crack open. If one concentrated, said the caretaker in the striped robe, one could crack open thick eggs the size of a child's head, and one might even tear open the heavens.

"The time has finally come for you to be a mother ostrich, sweetheart," Katrina said and handed me her coat so that I could help her get it on. "It's an indispensable trait for writers."

Translated by Binyamin Shalom

ESHKOL NEVO was born in Jerusalem in 1971. He studied copy-writing, and then psychology at Tel Aviv University. Nevo teaches creative writing and thinking at various academic institutions. He has published a collection of short stories, a non-fiction book and two novels. His novel, *Homesick*, on the bestseller list for 60 weeks, was awarded the Book Publishers Association's Gold Book Prize (2005), and has been published in Italian and German. Forthcoming in French and English.

Israel between the two Intifadas. Four friends, who served in the army during the first Intifada, gather to watch the 1998 World Cup Final, and write a secret wish list. At the next Cup Final, they will see which ones they have fulfilled. The novel follows the four, close but also competitive and driven by their passions. And around them, a

tense, stressed-out society, in which repression has become a way of life. When the second Intifada breaks out, the main question becomes clear: in a society and a reality like ours, can wishes be fulfilled?

World Cup Wishes

Tel Aviv, Kinneret, Zmora-Bitan, Dvir, 2007. 336 pp.

Eshkol Nevo

World Cup Wishes

I *An excerpt from the novel*

drove slowly, real slowly. It seemed pretty stupid to me to die in a car accident when I was so close to making Ophir's dream come true.

When you drive slowly you notice all the different shades of green in the fields, the flocks of birds flying in swift-changing formations over the fish pools of Ma'agan Michael, and the new neighborhood they're building next to Neveh Yam, where there used to be a water park that had the bluest slides in the whole country; and as you slide down the slope of memories, other trips along this highway—whose official name is No. 2, though it's Highway No. 1 in your life—come floating up within you. Like that time Churchill helped you move your things to an apartment in Tel Aviv, driving his Beetle along behind you, and after a while he called you on your cell phone to say he was thirsty, was there a chance you had anything to drink in your car, and you told him there was mineral water but you didn't want to pull over, so he drove up alongside, you passed him a bottle through the window and he took a few sips and gave it back, still driving along the entire time. Then there were the night-time rides back from Haifa on Saturday nights, with all those songs on Army Radio, and your heart tightened with hope that there'd be some beautiful soldier standing at the hitchhiking stop, and just like in that Eran Tzur song, you'd pull over for her and "fall in love with her in an instant;" or the driver who picked you up hitching to your base when you yourself were a soldier who kept nodding off the whole way, until finally he fell asleep outright, and you jumped over and grabbed the wheel by force, saving both your lives; and he thanked you very emotionally and took your address to invite you for a free meal at his restaurant, but to this day he never got in touch. And there's that huge throne—God's throne—on the cliff across from Atlit, where one time, as you were passing it, Ye'ara asked if you knew who put it there, and why, and to your great embarrassment, you didn't know; then she suggested that on the way back the two of you go up to check it out, and if it wasn't a monument for the fallen or something sad like that, then you could make love there, because she really got off on unique locations. But on the way back she fell asleep and her cheeks were so soft you didn't have the heart to wake her. Now here's the moment the highway escapes from the limestone hills, and all at once you see the water, not some narrow strip but the entire blue expanse of sea. It's right here that you always want to forget about all your prior commitments and just pull the car over onto the shoulder, get undressed and run out into the waves. You remember that even on the way to Ilana's funeral, Ophir glanced to the left now and then, and said, look at the color of the sea today, but you didn't pull over because Maria was letting out these jagged, heart-rending sobs; anyway, how can you go to the shore on the way to a funeral. And you don't pull over now either, you keep driving straight ahead, because you've got to talk to your father, you've just got to, and on Sundays he closes at five on the dot because he believes that printing machines are fated to break down on Sundays—they're a little sleepy after taking the day off Saturday—so you've really got less than an hour. If you're late, you're going to miss a day's work, and every day counts because the World Cup is getting closer.

When I walked into the print shop my eyes still scanned for my mother, out of habit. Twenty-five years she worked next to her husband, handling the layout: photography, editing, plates. When things were going well, she had four employees under her, but in recent years the whole process became computerized, which made her and her employees superfluous. At first my father tried to stand firm against change and held off buying the advanced equipment (perhaps his heart prophesied what would happen?), but after his clients and commissions threatened to go elsewhere if he didn't modernize his operation, The Lark at last joined the new, less romantic era in publishing. And one day, a little before six in the evening—closing time since forever—my mother got up from her seat and started putting all the little optimistic signs always fluttering over her desk into a cardboard box:

An apple a day keeps the doctor away

Smile—it's a curve that makes everything straight

Smile and the world smiles back at you

In God we trust. All others pay cash

My father sat and watched her silently. When she went ahead and took down the books and notepads from the shelf behind her and placed them in the box, he added a raised eyebrow to his silence. But when she began to clear off her many photographs of Princess Diana (with Harry, with William, with both sons together) he found it difficult to hold back his emotion, so he cleared his throat.

She turned to look at him. For a brief moment their eyes met, and were immediately lowered in shame.

That's it? he asked.

That's it, she said. There was no aggression in her voice. Or anger. Just quiet determination, the kind that makes clear there's no room for argument. And just like that, with those two words, twenty-five years of joint creativity, joint failures and joint successes came to an end. The live thread that bound my parents to one another was cut, the bond that forced them to talk at the shop even when they didn't exchange a single word at home, that made them get up and stand on their own two feet, together, after my little sister was not born; that prevented them—even then—from taking a vacation for more than a week, because, "it's much easier to lose a client you've got than to make a new one."

After she left the print shop, my mother tried to make all her dreams come true in one go.

She renewed contact with her friends from university after being out of touch for years while they all looked after their homes, and they met weekly for breakfasts that stretched into the evening, signed up for lectures on the New Wave in French cinema and went together on a heritage tour of Morocco even though not one of them was of Moroccan descent. At the urging of her new-old friends, my mother dyed the roots of her hair blond and changed hairstyles, though her face remained the most beautiful I'd ever seen. She smiled more, and wept more. And she joined a course for local guides offered by the Ministry of Tourism, despite my father's anger and skepticism—he claimed that no tourist would want an older guide when he could just as easily get a younger one.

But as it turned out, most of the tourist groups that come to the city are composed of older people, who actually feel more comfortable with a woman their age who has perfect English and a smile like sunshine. In fact, within less than a year, my mother became the star of the local tourism branch. Every day, you could see her striding along energetically in her worn-green health sandals, a winding-enthusiastic clump of people trailing behind her with well-brimmed hats and cameras. The route was set: from Panorama Street, via the Baha'i Gardens, down to the German Colony and the port, and returning from there via the cable car to Stella Maris. Except that my mother added a special new stop to the route at 49 Independence Street. The official reason for this was that the building once held a secret weapons cache of the Haganah, and this gave her the opportunity to unfold tales of hair-raising battles in her listeners' ears, tales so loved by tourists from countries where peace reigns supreme. The unofficial reason for the stop was the building next door, at 47 Independence Street, whose ground floor held The Lark print shop.

Almost every day my mother would position herself with her back to the place where she had worked for twenty-five years, turn on the little microphone attached to her collar and begin telling the history of the secret weapons caches and its use.

She knew well that from where he sat, the owner of the print shop could see her, and in order to be sure that he could also hear her, she would turn up the volume on her voice until it was almost a yell. Sometimes, when the spirit moved her, she would also finish off the visit by calling her listeners' attention to the fact that next to the building which once housed the weapons cache, you could still see one of the first print shops in Haifa, a local monument the likes of no other.

Think about it dear, she laughed, sitting across from him at one of our family dinners, in Japan there are now hundreds of people who have a picture of The Lark in their photo albums!

My father failed to see the humor in it. He thought that her public recommendation of the print shop was meant to ridicule him and remind him, in a particularly cruel manner, that she was now earning more money than him. Every day anew he would swear that as soon as he saw the nose of the tourist bus approaching he would take off for the back of the print shop, behind the machines, from where he couldn't see the street, yet every day he'd stay glued to his chair staring at her fragile back and listening to her talk. How fluent, full of life, and with all that knowledge. How patient she is, too, so open to the questions of the group.

Truth is, your mother is a terrific guide, he admitted to me one Friday evening, after she'd already gone off to bed. But he was incapable of saying it to her.

For her part, from the time she left she never once came in to say hello to him. Not even once!

And he, for his part, filled her spot with pretty young design-ers in the hope that one day she *would* come in and see them, and eat her heart out. But not one of these designers lasted more than a month. He would pay them pennies and tyrannize them with regular diatribes, complaining that their work ethic was poor, they had no soul, no real love for the profession, and in the end they would just get up and leave—which left him amazed time after time, for "*once people knew the value of a regular job.*"

After four different designers had fled within a year, he "came to the conclusion that, essentially, he doesn't need a designer, since he knows how to do the basic things himself, and what he can't do, he can always outsource."

That was the explanation he gave me when I asked him why mom's chair was empty. After a brief silence, during which he looked me over along with the bundle of papers under my arm, he wondered aloud whether a graduate in bumming around like me even knew what outsourcing was.

With outward cool, I threw out the Hebrew term, which I knew well from dozens of translations, and held myself back despite the disdain hidden in his question (you didn't travel this far to fight with him! I checked myself silently).

To what do I owe the honor? he asked as he occupied himself with a checkbook lying open on the desk. He always busied himself with the checkbooks when he was embarrassed, the palms of his large hands—they wrapped me in towels on that rainy day—touching the pads and his fingers straightening any wayward crease.

I wanted to ask you something, I said and sat down.

That's what I thought, he said, and signed one of the checks. I mean you wouldn't come all this way just to see how your father's doing, right?

How *are* you doing? I asked.

His eyes flashed up at me in surprise. And were immediately lowered to the desk.

Business isn't good right now, not good at all, he said (my father always answered about his business when asked how he was doing. And business was never good. Overall I don't remember him ever expressing satisfaction. Or contentment. I once asked my mother about it and she said, "your father has many talents, but the talent for being content isn't one of them").

These bloody terror attacks, he went on, people don't feel like spending money. And this street is going down all the time. A week ago I got here in the morning and found some fat junkie in the doorway of the shop. Tell me, aren't junkies supposed to be skinny? Three police officers could hardly move him!

So maybe you should go up to the Carmel already? I made the usual suggestion.

Maybe, he answered with the usual response. At any rate, I have to find a buyer first. Rule number one, son, never buy with money you don't have! He waved a finger at me. I stayed silent, duly rebuked. Meanwhile, he signed another check. All the machines in the print shop had fallen silent except for the Roland Galley '72, which labored on robustly. It was the first printing machine my father had bought when he opened the business, and through all the years he never let anyone else get near her. At the end of every day, he would oil her, clean her and wipe her down. A few times I even heard him talking to her.

Tell me, Dad, I tried to renew the conversation, how's that writer doing, Miron-Michberg?

Why do you ask? My father raised suspicious eyebrows over his glasses.

No reason, I said, I just suddenly remembered him.

He went crazy, the poor bastard. I called him a few weeks back. I noticed he hadn't come in with his book like every other year, so I wanted to see how he was doing. His wife answered. Said he was institutionalized at Tirat Hacarmel. She committed him, she had no choice. He bought an aquarium the size of a closet, and decided he was moving into it. Two months he lay there in the living room, inside the aquarium, ate his meals there, slept there. Wrote there. Watched TV from there. Can you imagine? In the end she broke down and had him committed.

Wow.

She says it's because of what happened to him in concentration camp, that he never managed to get over it. I don't think so. I think that any person who sits at home all day and just writes, and doesn't have a job and doesn't see people, is bound to go crazy in the end.

I nodded hesitatingly, and remembered Ophir's words about the depths of fear lying in wait for every artist. I stepped on the bunch of pages I'd placed under the seat and pressed down hard, hoping the fear would shrink. Shrink until it disappeared.

So what...what did you want to ask me? my father asked, putting aside the checkbook and going to work on a stack of receipts.

"Forget it," that's what the hero of an American series would say, creating a bittersweet sense of missed opportunity, stretching the plot out a little further, another episode, another season even, if the ratings are high enough. But me—I had the World Cup on my mind.

Translated by Binyamin Shalom

photo © Dan Porges

BORIS ZAIDMAN was born in 1963 in Kishinev in the former USSR and immigrated to Israel in 1975. He holds a BA in visual communication from Bezalel Academy of Art and Design, and also studied copywriting. Zaidman has worked for many years in advertising and marketing-communications, as a graphic designer, art director and copywriter. He also teaches communications at several academic institutions. Zaidman was awarded the ACUM Ashman Prize in 2005. *Hemingway and the Dead-Bird Rain* is his first novel, soon to be published in French, German and Italian.

Tal Shani, a typical rough-edged Tel Aviv youth, is invited to go to the USSR. The moment he boards the plane, however, Tolik Schneiderman appears, a Russian-Jewish child who sat alone in a tiny

apartment, fearing to be "taken away" like his grandfather. From then on, the novel alternates between Tal's Israeli self and the "foreigner" hiding within him. With a style as finely honed as a laser beam, Boris Zaidman lays before us—perhaps for the first time in Hebrew literature—the double inner life of the "Russian immigration" to Israel.

Hemingway and the Dead-Bird Rain

Tel Aviv, Am Oved, 2006. 221 pp.

Boris Zaidman

Hemingway and the Dead-Bird Rain

R osa's front yard always reminded Tolka of summer
An excerpt from the novel

vacation. Even when he and his mother were sucked into it on the
raging wings of December gales that lashed fiercely at their backs and
slammed the gate shut with sharp, dry cracks of frost. Tolka and his
mother would step between the mounds of snow on the path Rosa
had dug in preparation for their arrival. She had scattered handfuls
of dry sand along the twisting wadi between the white hills so that
her guests wouldn't slip on their way to the house. The brown trails
of sand looked to Tolka like small, thin snakes slithering along with
them to the front door.

Rosa's comfortable house lay sleepily in an old quarter of the
city. Tolka lived far away in the stomach of one of the gray concrete
soldiers that lined the streets of his neighborhood. Rosa's house was
an enchanted desert island run solely by Rosa-Robinson, and only
Tolka-Friday was allowed set a bare foot on its land, during summer

vacation, and the untended yard became an ocean that surrounded them completely, cutting them off from the world.

The enchantment would begin right at the old gate. Its hinges squeaked menacingly the minute someone dared touch its rusty handle, which had been cast in the shape of a horse and protruded from the forehead of the gate like the prow of a Viking ship. Undaunted, Tolka would boldly grab the horse's head and press it down hard like a mighty cavalryman subduing a wild pony. He would push the heavy wooden door with his shoulder until it yielded, then slip through the narrow crack. The gate would slam itself shut, leaving behind the noisy, sweaty world of urban summer. There, in the sea of weeds, the air was cool and pleasant even in the hothouse of late August, and the smell of mildew, nettle and cat piss enveloped him, piercing his nostrils, tickling his nose and making his eyes water, stirring his spring fever from its summer sleep. Tolka would peel off his sandals, run barefoot along the stone path to the front door, forgo the nicety of knocking on the door, run straight inside, float through the living room to the kitchen, press his pug nose against the small window facing the street and wave to his mother. She would blow him a kiss, "a wind kiss," swivel around on her heels and clack her way back to the tram, trying to grab the tail of another panting day.

Rosa was already in the kitchen, still wrapped in her long, flowered nightgown, her breasts and hips imprisoned in an apron, bent over the large pots on the stove. She was a big woman in her mid-forties, and in her unrestrained lushness reminded Tolka of one of Rubens's or Renoir's soft, huge women. The ones who looked shamelessly out at him from the yellowing pages of the potbellied art books that stood on the shelves in Rosa's living room. Her body, steaming through the folds of cloth, her tight apron and the aromas of the food cooking in the pots made his head spin hotly, and he tried to hide the embarrassing results by thrusting his hands into his pants pockets, blushing to the roots of his straw-colored hair. Rosa's buoyant laughter was spiced with thick sadness, the love of body and soul, many small secrets and one large one all blended together and living peacefully in the large garden of her spirit. Moving apart and brushing against each other, touching and overlapping, converging and endlessly invading each other's space.

Aunt Rosa's big secret was "him." Uncle Niyuma. Sometimes, when she was in a good mood, it would become "Nayum," "Niyumchka," or just plain "Niyumka." But usually, it was simply "him." And for Tolka, despite the portrait hanging on the wall, despite Rosa's stories or maybe because of them, he was still a big secret. With time, Tolka turned him into a secret grandfather, and Niyuma let him: one night, after one of their long conversations, Niyuma nodded quietly to him with his colored eyes from the black-and-white photograph and consented to be his grandfather.

For Tolka had no grandfathers, neither his mother's father nor his father's father. His mother's father left her and his grandmother, evaporated at some point in the twilight of Tolka's babyhood, and during the first years of his abandonment, was a flash in Tolka's consciousness in the form of small white envelopes, their edges adorned with red-blue diamond shapes and the silhouette of an airplane on the upper left-hand corner. When his mother took them out of the mailbox, she didn't even open them. But she didn't tear them up either. She'd put them into the bottom drawer of the wardrobe, the only drawer that had a key. Once, she told Tolka that if he wanted to, he could read them someday, but not now. And that "not now" and that "someday" turned into an eternity that had no beginning and no end. Whenever he'd ask her when that "someday" would start and that "not now" would end, she'd turn her back on him, but not in anger, he knew it wasn't in anger, even though he didn't see her face. She'd go into the kitchen or onto the small balcony, and he saw her eyes through the pale back of her neck, as if she were transparent. He saw them grow moist, ripening for tears. Sometimes, when she was standing that way, her back to Tolka, she'd run her hand over her cheek, sometimes wipe her nose with a perfumed white handkerchief, and that was it. She'd turn back to Tolka, her old-new self, the omnipotent-omniscient-forgiving-life-goes-on-as-usual Momma.

His father's father, Tolik, whose name Tolka bore, was murdered by the landowners. They killed him in the same war that Niyuma managed to come home from. And he didn't just come home; he came home with a medal of valor. That medal sat in a small, square, red velvet box. Sometimes, in the evening, when Tolka slept over at Rosa's, she would open the glass door of the breakfront and take it out, hold it in her hand, open it carefully and let Tolka touch it. And Tolka was proud of Niyuma for settling the score with those landowners, those fascists, for what they did to his original grandfather.

Not only wasn't Uncle Niyuma Tolka's uncle, but Rosa wasn't his aunt either. Momma told him that she and Rosa met after the war, when they came back to the city, or what was left of it after the German steamroller—after four years of darkness—she'd say. When they returned, the two families lived in one of the summer dachas in the center of the ruined city. Two families that had survived, in a house that had survived, in a city that had survived, she'd say. As the words streamed from her lips, she'd smile, as if she were remembering something pleasant. "Back then?!" She'd ask-declare. "Only survival! Only the body's survival! No one talked about the mind. Two slices of gray bread with a piece of salami hiding between them was the best psychologist!" Here, Tolka would lose the thread of her story, seized by a sharp, demanding hunger, as if he himself had just come back from there.

"We were always bumping into each other," his mother would say, "all of us in two little rooms, one communal kitchen for six families and a rotting, falling-apart doghouse-outhouse-hole at the far end of the yard. Once a week, Rosa and I would go to the *banya*"—the city bathhouse next to the bakery—and Rosa took the *debchoska* under her wing.

"The *debchoska*, the *maydeleh*, was me," she'd laugh as Tolka listened open-mouthed.

"I was skin and bones, a twelve-year-old stick. It was a miracle that I survived Hitler and his henchmen, hunger, tuberculosis and typhus. Rosa took me under her wing, also pretty well plucked then, and taught me a thing or two about life. And ever since," the lyric flow of her words halted, "ever since, despite the age difference, we've never parted."

In addition to Tolka-Friday, two other natives lived perma-nently on Rosa's island. The first to welcome Tolka when he slipped into the yard was the cat, Vaska. Vaska was the name of all Russian yard cats. Vaska was short for Vassily, just like Tolka was short for Anatoly and Jenka, his friend's name, was short for Yevgeny. Even Sashka, Jenka's little brother was a young seedling that would grow into Alexander. That specific cat's name was actually Vasco, Rosa told him, after Vasco da Gama, the Portuguese explorer, and he was given the name because of his tireless curiosity. But with time, the whiskered tomcat lost his noble title and was demoted to the common Vaska. He would curl his tail around Tolka's ankle, rub against him, his nostrils quivering and the ends of his whiskers pricking-stroking his bare feet, reconstructing the stories of Tolka's voyage through the ocean of the city. Then, purring with satisfaction, Vaska would lead his guest to the house, the hair of his upright tail standing on end, clearly visible to all the females they might meet on the way.

The name of the other native living on the island was Sharik. Sharik was a huge, tired German shepherd, his once luxurious fur thinned by the years, his tail hanging permanently between his legs. Most of the day, he lay in his doghouse at the far end of the yard with his front legs crossed at the opening. He looked out at his surroundings with disgust, as if to say, nothing in this screwed-up world of yours surprises me anymore, and as he did so, stuck out his pink, quivering tongue at both Tolik and Vaska.

Even when it came to guard dogs, Rosa told him, Niyuma had cosmopolitanism bursting out of every pore. She explained to Tolka that a cosmopolitan was a citizen of the world, and in the good old days, people were put away for that too. When he asked her what those "good old days" were and who was put away and for what, and why Niyuma wanted so badly to become a citizen of the world in addition to being a citizen of the Soviet Union, she just waved her hand with a "you're too young to know" gesture. Tolka was familiar with that "you're too young" from home and had figured out a long time ago that it was an obvious disguise for sorry-but-I-have-no-real-answer-and-when-you-grow-up-maybe-you'll-understand. Or maybe not, like me.

And so, Niyuma the cosmopolitan called his dog Sharik. After General Charles de Gaulle, the French president whose height would not have put any CSKA Moscow player to shame, and whose face was adorned by a magnificent Jewish nose. It was very important, Rosa said, for Niyuma to have a German shepherd. Because if a Jew takes a guard dog, he used to say, then it should be German. No one has ever guarded us better.

"And why Charles de Gaulle?" asked Tolka, an excellent student in the faculty of the grown-ups' "you're too young" stories.

"Because of his defeatist character," she explained. Niyuma said they tricked him, and instead of a German shepherd, they stuck him with a French sheep. He would always make fun of him for barking at the whole world from inside his doghouse and coming out only when he smelled his dish. And that was just like Charles de Gaulle, he'd say, who barked from his doghouse in London while the Germans shit in his front yard. Only after the Americans cleaned up the occupier's shit and served him the *pulkas* of Paris in a dog's dish, only then did he run to "liberate" the city while he waved his *fransoizische* tail and barked loudly, "*Paris est libérée.*" And actually, at that point, Tolka had to agree that he really was too young for all of that.

After they took Niyuma, the dog also lost his noble status and was demoted from Charles to the country-*mujik* name, Sharik, and no one remembered he was a member of the Aryan race.

On their way to Rosa, Vaska and Tolik walked past the old wooden storehouse, his storehouse. No one had been allowed to enter it until he came back. The storehouse had already sunk into a sea of nettles up to its window-eyes. And the broken panes, which no one had taken the trouble to fix, winked at Tolka with the inviting-forbidding menace of evil. And sometimes he thought that someone (maybe even he himself) was looking at him from behind them, as if through dark gun holes, watching every move he made on Rosa's island.

There was also a large cellar that emitted winter breaths even in the middle of August. Right under the three steps that led to the front door. That's where Rosa kept sacks of *kartoshka* and the huge jars of pickles she made from all the bounty of mother earth: cucumbers and cabbage, carrots and tomatoes, even apples and watermelons.

"She pickled her life too," Mama would say and sigh the way only she knew how, from the depths of her lungs and her heart, as if she were singing a hymn to guilt, to a stricken conscience, to sorrow, longing and memories. A hymn to Rosa's aloneness, and to her own early orphanhood.

The space in Rosa's living room had an inner lining. It was like a soft, warm fur lining inside a thick, rough zip-on: wooden shelves packed with books covered all the walls from the faded wood floor to the peeling ceiling that had seen neither brush nor whitewash since they took *him* away. A wooden ladder leaned against one wall, and Tolka was allowed to climb it, but only when Rosa watched him from below, holding the legs of the ladder and supporting the base with her large body. When Tolka had first learned to read, he would stand dumbstruck for long minutes in front of the rows of books, twist his neck and tilt his head to the side. Soundlessly, he would weave the letters into the titles imprinted vertically in the direction he was used to reading from Azbuka, the Cyrillic alphabet.

They all stood to attention in the straight, crowded rows, his soldiers, the "collected works:" in the center of the middle shelf were the bottle-green bindings of Chekhov supported on the left by a company of gray Gogols. A battalion of grim-looking Dickenses in chocolate brown squeezed them from the right, volume pressed up against volume in tight British order. And from within all that dark brown-green, a youthful Mark Twain suddenly winked at him with a boyish smile in orange letters dancing on shiny bright blue spines. The glittering Pushkins glowed in gold print on fiery red, and above them, a whole division of Tolstoys in soft café-au-lait uniforms.

First, he learned to recognize the "collected works" soldiers according to the color of their uniforms. Then, slowly, he became familiar with their contents, discovering new worlds in their silent pages. Some were unclear to him, others completely incomprehensible. But he never stopped pounding on their unyielding gates, waking them with naïve insolence from dusty years of sleep. And they began to open before him, first slowly, grudgingly, spilling words into sentences, revealing lines, paragraphs, then whole pages. And finally, they would yield and unfold their plots before him in a huge flow. So he got the rainy Dickens to talk, easily became friends with Twain, tried the magic of his naïveté on Chekhov's short stories, which acquiesced with provincial openheartedness, but when he couldn't crack the wall of Balzac's *Human Comedy*, he gave up, folded his bespectacled tail and promised to revisit it in a year or two.

The portrait hung on the wall above the top shelf. His portrait, the one of Uncle Niyuma (in his mind, he already called him just plain Niyuma, without any uncle-nephew niceties, and Niyuma heard and was not offended. On the contrary, he looked down at him from the wall with an approving smile). It was a gray, faded black-and-white photograph of his face, neck and shoulders squeezed into a simple wooden frame that had darkened with the years and was heavily dotted with greenish spots of mold. Looking out at him from the photo were knowing, mocking-smiling eyes entrenched in the deep caves that had been carved out under the rock of his forehead. A tanned, warm rock etched with lines of laughter, irony and even open mockery. Or maybe they were just smile lines, the lines of an embarrassed, all-knowing smile. Then Tolka would go back to the eyes. Sometimes they were open to the world in amazement and other times they were narrowed to cracks of frozen skepticism. Beginnings and ends were intertwined in them, flashing at him, telling all they could tell to the walls of the house and to a child-adult like Tolka.

Two lone soldiers stood under Niyuma's portrait, squeezed together in the middle of the top shelf, lost among all the Russian divisions, the top of their spines touching the picture frame. Two soldiers in wintry melancholy-black, as if they had been attached to the Cyrillic army from a distant front, a different war. They huddled together there like two brothers, twins who had only each other left on those snowy shelves. From the silvery letters printed on their spines, Tolik was able to make out a new, strange name, and he breathed the sharp, still sounds that pulled his lips in unexpected directions. That name didn't have the round Russian fullness, so close and warm, or the French delicacy that rolled on your tongue, almost slipping down into your throat. It didn't have anything familiar or known. Slowly,

Tolka read the two words, one short and the other long, pronounced them carefully, their sounds filling his palate, turning his tongue over, rolling in his throat. He repeated them again and again, until he managed to pronounce them properly: "E-R-N-E-S-T. H-E-M-I-N-G-W-A-Y. Ernest Hemingway."

Translated by Sondra Silverston

photo © Dan Porges

ASAF SCHURR was born in Jerusalem in 1975 and has a BA in philosophy and theater from the Hebrew University of Jerusalem. He has worked on the editorial staff of the magazine *Kahn* for human and animal rights and environmental issues. At present, he is an editor for the culture, art and politics website *Maarav*, writes literary reviews for the press and is a translator. Schurr received the Bernstein Prize (2007) and the Minister of Culture's Award (2007) for *Amram*.

Amram and Avichai's lives revolve around their love for a woman—for the one it is his motherless daughter, for the other his childless wife. Yet in this novel, gestures of love are slowly replaced by black masks, blunt objects and crushed bones as the two men, unknown to one another, hide their faces and wreak havoc throughout the city. Their love drives them to terrible acts in protection of their loved ones,

carrying out summary justice on rapists, drug dealers and other criminals. And as confusion takes over, we no longer know which face hides behind which mask.

Amram

Tel Aviv, Babel, 2007. 227 pp.

Asaf Schurr

Amram

An excerpt from the novel

Every evening Avichai and Ella sit down to eat together. The TV is switched off, the newspapers lie folded on the third chair, and they sit facing each other and eat their salad and omelet. A lot of time and effort was demanded from both of them in order to maintain these meals on a regular basis, and now they are very dear to them both. Once he hardly ever said anything to her about what his day was like and what he had done. He was afraid the details would bore her. 'But Avush,' she said to him maybe ten years ago, 'what do you think people talk about? If you only keep your most remarkable thoughts for me, we'll end up talking maybe once a week.'

Another five years passed until he was persuaded. In the middle they almost split up; Ella fell in love, in retrospect perhaps she only thought she had fallen in love, that's what was said afterwards, by somebody at work. Avichai was strong and resolute, it nearly drove her crazy, but in the end he broke down and cried all night long. Ella held him then, trembling, and from then on she didn't stop. If he had been forced to say it clearly in words, Avichai would have said that something cracked in him that night, when he lay in the empty bed (at that precise moment Ella was brushing her teeth) and thought that soon the bed would be empty forever, that he would be without her for the rest of his life. Something cracked in him and remained cracked, and suddenly there was (through the crack) a way out of himself.

Not everything comes out, in any case. There are things he hides. Not because he's ashamed of them (okay, maybe a bit because of that: not exactly ashamed in his own mind, but aware that he'll feel uncomfortable if anyone else knows, even Ella. Especially Ella), but still.

In any case, ever since then he talks more. Not without stopping, but a lot more. Sometimes it's as easy as spreading his hands in the wind. Sometimes it's more of an effort. Even things that are, theoretically, very general and abstract can become terribly personal. Things like heredity versus environment, for example. Once, Avichai would tilt his head slightly sideways and purse his lips in a near smile when he read about identical twins separated at birth, and lo and behold, thirty or forty years later, it turns out that both of them are firemen or accountants or refrigeration engineers or whatever; not because he necessarily believed in it, not because he thought it was some undeniable proof of something or other, but because he took pleasure in the possibility of clear patterns and lucid solutions (the same sideways tilt of his head accompanied the reading of books about quantum mechanics, for example, and it isn't entirely clear whether because he was astonished at the world being the way it was, or because he was astonished at our ability to comprehend the world being the way it is or to invent such a possibility at all).

When they talked about the treatments, in any case, he didn't tilt his head anywhere. He lay on his back and looked at the ceiling, the pillow cool and pleasant on the nape of his neck. Ella lay her head on him (only a minute ago she was still moaning, now she was so relaxed) and played absent-mindedly with the hair on his chest. "But don't tell anyone it's from a donation, okay?" Avichai requested, and he didn't really know why. If anyone had asked him, anyone else who was in his position, he would of course have made clear that being a good father wasn't a matter of providing good genes (at least not first and foremost). Love didn't come from there, or not only from there. And he more than anyone should know that this wasn't a guarantee of anything; the things he'd seen, the things he'd been told, they were enough to make it quite clear. Sometimes it seemed to him that people put out cigarettes on their children no less than they were ready to die for them. Sometimes they were the very same people, and you had to admit it was a little confusing.

So Avichai lay on his back. He felt relieved that the lengthy tests were over (those interminable waiting rooms alone were enough to drive you out of your mind). Knowing that there was no further need for the pills was a relief too, all those hormones couldn't be a good thing, but there was really no need to apologize or explain: before, there was a possibility that they would have a child who was both of theirs from beginning to end, and now that possibility was closed. What really frightened him wasn't the possibility that in the future this child would look at him and say, you're not my father. What frightened him was the opposite: the possibility that he himself would look at this child and feel it to be alien (but how could that be, he thought to himself, when in any case it would be Ella's child? Nothing that was Ella could be alien to him, he wanted very much to believe this, and he was sure it was true. Even the things that he didn't yet know he loved, even the women she would still be in the future). And in all honesty, how could he now suggest that they adopt a child and be done with it? It was already clear that the question of the genes was not insignificant to him, as he could have argued with complete honesty before the tests were concluded, and with very partial honesty now that they were over and everything was known.

Ella didn't say anything, but he had to say it again even if it wasn't completely clear to him why he was asking and what was supposed to come of it. "Don't tell anyone it's from a donation, okay?" Avichai had already seen enough of himself and others to know that you couldn't always know what to expect. You couldn't always even trust yourself, and people sometimes did things that were simply unbelievable.

Amram thinks it's important for Tikva to get almost everything she wants. He thinks she should be happy, and that this is the most important role he has in the world. For her to be happy. For her to be satisfied, but not spoilt. For her to have everything she wants, not because anyone is at her beck and call day and night, hearing whatever she asks for and guessing whatever she doesn't ask for, but because she wants the right things. He will help her to be a person who always wants the right things, and always wants only a little more than she has: enough to draw her forward, not enough to make her fall down.

And therefore Tikva is a flower given exactly the right amount of water. Not too little, so it won't straggle, but not too much either, so the leaves won't droop. She grows in unexpected directions, and he is proud of her for it.

One evening, for example, when she was small, five or maybe six, they sat down to have their supper in the kitchen. In the dining nook stood a big wooden table that Hava had brought with her from her parents' home, and they sat there when they had guests, family or friends of Amram's from work, or even if Tikva's friends from kindergarten wanted a slice of bread with something on it or stayed for supper, but the formica table in the kitchen was just for them. Almost every evening, never mind if Amram planned to go out later and never mind if there was a lot of pressure at work, the two of them would sit there. One Saturday, when Tikva was four, Amram made a whole operation out of it: he emptied out all the kitchen cupboards (they were coated with ghastly green formica), cleaned them, used up an entire box of tacks to pin flowered paper to the shelves, and then switched everything round. All the pots and pans, bowls and baking tins went upstairs, all the plates and cups, even the unopened dinner service they got for a wedding present, went downstairs, so that now Tikva could reach them easily. Every evening at six they would meet in the kitchen (there was no need for a watch or a reminder, they simply met there), Amram would fry an omelet and cut up vegetables for a salad, sometimes he would heat up chicken or something left over from Friday dinner, and Tikva would set the table with remarkable concentration.

They would work in absolute silence, preparing for their supper. From time to time their eyes would meet, and then they would smile.

In any case, on the evening in question Tikva finished setting the table (she chose the blue checked tablecloth and the tall glasses with flowers on them) and sat down to wait for him to finish frying the omelet, contemplating the bowl of salad that was already standing on the table (her additional task was to mix it, but only at the last minute). Amram divided the big omelet down the middle, then he put half on Tikva's plate and half on his plate. He replaced the frying pan on the stove (even the frying pan reminded him of Hava, the way she wiped it carefully, so as not to scratch the Teflon) and sat down. But when he wanted to put a piece of chicken on Tikva's plate, she covered the plate with both her hands.

"Don't want chicken," she said. "Tikki," said Amram in an almost scolding tone, "don't be spoilt." "Don't want chicken," Tikva said again. "How about schnitzel?" Amram tried. "Don't want chicken and don't want schnitzel," Tikva said, obstinately. "I don't want chicken and I don't want schnitzel ever ever ever." She folded her arms and pouted resolutely. "Why not?" asked Amram, and Tikva said, "Because they killed it."

It didn't come from him. He had never even considered abstaining from meat. It didn't come from him, but the jealousy that flooded him for a moment was nothing compared to his tremendous pride in this big daughter of his, who was already thinking for herself. Who decided for herself and stood by her decision. For a moment he still thought of making an issue of it, to see her stand her ground, but then he decided it wasn't such a good idea. "So maybe just this one little piece and that'll be it?" he tried anyway, wondering who he knew that didn't eat meat and would be able to tell him what he could give her instead, so her growth wouldn't be stunted. But Tikva said no, and he nodded gravely, because if he laughed she would be insulted, and then he took the oven dish and emptied it all into the trash. When he stood with his back to her he smiled anyway. How many times he had been proud of her since then, and he still couldn't look at the tablecloth (which was still folded up in one of the drawers) or think of the table without smiling that proud smile again.

Even though the story isn't about her this time, Hava is present, a bit like Eurydice in Gluck's opera: the curtain rises and she is already dead. Precisely for this reason she is important (you could almost say, precisely for this reason she is loved, but no).

Translated by Dalya Bilu

SAMI BERDUGO was born in 1970 and studied comparative literature and history at the Hebrew University of Jerusalem. He teaches creative writing at Tel Aviv University and Bezalel Academy of Art and Design, as well as holding writing workshops for youth. Berdugo has published a book of short stories and two novels. He won the *Haaretz* Short Story Competition (1998), and has received the Yaakov Shabtai Prize (2002), the Peter Schweifert Prize (2003), the Bernstein Prize (2003) and the Prime Minister's Prize (2005). Berdugo is the first Israeli to be awarded a Sanskriti Foundation Residency (New Delhi, 2007).

Both novellas in this book deal with men of North African descent, who feel excluded from mainstream Ashkenazi society. Here, 18-year-old Yechiel, the first *sabra* in his family, is about to be enlisted to the army. However, unlike the classic *sabra* in Hebrew fiction, he is

a hesitant and wary person, torn between the desire to prove himself "a man" like his older brother Shiko, and his fear of the years ahead. His mother's unexpected pregnancy at age fifty-two, which triggers conflict within the family, only increases his sense of alienation.

Orphans

Tel Aviv, Hakibbutz Hameuchad, 2006. 196 pp. 2 novellas

Sami Berdugo

Orphans

An excerpt from My Younger Brother Yehuda

A miracle happened in our family. Mother became pregnant at the age of fifty-two. I think that she's in her second or third month, and she still doesn't show, she's still the way she always is and is not showing any signs of change. We don't talk about this situation at home and are accepting the surprise as though it were something ordinary. Two weeks ago I heard her tell my father on the balcony, "There's nothing we can do, a miracle has befallen us, Mardosh, a miracle." Afterwards she looked straight ahead, sat upright on the sofa and didn't wait for Father or anyone else to answer her.

Father knows that that's how it is. He barely speaks in his thin voice. Mother loves him and she's good to him during these silences. I can't guess who started out the stronger in our family. Maybe Mother made Father like that over time, slowly turned him into the person he is. They get along together and you can feel Mother knows Father isn't weak, because he's always ready to listen to her and stand by her side, as though saying to her silently, "What should we do now, Julie?"

and he's waiting like all of us to see what will happen with the new child in her belly.

The baby is supposed to arrive in a few months and maybe the miracle will take place without a hitch. We haven't spoken yet about the physical complications that Mother could have. We all know that the situation isn't natural and it's dangerous to have children at her age. Until now I was sure we would stay as we are, only three siblings with Mother and Father and Grandma Yakota, who is always here. I thought that we would keep the family small, even smaller after Dina got married and left home, and Shiko is in the regular army, coming only every two weeks for the weekend. I already got used to these days long ago. Aside from me, there's also Yakota. But she barely leaves her room, and most of the time I'm alone in the big house that spreads out just for me. The empty rooms with the long corridor, and the living room that opens out to it and invites me to pass through. Every day I rediscover the decrease and the pleasant emptiness.

It's almost unreal to think what it was like once, when we all lived here without paying attention to where we were headed and what the future would be like. Dina, Shiko and even I saw Mother and Father in their permanent state of slight apathy. As though nothing shakes them up and they only know how to live in a straight line. Even now, with the miracle, they don't seem to worry about what will happen very soon, after the new child arrives and I'll have to join the army and leave home.

Meanwhile everything is all right. Mother continues to get up at five thirty, dresses quickly in her room, drinks hot tea in the kitchen and doesn't make much noise—she tries to make sure the house won't feel she's leaving it when she quietly shuts the door and goes out through the yard, walks to the bend in the road and waits on the sidewalk for the ride to Tadiran. Father gets up twenty minutes after her and walks hunched over. He drags himself to the kitchen, sits on the chair and drinks the leftovers from the pitcher that Mother prepared earlier. He sits without moving and waits for Yakota to wake up and call, "I'm up, Mardosh." Sometimes I hear her because her room is opposite mine and has no door either. I pull the blanket over my head, trying to hide from her voice and the light that comes in between the slats of the shutters, mingles with the darkness that is over and throws heat above my bed.

That's what's been happening to me every morning lately. If it weren't summer, maybe I wouldn't notice the noise and the shadows. I fight a war against them on the bed, trying hard to get rid of the disturbances. The best thing is to stretch out the sleep until noon, without seeing what's happening in the house when Father has already left.

I've turned my bed into a bunker. I toss out anything that's bothering me, and try hard to stick to the good part of the oppressive heat and bright darkness in the room. My eyes are closed and I'm still grabbing the ends of dreams, trying to enter them and convince myself that this is a time of not-here. I succeed in almost everything, but Fivefirst starts in with his sounds and his barking. Only he interrupts my attempts to continue sleeping and reminds me every morning that it's already late. He doesn't stop the noise that is repeated like a broken record; it comes from the balcony, passes through the front door, streams along the entire corridor and enters my room without difficulty. On the bed I'm already moving, very annoyed.

"Smelly son-of-a-bitch, shut up, Fivefirst, shut up already, you little shit," I curse onto the pillow. He should be killed now. I pray and kick at the blanket. "May you burn with your fucking barks," I say in a weak voice, with my eyes already open. Now all is lost, another late morning is over, my free time keeps getting shorter. Only the house and the coming day are waiting for me. On the balcony the barking continues. I throw off the blanket and get up to open the shutters a little.

I'm in the house almost all day. I hear the quiet of late morning and of the dark afternoon. The shutters in the living room are closed and give a feeling of coolness. They're always left that way, because the sun falls right on them and heats up the room as though we had only summer here. After eleven o'clock you can really feel it. I stand in the kitchen in underpants and a T-shirt, prepare instant coffee and take it to the living room. The dark light is pleasant and nobody sees me. During these hours I don't even hear Yakota. Sometimes I almost forget that she's there on the right side of the corridor, right at the end of the house. She won't leave her room until Father comes home from the local council at three o'clock.

The hot taste of the coffee convinces me that I'll always be here. The hour is stuck in my mind. There is nobody to come in and disturb my boiling hot drink. That's how the days begin. Everyone knows that very well and it's hard for them to understand how I can spend all these months before the army without doing anything. I reject every suggestion that they throw my way, especially when Mother asked me last week to come with her early in the morning on the Tadiran ride to ask if there's something for me in the factory for just a few months. I told her to forget it, I didn't understand how she even got this idea for me, especially now, with the whole new situation of the pregnancy that's progressing and still having no effect on her. When will we see the changes in her already. Father is keeping the tension inside him and hopes that Mother will manage to hang on to her belly and herself in her elderly body.

The excitement and fear come and go. At home they help me see that nothing is happening. Mother perspires a little more and comes home from work with circles on the underarms of her dress. Maybe that's the first sign of the change, but it may also be from the heat of late summer. Things are in their place. Only my memory of the house, and of the shape it used to have, change something in my mind.

My room brings strange feelings and mixes up the times. The walls seem to be talking to me about my time with Shiko. Since he went to the army the room is mine alone. Shiko gave up his part without a fight, and now he agrees to sleep in the living room when he comes home on Friday-Shabbat. It's even convenient for him. After he went out last Friday night, he came in late, lay down on the sofa and turned on the television low until he fell asleep. After that I heard Father go into the living room and turn off the television. Shiko sensed him and said, "Quiet Mardosh, quietly, Mardosh." Father went back down the corridor, walking slowly. Only then did I know that everyone has surrendered to the house, everyone is in his own place and there are no movements or changes. Within this silence I had memories about me and Shiko, and the darkness of the weekend brought new rules. Time could not be understood in my brain and my heavy body.

When I turned over to the other side of the bed, I pressed hard and dug into the mattress, that way you couldn't see the spot, and something strange began to come over me. It was almost weird when I remembered how Shiko used to sleep on a short bed opposite me. He would come into the room late, close the door quietly, take off all his clothes and lie naked under the blanket. He knew that I was awake and saw everything. I didn't speak, and I waited to see when he would fall asleep. But Shiko was wide awake. He bent down to the floor to take a cigarette out of his pants pocket, lit it with a lighter and took a hard puff, so its light came out over his face. He looked up at the ceiling and blew out smoke that stretched in a long line above him. "Go to sleep, Yechiel, I'm almost finished," he said. I was scared and didn't answer. Shiko took another puff, which looked like the spot of an orange lamp but with a stronger, more beautiful light and again I saw his serious yet happy face. I didn't understand where such maturity came from or how he was developing so fast and becoming a big man. Shiko drew on the cigarette and exhaled balls of smoke that he was proud of. The smell reached all the way to me. Mother and Father and Yakota were in the other rooms sleeping soundly and they didn't know anything. "That's it, I'm finishing," said Shiko, and he continued lying on his back with the cigarette between his fingers. I kept my eyes on the burning point that moved slowly, then he pulled out a stainless steel ashtray from under the bed, put it on his stomach, and waited a little longer in order to save the last puff. I waited with him quietly and didn't move, until he inhaled the end of the cigarette hard, loudly blew out smoke and crushed the cigarette in the ashtray.

I thought that Shiko was really grown up in those days. I don't smoke like him. I keep my lungs clean. The feeling of heat in my mouth disgusts me, especially now, at the end of the summer. Yakota sometimes mentions the tar that Shiko is putting into his body. Last Friday she also smelled the cigarette smoke and started to talk out loud from her room, "Trash, tar, tar." That's what she muttered to herself, and we all heard and wanted her to stop, but she continued, "Trash, Moshiko, tar, trash." Shiko got angry. He deliberately lit up a new cigarette, and Yakota reacted as though her sight had come back and began to shout louder, "You-have-to-keep-the-house-clean-of-Moshe's-tar-why-Julie-is-breathing-and-putting-it-into-her-belly-straight-into-the-body-of-a-sick-baby." Then Father intervened and tried to calm down the atmosphere and said in a loud voice for her to hear, "Everything will be all right, Yakota, everything's okay. "No-Mardosh-poor-Julie-now-it's-not-good-now-Moshe's-smoke-like-that. "Don't call me Moshe," Shiko shouted to her; he was not ashamed of anything, he said that he hates her with a passion and is only waiting for her to die. Then he approached the beginning of the corridor and shouted in the direction of her room, "That's how it is, Yakota, that's how it is, tar your black life," but Yakota was indifferent to his shouts and continued with herself. So Shiko got even angrier and shouted "You're tar, you hear, black tar," and only then did Mother intervene and shout at him to keep quiet already and leave her alone. "Let her leave all of us alone already," replied Shiko returning to his cigarette.

These shouts began from the time that Shiko was fourteen and began to smoke in the house without getting permission. He wasn't afraid of Mother. My father didn't say anything to him, Yakota was the only one who intervened a little. In those days she could still see with her eyes and tried to educate him to stop smoking because he was ending his future like that, starting with one cigarette, after that drugs, and straight to prison. Nobody intervened, and Shiko only gave her the finger and stayed away from her.

Almost a week has passed, and I'm already less worried about the army. I'm a little bit happy about the order in the house, but I feel like going outside and thinking about my luck, how it's the opposite of Yakota. I open the door and go down the low stairs straight into the yard. I can go to Rami, he lives near me. I walk barefoot in the direction of his house, which is located exactly where the road curves.

Something has changed in the atmosphere surrounding the houses that I pass. They're strange and have become quieter, as if deserted. The elderly people who live in them give you a feeling of something old. Rami was almost the only child in the area, and that's why I was with him from the beginning, even though he was a year and a half older than me. Shiko had friends from other neighborhoods, and from the city too. I didn't know a single friend of his, and he didn't bring them home either. Dina always hung around with two girls who grew up together. They remained good friends, until one of them went to work in a hotel in Eilat, and Dina was left only with the second one. But she left too, and then Dina met her boyfriend when she was nineteen. Two years later she married him and went to live in his town, in Nahariya.

Rami is still here and nobody knows what will become of him, not even him. I see the thin tree in his yard and peer inside through the window with the yellow panes. You can't see anything. I enter the paved path, reach the door and knock. There are noises in the house, but nobody answers. I knock more softly and begin to worry and hope that they won't open the door. Everything is still the same. I can hear small sounds. I stand without moving and try not to be noticed in front of the door, I walk backwards quietly and quickly get off the path, without peering into the window and discovering that someone has seen me.

Before I enter my house again, I remember that tomorrow is already Friday and a weekend is coming up. How much time like this do I still have?

Translated by Miriam Schlusselberg

YOSSI AVNI-LEVY was born in Israel in 1962 and served as an officer in the Israeli Defense Forces for several years. He then studied Middle Eastern history and law at the Hebrew University of Jerusalem. Avni-Levy has published two books of short stories and novellas, and two novels. He received the Prime Minister's Prize in 2007.

The life of Yonatan, an Israeli envoy to Berlin, changes dramatically when a young man named Sebastian asks him for help. The police come to his house, and his phone is tapped. While the net tightens around Yonatan, Sebastian's story unfolds, revealing his harsh youth in East Germany and, later, his recruitment into espionage. His past also revives Yonatan's childhood memories—the rundown neighborhood, the aroma of rice and mint, and Grandma Nana spitting out old love songs. Yet there is a subtle tension between the two men: is Sebastian friend or foe? The borderline between fact and fiction is more deceptive than ever.

איש ללא צל
יוסי אבני־לוי

A Man without Shadow

Tel Aviv, Kinneret, Zmora-Bitan, Dvir, 2007. 478 pp.

Yossi Avni-Levy

A Man without Shadow

An excerpt from the novel

Impatiently, he kept the appointments that the foxy secretary had made for him. He left his mobile phone in the middle of the table, as though it were some ritual object whose presence was necessary. But there were no calls.

At the end of the day he returned home and sprawled as usual in the yellow armchair, beneath the burnished grandfather clock he had purchased in Pforzheim. The spider web is closing in, he said aloud, something has to happen now.

When the phone rang he pounced on it like a hungry hawk on a field mouse.

"Are you alone?" a voice asked quickly.

It was him! Sebastian.

"Yes. And you? Are you alone?" he asked in a hostile voice.

"I ask the questions here," said Sebastian, interrupting him sharply. "Do you remember where you were standing when we last spoke on your mobile phone?"

"No, I don't remember a thing. Don't you think the time has come to…"

"Shh…" Sebastian silenced him. "Don't get emotional, okay. I'll ask you again, so concentrate. Do you remember where you were standing last time I called, dear new Mr. Conrad who went looking for me in cafés?" he asked impatiently.

"Yes, I do." Between Wittembergplatz and Nollendorfplatz. The broad shaven face of the waiter stared at him like a rodent. A short rat made a beeline for the bushes. A sausage bursting with fat sprawled in a tin skillet.

"Be there tomorrow at one P.M."

"But tomorrow I…"

"One P.M. or never!" he shouted.

Never. He turned over the new word with perverse pleasure.

That's that, he decided.

There's a limit to chutzpah.

The end of the chase, the pacing back and forth from room to room. Finito! I'm tired of him ordering me around. I'm tired of the way he controls my life and ignores my schedule. I won't go to any meeting place tomorrow. No way! He fell asleep with the broadest smile in the world.

He was already there at five to one.

Loads of people passed by in the street. Elderly women with expensive Gucci bags. Pretty girls with long hair carrying fruit and low-fat yogurt in their little baskets. Young American tourists in tattered sneakers photographing buildings and squares. Someone was dragging a strange creature behind him on a leash—a human-like dog that was wearing tight black leather clothes and moving along the sidewalk on its four extremities. Its chin was set in a mask with only three openings—for its eyes and nose—and it marched obediently behind its master. This is Berlin, he thought with a mixture of disgust and admiration. People glanced at the strange couple with apparent indifference. As long as it doesn't crap on the sidewalk, they bypassed the man and his dog and continued on their way.

His mobile rang again.

"Are you there?"

"Maybe," he said, bringing the phone close to his ear because of the noise.

"Of course you're there. I can see you. Now get on bus No. 119, going in the direction of Mehringdamm."

"But...where should I get off?" he asked, complaining. "And why do I have to listen to you all the time?"

The phone was silent. Sebastian had hung up long ago.

Bus No. 119 arrived two minutes later, a yellow double-decker like its hundreds of fellows that travel all over the big city.

He got on and sat next to the exit door. The more people got on and off at the stops, the more foolish and annoyed he felt. If there were an international competition for the stupidest person in the world, I'd come home with a shiny medal, he thought, hating himself. Deep inside the Kreutzberg area, among the signs in Turkish and the shwarma stands and the women wrapped in scarves, the damned phone rang again.

"What's the next stop called?" asked an impatient voice.

"How should I know?

"Your attitude is starting to annoy me. What does it say on the electronic sign at the front of the bus?"

He screwed up his eyes.

"Katzbach Street," he said without hiding his annoyance.

"Very good," Sebastian said with satisfaction.

"What's so good? Have I won the lottery?"

"No. Get off at the stop after that, Mehringdamm, and switch fast to the underground, No. 6 in the direction of Tegel. Make sure you don't get on in the opposite direction, Mariendorf. The train comes every two minutes. Is anyone following you?"

"I really hope so! Am I allowed to know where I'm going?"

He had hung up.

Son of a bitch, shit, he cursed him furiously.

The chase continued. He was told to pass three buildings and cross a road. Afterwards to go into an inner courtyard and enter an elevator concealed at the end of it.

The elevator moved upwards and stopped suddenly. "Get out," the voice ordered in his ears.

I'm on my way to an apartment that isn't listed anywhere; he smiled in spite of himself. Even Iran's nuclear secrets are less complicated than this journey.

"Don't move," he heard the voice say.

I'm going to die now, occurred to him as a transparent thought. They'll never find my body. I'm imprisoned in a country that's hidden between walls. In just a moment a sad yak will stick out his frightening head from inside the wall and chew up the remains of my life.

"Do you see something gray near you? Don't say aloud what you see! Just look!"

A simple-looking electricity box stood in the corridor, perhaps a little larger than ordinary.

"Yes, I see."

"Open that thing."

"But how? How do you open it?"

There was a very simple key in the door of the electricity box.

"Yes, with that thing you're touching. And don't say anything."

A buzz.

"Coffee is ready!"

A young man with a huge smile stood facing him, wearing a white apron. "You can turn your mobile off now." He locked the door carefully. "Welcome to my kingdom," he said as he shook my hand.

I stood breathless. Light flooded my eyes. There was a large mirror leaning against the wall. I saw myself in it. No more masks, I thought. It's me standing here.

Hello, me, I murmured.

"You look good," Sebastian laughed, leading me inside.

A lovely penthouse spread out before me, furnished in wonderful taste. A very spacious living room with white leather furniture. Light-colored clay flowerpots and a serene pastel painting. Large windows overlooking a landscape of roofs. The dome of the Reichstag, the green cathedral, Unter den Linden, the concrete towers next to Alexanderplatz—they could all be seen through the sealed window pane.

"I love Berlin." He was next to me.

I'm standing face to face with the anonymous man who's invaded my life in recent months, I thought. The man who is being followed by so many people is holding a metal urn full of coffee and smiling like an elevator boy.

"Shall I pour fresh coffee for his honor?" he bowed. "Or is his lordship still angry at me?"

"Yes. Thank you," I stammered.

There was fresh orange juice on a small sideboard, and next to it a basket of fruit and a tray with thick slices of poppy seed cake, plain cookies, apple cake and plum cake.

I'm avoiding looking at him, I thought, surprised. As though I were afraid something would happen to me.

"Sit down," he said, leading me. "I don't bite. Unless you ask me nicely." He laughed again.

In the corner of the living room stood a beautiful white piano. When he noticed that it had caught my eye, he sat down in front of it without delay and lifted the gleaming white lid. I had never seen such cleanliness: not even a speck of dust had entered this house. It was not a human apartment.

His fingers ran across the keys with surprising agility. "Do you recognize this?" He played a few opening notes and looked at me.

He has the gaze of a cub, I thought. A wolf cub. I listened to the notes, but shrugged my shoulders.

"Only few people remember it," he nodded sadly. "Listen." He leaned his head back and closed his eyes.

Risen from the *ruins*
and faced towards the future,
Let us serve you for the good,
Germany, united fatherland.
Old woes we will have to conquer,
and, united, so we shall,
For it lies within our power
that the sun, beautiful as never before,
Shines over Germany.

Longing quivered within the words like a small trapped animal.

"It's the old anthem, the anthem of East Germany," I said. "Right?"

"Yes." Light and water mingled in his eyes. "The words—Johannes Becher. The melody—Hanns Eisler. A Jew," he suppressed a smile. "It's a kind of longing, you know. A longing for something that will never return." He looked at me inquisitively. "And perhaps never was. Are you familiar with that type of longing?"

"Yes." I felt myself turning pale.

"I'm trying to run, but my feet are rooted to the ground. A long time has passed since then, but I still want to take revenge. To punish. Only afterwards will I be able to start my life again. Do you understand?"

"No." I didn't understand a thing. Not yet. "Revenge against whom? Why?"

"Let's have a drink." He poured something. "Lechayim," he said in Hebrew. "Lechayim."

He was strong, and his feline gait testified that he spent hours doing exhausting exercises. As the minutes passed I noticed details that my eyes had missed at first: the fashionable pants he was wearing, in a wonderful shade of gray, the well-cut jacket. And that good smell, not too sweet but definitely pleasant, which I still remember from the taxi that took us to the destroyed factory in Erfurt.

"Why me?" I asked quickly.

He looked at me.

"Why you what?"

"Why are you telling me of all people, and not the others?"

His eyes filled with sea sand. His strong knee moved a little, almost shaking between us.

"And what if I'm telling the others too?" The mischievous gleam came back. "Don't worry, soon you'll understand everything." He got up and walked round the room. The sun was setting over the roofs like a huge orange ball. "There are things I haven't told you yet." His jaw was clenched. "I want you to listen, some of what you'll hear will not be pleasant to your ears. If you want to get up and go, I won't stop you. In any case, I thank you for everything you've done for me."

"I haven't done a thing."

He laughed wildly. "You have, and how. Shall we begin?"

"Yes." I looked at his hands. "Let's begin."

"From the beginning I sensed that you were a good guy," he smiled.

There was something magnetic about that look. He knows, I thought immediately. He sees me as I am. He reads all the secrets and unravels all the knots.

Suddenly, he took a cookie from the tray, stuck his thumb into it and divided it into two. "Take it," he offered me half.

I looked at him in surprise.

"A private joke," he smiled. "A sad one, like all private jokes." He bit into the half cookie. "Do you remember where you stopped reading?" He adjusted his position in the armchair.

"Of course I remember," I answered, afraid he was setting a trap for me. "You prepared the table for the meeting with the elderly couple who wanted to sell you the old house. This house, I presume." I paused for a moment.

On a rainy day his eyes are gray-green like seaweed strewn on the beach, I recalled. In the summer they're as blue as a sea. And now? Now they are all the colors together. They are the eyes of Satan.

He watched me, amused, his large hand resting casually on his knee.

"Suddenly two policemen appeared. They demanded that you leave of your own free will and gave you two minutes to decide."

"Yes," he nodded. "Two minutes. That's exactly how it was."

Translated by Miriam Schlusselberg

Poetry

YONA WALLACH (1944–1985) was born in Tel Aviv and was raised in the town of Kiryat Ono of which her father was a founder. He died when she was a young child. Wallach was active in the circle known as the Tel Aviv Poets which emerged in the 1960s around the journals *Achshav* and *Siman Kriah*, and was a frequent contributor to Israeli literary periodicals. She also wrote for and appeared with an Israeli rock group, and in 1982 her poetry was set to music. Characterized by "an abundance of nervous energy," Yona Wallach's poetry combines elements from rock and roll, Jungian psychology and street slang in a body of work known for its break-neck pace and insistent sexuality. Refusing to be limited by conventional poetic structures, Wallach took upon herself the women's revolution in Hebrew poetry, and became a stylistic model for many women poets.

Yona Wallach

Three Poems

THE MAN TURNS INTO A STREAM

The man turns into a stream
his head is round
his body long and continuing
and between his spread legs
two brooks splitting
his banks of different shades and his color also
like the color of my feelings at the same time
shades of pink pallid green
shades of sky-blue a lot of light red
like in an ancient myth
the man turns into a stream in my feeling
when my vision gets weak
and my awareness weakens
the man turns into a stream
and I didn't know
only after a time—
it became clear to me
oh this is the man changed

here is his splendid body
long and his full contours
here is his innocent beautiful body of
what was so lit
that turned the man into a stream
and I didn't know.

THE EVENING

The evening has no end
tears of children
hang
from the beam of night
cutting a cross-section
dark emptiness
like a cross-section
of my memory
the evening has no end
and it's short
it is a dwarf
like a child's evening
exaggerated
like the possibility
of thinking

DON'T WATCH THE OLD MAN EAT

Don't watch how the old man eats
pieces of paper like colorful stickers fly
between the shoots of his vine his head in the clouds and his hair
     on the ground
his giant pipe above it smoke at the edges of a distant plain
not to see how the old man eats his saliva drips from the sky
his hands dropping remnants of food identify mouth lips
colorful stickers fly between the shoots of his vine to pass
to sit between the ash-heaps not to see how the old man eats
with his hands sucking remnants of life he sees as he feels

Translated by Linda Zisquit

HAVA PINHAS-COHEN, born in 1955, studied Hebrew literature and art history, and holds an MA in Hebrew literature from the Hebrew University of Jerusalem. Over the years, she has been a book reviewer, a translator, a columnist for the daily newspaper *Maariv* and a Research Fellow at the Hebrew University. At present, she lectures on literature and art, and is the editor of *Dimui*, a journal for Jewish poetry, fiction and culture which she founded in 1989. Pinhas-Cohen has published six collections of poetry. She has received the Israel Efrati Prize, the Prime Minister's Prize (1995), the ACUM Prize for her poetry collection *A River and Forgetfulness* (1998), the Kugel Prize for *Orphea's Songs* (2000), and the Alterman Prize for *Messiah* (2002). Her poems have been published abroad in 10 languages.

Hava Pinhas-Cohen

Three Poems

WOMAN BREAKING

The woman breaks. How does a woman break?
From the waist.
She breaks from the waist
her torso inclines like a metronome—
times her head touches the ground and swings back
times her forehead touches the sky falling down to her.
Sometimes her forehead breaks on the ground and
her breasts pull out like two linen bags
shaking milk to cheese.

How does a woman break—
from the waist
from the waist a woman breaks and her torso
follows her throat backwards
her hair coils to the ground
as she turns on her axis with a weird
movement of pain, as if her father in heaven
were ravishing her

That's how Astarte looked to me—
incense and idol of a broken woman
in a display window.

THE LAST AUTUMN

I returned to that last autumn's place
thorns still spread the path to the hill
lamenting Elul's crisp furrows gaping for seed
drawn on I carried in me
an offering of tranquility.

Not an offering of resentment and not
an offering of remembering. The smell
of an innocent sheep would not dispose
of the layer of things hidden
in household utensils: clay, iron and glass.

Not an offering of resentment and not
an offering of remembering, even
a High Priest laying his soft palms on my
small hands would not prevent
the body's confession:

Falling thigh swelling belly a crack in the soul.

IN THE RHYTHM OF LOVE

B
In the narrow white cubicle
between toilet bowl, basin and shower
enfolding my soul in a towel
I am able to bring both my faces to you
to prepare my body with soap and perfume
and oils for my man and spill my soul
with the water down the drain
at twilight

from this place nobody drives me
out of my mind
without my consent.

Translated by Riva Rubin

credit Micha Simhon

SARA FRIEDLAND BEN-ARZA was born in 1960 to a Hassidic family in Jerusalem. She received a BA in Hebrew language and musicology from Bar-Ilan University, and an MA in Hebrew literature and Hassidism from the Hebrew University of Jerusalem. At present, Ben-Arza researches Hassidism as well as teaching Hassidic studies, liturgical music and *midrash* (homiletic interpretation) at religious study centers for women. She also organizes a women's prayer group. *With the Name I Pray* is her first collection of poems.

Sara Friedland Ben-Arza

Three Poems

BE'ER LAHAI ROI

An angel of the Lord found her by a spring of water in the wilderness, the spring on the road to Shur, and said, "Hagar, slave of Sarai, where have you come from, and where are you going?" And she said, "I am running away from my mistress Sarai." And the angel of the Lord said to her, "Go back to your mistress, and submit to her harsh treatment." And the angel of the Lord said to her, "I will greatly increase your offspring, and they shall be too many to count." The angel of the Lord said to her further, "Behold, you are with child…"

    And she called the Lord who spoke to her, "You are El-roi," by which she meant, "Have I not gone on seeing after He saw me!" Therefore the well was called Beer-lahai-roi…

Gen. 16:7–14.

An angel was sent by my man
To find me
Between the Wilderness of the Blind and the Gaping Sky.
I appeared to him, gazing,
For mighty waters surged in my belly

247

Eyes, eyes too numerous to number,
I was seen
On the road to Shur
Washing in the white of His divine eye
Naked

SUDDENLY LIGHT

Suddenly light, my legs bird-like,
I didn't recognize them,
For years they penetrated, pillar-limbs burrowing
Into earth
Descending and seeping into bed-rock,
And knowing rises in them to my belly, my heart, my neck and
     higher.
My relics couched in mighty waters—
Not wayward, not wanton.
From here I'd drink.
How have my legs become birds,
And how could the Great Deep, couching below,
Be so light, its waters cavorting like this,
Perhaps secretly my hands brought
Earth of dread here to seal up my wells
And my arms carried broken tap-water in buckets,
Buoyancy for my ankles, buoyancy for my knees,
Or my springs they prance,
Going forth in the Circle-Dance of the Righteous
They come singing, playing music, and gesturing with their finger:
"This"

The Shore of Achziv

SHTUKIT*

As a daughter to Mordecai
Wife to Mordecai
From his embrace to immersion in myrrh
From perfumes to the king's embrace
And from the king to immersion in water
To return to the embrace of the first
She returns and circles back
submerging and embracing.
And the immersions rinsed away her men's traces,
Blurring pleasure, blurring lesions.
And the memory of her people and her progenitors in wine was
      erased.
Orphan of the dispersed—
Esther said only:
Write me down

Translated by Rachel Adelman

---

* Silenced one; whose father is not known

Review Essay

Hadar Makov-Hasson

Compelling Reading

Risa Domb, ed. *Contemporary Israeli Women's Writing*, London & Portland, Vallentine Mitchell, 2007. 339 pp.
Vol 2. of *New Women's Writing from Israel*, ed. Risa Domb. London & Portland, Vallentine Mitchell, 1996.

Women writers have been notoriously absent from the history of modern Hebrew literature and those who managed to make their mark, often represented an entire generation: from Dvora Baron in 1905 to the poet Rachel in the 1920s through Lea Goldberg's works and Amalia Kahana-Carmon's first short story collection in 1966. But it was in the 1980s that we witnessed a flux of talented women writers who suddenly began invading the Israeli literary scene. Some of these voices were captured in *New Women's Writing from Israel*, the first anthology edited by Risa Domb in 1996.

The recently published *Contemporary Israeli Women's Writing* captures some of the more interesting, and less traditional, voices of Israeli women writers today. The anthology presents an appealing mix of well-known writers like Ruth Almog and Judith Katzir alongside newer voices such as Orna Coussin and Shva Salhoov. Thematically, these stories portray not only the voices, lives and struggles of Israeli women, but also the fragmented narrative of Israeli society in the past two decades. Broken ideals, gender roles, religion and ethnicity all receive a probing examination by the different writers. Interestingly, the anthology features a prominent number of stories by and about Orthodox women, whose concerns and struggles within Israeli society are amplified by their unique position as women in a religious environment.

Indeed, the different stories tend to depict the voice of the other in Israeli society, be it women, Orthodox Jews, newcomers or children caught in an unexplained adult world. Some of the stories deal with familiar themes within modern Hebrew literature. Such is the case with Ruth Almog's "Dwarves on her Pajamas" and Savyon Liebrecht's "Kibbutz." In the first story, Almog treats the topic of Holocaust survivors from the unique point of view of a broken family that deals with the haunting memories of their past. Maya, the daughter, longs for her parents' attention and could not be happier when her brother runs away from home. When her distraught mother leaves the family behind, Maya—although born and raised in Israel—begins developing disturbing symptoms as a result of second-generation trauma.

Liebrecht also adopts the point of view of the child, yet presents a different take on the integration of Holocaust survivors in Israeli society. "Kibbutz" is a powerful story about a mildly retarded Holocaust survivor, David, who moves to a kibbutz, where he unknowingly serves as the local fool. Two contradictory narratives clash within the story—the real, and cruel, story of David and that told by the kibbutz nurse to his son, Melech. The latter is a fairy tale of how his parents met, how he was conceived and how they were all loved by the kibbutz members. As an adult, Melech meets with Dvora, forcing her to confront the truth by making her retell the fairytale while he adds the sordid details of his parents' life and death. The cruelty of the kibbutz members is masterfully portrayed in this story, where

Liebrecht proves, once again, that she is a sensitive narrator of the Israeli margins.

Other stories also focus on children, but as part of their struggle within the nuclear family. Nava Semel's beautiful "Boukitza" is the story of a mother's mental deterioration and death as told through the eyes of her daughter. The child longs for her mother to wake up while a strange woman whom she refuses to acknowledge and calls only "the woman I didn't know," takes care of her and her younger brother. The little girl finds solace in a book about trees, where she discovers the boukitza, a beautiful yet distant tree which cannot be found where she lives, just like her own mother. Although she resents her mother's lack of will to live, she too longs to "rest" forever as her mother dies with her drawing in her hands. Erna Coussin's "Tequila-Mama" presents a different narrative of a child-mother relationship, both in content and in style. Here the narrator is the mother who just broke-up with her (female) lover, a woman her son will only acknowledge as "her." As she struggles to recreate a routine for him, she takes him out to dinner at the local restaurant while ordering drinks for herself. There, both mother and son toy with the idea of replacing the missing lover with an animal, whether a dog or an elephant. The laconic, almost bitter style in which the story is written painfully portrays a different parenthood, one which is deeply rooted in the alienated environment of the big city.

As mentioned earlier, many of the stories in the anthology depict the lives of religious women and the struggles they encounter within their society. Most of these are written by Orthodox or formerly Orthodox writers (Judith Rotem, Chana Bat Shahar, Shva Salhoov and Michal Govrin). Interestingly, while capturing some unique traits, their narratives are often similar to the other texts in the anthology. Judith Rotem, for example, follows the unfulfilled attraction between two cousins who long for each other and share the love of reading (forbidden) books, but when the woman decides to divorce her husband, she finds that her beloved cousin is already engaged, thus "missing the train" as the name of the story suggests. Another pair of cousins in love is found in Shva Salhoov's "Rainbow." Here, the two share the covenant of the rainbow ("keshet" in Hebrew is also a hair band, a gift she receives from him as a token of their bond) just like Noah with God. One of the most intriguing stories in the anthology is Chana Bat Shahar's "The Ram of Nazirite." Interestingly, the story does not necessarily focus on religious issues but rather touches, once again, upon the unfulfilled love between two relatives. As the woman takes in her step-brother, and former beloved's hallucinatory son, she must deal with her past as well as her future. Bat Shahar delineates a complex narrative of family, memory and delusion, providing her readers with searching questions rather than firm conclusions.

Read together, these stories weave an intriguing pastiche of postmodern life in Israeli society as told by those who were often found in the margins of what Gershon Shaked called the Zionist meta-narrative. However, as is often the case with anthologies, the image captured here is a fragmented and multifaceted one rather than a comprehensive account. This is perhaps is what makes it such compelling reading material for those who are interested in contemporary Israeli literature.

Reviews

Don't Envy the Author

Amos Oz, *Rhyming Life and Death*
Jerusalem, Keter, 2007

One might expect the reactions to Amos Oz's new book to be half-hearted. What did he need this for, his admirers may ask? After all, he already has his glory: there is so much beauty in *A Tale of Love and Darkness* that it has been translated into numerous languages. So much love, so much praise, so many awards have been bestowed on the author, why must he pick at the embarrassing wound of the creative process with this pointed scalpel? This question, however, is not what *he* needs, but what we, the readers, can absorb from this short, condensed piece and why it is so difficult for us to follow its mocking gaze.

We can read this book from three different perspectives: as someone who is involved in writing and literature, as someone who examines them from the side, or as someone who spreads an ironic, surreptitious net over Oz's work and literature as a whole. It is almost impossible to think of another author who has offered such an honest and sophisticated key to his work and perhaps to his life. This devastating courage—which insists, like a stubborn grumpy child, on tipping over the bucket he has just filled, to reveal the crack blighting its depth—is not easy to accept. But it is this very quality that makes Amos Oz what he is.

Rhyming Life and Death narrates one evening in the life of a nameless man, the "author." The narrator's laughing eye does not spare the protagonist any stupidity, arrogance, inferiority or humiliation, at times making you laugh to tears and at others to revulsion, yet it also enfolds the bitter, desperate pain of the writing self. The author thus provides a certain unpleasant scrutiny of writers that they would prefer not to see. He exposes them as horribly self absorbed, detached from life and from others' feelings, and at the same time filled with an excessive, obsessive sensitivity that picks up every shred of life, like a starved bird. This is a brutal description of a process through which the lives of others are drawn into the author's consciousness against his or their will, and they stop recognizing themselves even while it is happening. Who knows which part of them is truth and which fiction? Even when they are recreated in the book, and even if their spirit reverberates within the characters, the author will not be able to tell exactly when he finished drinking their blood and when, or how, he re-emitted them in a spectacular golden fountain.

This is what Oz offers in *Rhyming Life and Death*: that precise and ruthless tone most of us would rather deny. Do not envy the author, whose sensors scan all underlying tones and walks the world all eyes and ears. He has to maintain a clever, smiling, normal appearance, but his soul cries out from the excess of noise always knocking at its edges, and his oversensitivity which turns it into a blessing and a torment.

A weary jester, this author—one eye laughs as the other bleeds. The audience demands beauty, more beauty, and all the magic tricks in the circus. But the jester, as though to infuriate us, flashes his ugly, embarrassing and loathed behind. Even our coldness and our scorn cannot stop him, for he has no other choice.

Avirama Golan

Of Mixed Descent

Aharon Appelfeld, *An Entire Life*
Jerusalem, Keter, 2007

Aharon Appelfeld's most recent book joins the long list of excellent Applefeldian novels and novellas which are written with restraint and verve, simplicity and sophistication, and focus on the epic of the Jewish people in 20th century Europe. This time the heroine is a young girl named Helgaleh, the daughter of Gizaleh, a Jewish mother who converted to Christianity, and Zingfried Schönbach, a Christian who is also a well-known landowner. When the Nazis come to power, Gizaleh is arrested and Helga is taken to a sister of her father's, Brunhilde, but then runs away in search of her mother. Finally, Helga goes to a concentration camp of her own accord, and manages to survive until it is liberated, when she and her mixed friends open a center where they take care of Jewish refugees in need.

The novel is dedicated to Appelfeld's mother, Bonya, who was murdered by the Nazis, and it accordingly places Helga's mother center stage. However, although the novel opens with Gizaleh being taken to the camps, her funeral takes place only during the final chapters. In between, her dignified personality is mirrored through friends and acquaintances who knew her during those years. Thus Helga becomes acquainted with her mother through various mirror images. As in many of Appelfeld's novels, the narrative conceals a coded network of motifs that conduct a dialogue with Christianity. Helga says, for example, "Sometimes I feel as though Jesus' fate, which the priest talks about in almost every Sunday sermon, is nailed onto me and I too will be crucified." There is also a similarity between Mary and Jesus—the Jewish foundation stones of Christianity—and Helga's mixed descent, which helps articulate the complex Jewish-Christian link presented in the novel. Appelfeld also creates a fascinating symbiotic equivalence between Jesus and the suffering Jews: when Helga meets a Jewish woman in prison with her children she says,

"The scenes come back to me slowly. I saw the woman and her three children again. They reminded me of a painting I had seen in church." It is worth noting that *An Entire Life* will be joined in the next few months by yet another link in the Appelfeldian chain.

Ktzia Alon

The Multifaceted Self

Yoel Hoffman, *Curriculum Vitae*,
Jerusalem, Keter, 2007

Particularly in the academic world, the title of this book usually refers to a short personal history accompanied by a list of publications and achievements for the purpose of professional advancement. However, these do not interest Hoffman at all, and anyone familiar with his work will not be surprised by the mockery and the ironical smile of the narrator, who presents himself—in the plural "we"—in what is ostensibly his life story. Because the narrator's identity is multifaceted and dynamic, or in Hoffman's singular view: "We were so many in one body, and even that was concealed by clothes" (33).

For a moment this book seems accessible, more readable than its predecessor, since the events unfold in chronological order. But this is also deliberately misleading. Not only is it impossible to introduce order into life, or to organize it according to certain rules, even the very "writing of life" is an illusion, since "one can write only by not-writing. When things come from the opposite direction." (83). This is a typical Hoffmanesque moment, like writing on one side of the page, waiving conventional pagination, and even the minimalist drawings included in the text. Everything is reduced.

Anyone who wants to summarize the plot—a boy who was orphaned of his mother at age three and a half, who grew up with his father and his stepmother Ursel, raised a wild pigeon, attended a typical Israeli school, was attracted to philosophy, spent a long time in Japan etc.—will miss the essence of Hoffman's work. Because what is important is the experience itself, the specific moment, which remains as a memory or a dream. "What do we remember? Biva Lake and the houses beyond the lake. The flowering of the cherry tree and Auschwitz and Treblinka and Maidanek" (73).

Hoffman views the world with great, almost childish wonder. The episodes, which are like a patchwork, excel in associative imagination, bizarreness and charming humor. "A woman named Mina Katznelson, from Kvutzat Kinneret, sold me five swarms of bees. I put the swarms into five wooden boxes and placed the boxes in an open field next to the village of Gush Halav. The bees, who must have heard of onomatopoeia, buzzed incessantly. Sometimes they congregated in front of the opening of the box like Jews in front of the synagogue on the High Holy Days" (27).

As in his earlier books, here too Hoffman sketches European Jews who are alien to the Israeli environment. He also calls attention to this alienation by the use of German words and grammar (making mistakes typical of the *Yekkes*, the German Jews). And as in earlier texts, Judaism does not lack Christian signs ("the baby Jesus"). There is no question that Hoffman is one of the most original writers in contemporary Hebrew literature. Only Hoffman's language is capable of breathing life into the following image: "Imagine a Jew and the Jew is sitting on a chair and the chair is in the world. The great loneliness of the Jew. How much space does a man with a chair need, and how much space is he given?"

Anat Feinberg

In Times of War

Tami Shem-Tov, *Letters from Nowhere*
Tel Aviv, Kinneret, Zmora-Bitan, Dvir, 2007

Letters from Nowhere, written for teenagers, presents the memories of a woman today named Nili Goren and living in Israel, but who in the terrible times of World War II was torn from her daily routine in Utrecht, Holland and forced to spend the rest of her childhood hiding in various places. The last of these was the house of Dr Kohly and his wife, who lived in an isolated village where Lieneke—as she was then called—stayed from 1943 on, pretending to be his niece. In 2006, Goren returned to Holland accompanied by award-winning author Tami Shem-Tov and to the places where she hid during her childhood. "There," Shem-Tov writes, "in all these houses and hideaways, Lieneke told me all that happened to her during the war and after it." The result is the book before us, a moving and powerful book that doesn't have a single superfluous word in it.

Lieneke's story is told in the third person and moves between different time-frames—skipping from her childhood before the war to the years of hiding and back again. The connecting thread between the chapters is the letters her father managed to send her from his hiding place. He was a top scientist at Utrecht's University Hospital, and through the Dutch underground he sent his daughter humorous and lovingly illustrated letters, bound together with a piece of string like a little book. Although he asked Dr Kohly to destroy them, the village doctor didn't, and gave them to Lieneke when the war was over.

These moving letters, which are an integral part of the plot, are supplemented by Shem-Tov's talent for storytelling. The seeds of suspense that she plants with great skill lead the reader from one chapter to the next, and her book is full of subtle humor and compassion for the characters. She also manages to avoid the literary traps involved in combining her difficult subject with the book's target audience.

The secret of her success is twofold: first, she refrains from explicit descriptions of horror (apart from one incident) and her book is free of any "Holocaust pornography." Her style is reserved, at times almost laconic, and she creates a sense of drama without using excessive emotionalism. When Dr Kohly reminds Lieneke that "she must stay in the back room and be quiet; she mustn't whisper, cough or hum when she hears people coming into the clinic or the pharmacy," we realize there is no other way to express what children went through in the Holocaust.

Shem-Tov's second accomplishment is the way she shapes the character of Lieneke. Lieneke immediately arouses sympathy in the reader, both because she is a real flesh and blood person, and because she is appealingly portrayed as a girl more or less the reader's age. Thus she, rather than the Holocaust as a whole, becomes the focus of the book.

Shem Tov's literary accomplishment is complemented by good graphic design. The text is accompanied by the father's colorful letters as well as other pictures and illustrations, and the whole exudes an atmosphere entirely of Shem-Tov's making—a mixture of subtlety and immense hope.

Osnat Blayer

Imbroglio

Yosef Bar-Yosef, *Not in this House*
Tel Aviv, Hakibbutz Hameuhad/Hasifriya Hahadasha, 2007

Bar-Yosef, who is known as a successful playwright (*Tura, Difficult People*), and is an Israel Prize laureate for Theater, is revealed in his debut novel as a skilled and original storyteller. From the medium of drama he "borrows" the unity of time and place, and tells the story of twenty-four hours in the life of a father and his son.

The father, Emanuel (Mano), a businessman and Don Juan who is addicted to money, philandering and sex, returns from New York after a financial imbroglio and settles in the house he owns together with his son Ami. Ami, a lawyer, is portrayed as a sensitive and eccentric young man, and unlike his adulterous father is still a virgin in his late twenties. The relationship between the two, which is already fraught with tension and clandestine battles, becomes more acute because of Nimi, a young mother who has left the ultra-Orthodox world in Jerusalem and rented a basement apartment in the Tel Aviv house.

Ami the romantic, who is looking for pure love, gradually falls in love with Nimi, but when she is willing to respond to him, he draws back. "Not in this house," he says—he won't sleep with her here. His father is also captivated by the young woman, who has taken control of her destiny in her search for the beauty that for her is embodied in fashion magazines. The battle over the woman, or over the great riddle: "How do you know you're in love?" is the main plot line of the novel.

The trio is joined by an interesting secondary figure: Hannah Levine, the energetic elderly woman who was the lover of Erich, Mano's father, demonstrating that the apple did not fall far from the tree. Bar-Yosef describes the world of the ultra-Orthodox Batei Ungarin community in Jerusalem and the urban loneliness in the hedonistic society of Tel Aviv. The chain of events, which excels in a dramatist's sensitivity to pace and tension, is interwoven with wonderful dialogues that shed light on the heroes' consciousness. The fluent style, which combines the comic, the realistic and the lyrical, undoubtedly contributes to the success of the novel as well.

Anat Feinberg

A Frustrated Othello

Israel Hameiri, *Actors*
Tel Aviv, Even Hoshen, 2006

Actors, we must say at once, is a novel overflowing with theoretical suspense whose plot is so full and dense that it almost bursts. In the first place, we have here a psychological novel written as the confession of one Benny Lachiani, a failed and frustrated actor who is aching to play a leading part on stage, but has to make do with small parts, such as waiters and servants. On this level, the novel deals with the impossible personality of the perfect actor, whose life becomes meaningful only when he steps into the shoes of the characters he plays. In these fantasies, and only in them, is Benny transformed from an inconsequential little man to an admired hero.

Secondly, this is a social novel whose characters have been carefully selected to articulate a variety of socio-cultural tensions in Israel, such as between Jews and Arabs, and the identity problems of *Mizrahim* (Jews from Arab countries and North Africa), who are trying to break through into mainstream Israeli experience. Social anomalies, rich and poor, kibbutzniks, artists and academics, Palestinians from Gaza and Arab Israelis from Jaffa and the Galilee—all are represented in the novel or at least mentioned in it. Third, this is a novel that has clear idealistic and political tendencies, since most of its characters can be linked to the radical left and some do more than just argue about their convictions in the living room—they are willing to take chances and act. Additionally, the novel addresses the tension between art and life, the issue of the egoistic artist who focuses on building his professional career at the expense of family, and the need to choose between high ideals and caring for those close to you. And that's without mentioning the discussion about the turmoil that exists in our deepest psyche—those erotic drives and tensions that undermine orderly relationships and social norms, but add spice and color to life. Without these and the various forms of sublimation we have created, our lives would be dull and boring.

Israel Hameiri does indeed know how to put together an interesting, dramatic narrative which, like his previous novel *Symbiosis*, has the features of a suspense novel and holds some dark secret that is worked out towards the end.

Haya Hoffman

The Legend of the House of Tott

Zvi Yanai, *Letter to a Lost Brother*
Jerusalem, Keter, 2006

A young dancer from a Jewish-Austrian family falls in love with an older, Hungarian-Protestant singer and joins him in a ten-year performance tour across Italy. The couple have four children who are raised by random nannies and whom their parents come to collect every so often. Except for one child, the first son born after two girls, whom they do not collect. During World War II, the singer leaves his partner and three children in a small Italian village and returns to Hungary where he disappears, presumed dead. The mother dies of an illness at age thirty-two, so the three orphans remain with the nanny. The fourth child seems to have been forgotten. And this is only the beginning of the incredible story of the Totts, as recounted by Zvi Yanai, the youngest in the family. Born Sandro Tott in Italy a few years before the war, he grew up in an Italian village as a poor Christian child who counted on the German-Nazi regime for survival. When the war ended, he discovered that he was actually Jewish and immigrated to Israel.

Letter to a Lost Brother is Yanai's first novel and it is wonderful. It's a one-way epistolary novel, very like a letter-monologue addressed to his long lost brother, whom he rediscovered in 21st century Italy.

But it is also an investigation that retraces his family history, searches for his long lost brother and examines the inexplicable reasons why a mother would abandon her child with a stranger. To retrieve this past, he uses a bundle of letters his mother had kept—from her mother, her husband, other family members and the authorities, and through them, he tries to map out his family life and the course it took.

Yanai's grandmother, who lived in Vienna, had two children. Her husband traveled to the US and never returned; her beautiful daughter, a dancer, lived in Italy, and her Zionist son immigrated to Palestine. While the world around her becomes ever uglier as war approaches, the grandmother sits in Vienna and sends letters full of complaints and instruction—a sort of Jewish lament—in every direction: "Fourteen years ago your poor father went into the great world and never came back. Seven years later you left me and we haven't seen each other since. Seven years after you left, Pauli is leaving me. Who knows when I'll see him again," she writes to her daughter, instead of packing up and leaving.

The family life that Yanai revisits exists only in letters. He tries to reach out and establish a dialogue, but has to do it all by himself—the other side left no trace. And although his narrative embraces many voices, his brother's is not among them—he cut himself off and refused to speak. Thus the author struggles to recreate a family from a mosaic of silent pieces.

Yanai's writing is clear and beautiful. He explores possible explanations for his brother's abandonment, and for Germany's descent into Nazism, with equal restraint and lucidity, interweaving the personal with the larger situation. The result is a story that is larger that life.

Liraz Axelrod

Suburban Oblivion

Yaniv Iczkovits, *Pulse*
Tel Aviv, Hakibbutz Hameuhad, 2007

The novel is a kind of journey into the heart of the "normal," well-fed, smug, cookie-cutter Israeli middle class, and especially into that part that calls itself leftist and humane, but which hears and sees nothing beyond the hollow, false clichés it keeps repeating to itself

The main thread follows the emotional turmoil of two central characters: Yonatan, a young accountant, who is convinced that the seven-week-old fetus his wife, Mira, is carrying has died in the womb; and Yehudit, Yonatan's aunt, who is struggling with depression and with the fact that her son, Udi, a shell-shocked and traumatized paratrooper, has decided to break away from his family and live in India. The story is filled with the texts and the vacuous acts that shape the protagonists' consciousness: from the pornography Yonatan watches on the Internet, to the political declarations that Amos, his uncle, mindlessly parrots: "But they want us to kill innocent citizens, so they will be able to show the world how miserable they are."

The shallowness reaches a tragicomic peak in Yonatan's mother, an algebra teacher who lives on Brenner Street and considers it her duty to own the complete works of Yosef Chaim Brenner. However, she uses the volume as a coffee coaster, because "It's really hard to read, old-school, you know, depressing, and the pace, oh God, so slow."

What causes the bourgeois family to disintegrate is the seeping of the political into the private space that the collective cliché is supposed to protect. And so Yehudit, chasing after the shadow of her beloved son lost somewhere in India, tries to understand at what point she began to misunderstand. She believes that her main role as a mother during her son's military service is to ignore the acts he has committed, while at the same time sheltering him from them.

In a charged encounter with his cousin Yonatan in India, Udi expresses the conflict clearly: "And all day long my father sits there and babbles about politics, but he has no idea what is happening just outside his door. No idea that everything that happens out there isn't happening in some Arab village, but inside his own son. Jenin has taken root in my heart, and it's crowded and stifling and crude."

Iczkovits is trying to tell his readers something vital and accurate about Israeli reality, and he does so bravely, with great talent, and, above all, with an enormous effort to be precise.

Haim Weiss

What a Meeting!

Avram Kantor, *To the Lizards*
Tel Aviv, Hakibbutz Hameuchad, 2006

The interest that Avram Kantor's new novel arouses lies in his ability to give convincing shape to the highly charged encounter between Nechama, a Holocaust survivor, her German daughter-in-law and her gentile grandson. As fate would have it, a couple who met while running from the Nazis, had a son who then married a German girl. Neither Nechama nor her husband Menachem recognize this marriage, and they reject their daughter-in-law—"No German will enter this house!" Menachem declares. As a result, their son moves to Munich and builds his own family there.

Years later, Menachem dies and Nechama, now an old woman, is left alone to confront loneliness, daily problems, the separation from her children, and the prohibition left by her husband. Meanwhile, Gil, her grandson from Germany, arrives in Israel as a volunteer and suddenly turns up without warning at his grandmother's house.

With great sensitivity, Kantor traces the gradual rapprochement between Nechama and Gil, the doubts, the struggle and the softening of harsh principle in face of complex reality. And then, in the middle, the novel becomes a suspense-filled drama. While Gil is away on a trip, his bus is involved in a terrible accident. There is no contact with Gil, and the fear that he has been killed catalyzes a family reunion, during which Nechama meets her German daughter-in-law for the first time.

Kantor is very skilled at creating older characters who undergo a major change in their later years. As in his previous books, here too he creates a character whose age is asset rather than a burden. *To the Lizards* is very well written, and combines good psycholinguistic drama with an appealing and suspenseful plot. Kantor is both acute and sensitive in his portrayal of the relationship between grandmother and grandson, as well as between Nechama and her daughter-in-law. He reminds us that, beyond all public discussion of historical events, there are private spaces in which the lives of Germans and Jews are once again becoming involved with each other.

Ofer Dynes

Under the Knife

Shachar Magen, *Backyard Slaughter*
Jerusalem, Keter, 2006

In Alan Rudolf's 1982 movie, *Endangered Species*, a local sheriff in western USA has to deal with a horrific mass slaughter of cattle, and in the process he learns a thing or two about himself. The plot of the film may remind one a little of Shachar Magen's fascinating first novel, whose heroine Rutzi Ya'acobi, head veterinarian at a slaughterhouse in Kiryat Amal, is accused among other things of illegally butchering cows whose meat is unsuitable for human consumption.

But it is another Alan Rudolph film, *The Secret Lives of Dentists* (2002), that actually comes to mind because this is what Magen does. He reveals before us the secret, deranged and wonderful life of veterinarians, or at least of that sector whose cheerful daily routine includes parasitology, tick fever, bull semen, testicle jars, testing for parasites and swabbing the spleen, implanting embryos, sanding hooves, and to wrap it all up, having a drink at the Red Cow pub. A cross between *Family Farm* and ER. This is a world in which the animals' organs may seem "like soup," but the starting point is still always a sense of awe provoked by the beauty of creation. Rutzi ("not Putzi or Mutzi") was barely eight when she first saw "an animal from the inside, like a garment revealing its stitches" and realized what her destiny was. It was a transparent jellyfish on the beach in Haifa, and Rutzi tried to guess where the brain was, assuming there was one. This is how the lifelong love affair began. Along the way, we are offered colorful landscape flashes: a canary that died of loneliness; sharks that steer clear of a dead shark's scent; a cute beetle with a little bug, eating trees from within; Persian fallow deer let loose in Nahal Kziv; monogamous squills mating eight times a night, and even a key ring that isn't complete without a raccoon's tail.

Rutzi is, in my opinion, one of the most impressive female characters in Hebrew literature, and her love for animals is boundless. Referring to a poem by Natan Zach, she is deeply moved by a beautiful calf whose name is Quietude, no less. The silence of the lambs as fact and as image, certain people's tendency to turn into rhinoceroses, as well as other known and concealed moral maladies of the human race, are constantly juxtaposed with the deadly innocence of the helpless animals. The book's strength lies in its ideas, and in the poetic but unembellished manner in which they are expressed. It's no wonder that Rutzi asks herself, "Is there any comfort in human company?"

I detected a certain cinematic appeal in the book, so I will finish with another analogy from the world of cinema. This novel may remind one of the scene in the *Godfather* where a man finds the severed head of a horse in his bed. But the kinky-bleak atmosphere of the book, its uncompromising exploration of suburban life and the horror seeping out of the greenest lawns are most reminiscent of David Lynch. And so, whether knowingly or accidentally, Magen has created in *Backyard Slaughter* a fine Zionist alternative to *Blue Velvet*.

Yaron Frid

The fonts used in this book are from the Garamond family

The Toby Press publishes fine writing and journals,
available at bookstores everywhere. For more information,
please contact *The* Toby Press at www.tobypress.com